Crime Unknown

Crime Unknown

A Buck Taylor Novel

Chuck Morgan

Printed in the United States of America

First printing 2021

ISBN 978-1-7348424-5-6 (eBook)

ISBN 978-1-7348424-4-9 (Paperback)

ISBN 978-1-7348424-6-3 (Large Print)

LIBRARY OF CONGRESS CONTROL NUMBER

2021901969

DEDICATION

To my Mom, Dottie, and her gang of readers at Cherry Creek Retirement Village

Contents

Chapter One

Melanie spotted Kevin on the other side of the cafeteria, his head down and his face glued to the book he was studying. She worked her way through the line, grabbing a salad and an iced tea as she went, paid her bill and raced over to the table. Her excitement was almost too much to control. She pushed her tray onto the table, bumping the book Kevin was reading and knocking it onto the floor. Kevin looked up and glared until he realized who it was.

"I've been looking all over campus for you. Where have you been?" she said.

Kevin slid the book back onto the table. "Right here studying. I have a philosophy exam this afternoon. I told you about it yesterday."

Melanie smiled, reached out and put her hand on top of his. She leaned into the table and whispered, "We got it."

Kevin just looked confused. "What did we get?"

She leaned in closer so no one could hear. "The gallows."

Kevin looked around the room, then back at her, and then it came to him. "For real? I thought that was reserved for special parties. How did we get it?"

Melanie pulled her hand away from his, sat back

in the chair and looked at him. She shook her head as if she couldn't believe he was asking such a stupid question.

"Carly was able to work it out with Josh. We've been dating for four months, and I wanted to do something special for us. The club must have agreed, because we can use the space tonight after nine p.m. Carly will have it all set up."

Kevin sat back in his seat and looked at her. He had heard about the gallows since he first came to this school several years back, but he didn't know anyone who had been allowed to use it. Supposedly, the gallows were used by special members of the club and by invitation only. It was called the ultimate prize by the club members he knew.

The reality of the situation finally dawned on him, and he felt a rush of nausea. He hoped the chicken salad he'd had for lunch wouldn't end up all over the table. They both enjoyed performing the rituals, but this was the pinnacle. He hoped he had what it took to last and make Melanie happy.

"That's awesome, Mel, but what about Josh? Won't he be jealous?"

"Josh only wants me because he can't have me." Her blue eyes absorbed all the light around them as she batted them and flipped her long blond hair back over her shoulder. Kevin stared into her eyes, and he felt himself getting larger. He picked the book up off the <u>table</u>, placed it in his lap so no one could see the bulge and squirmed in his seat.

Melanie was gorgeous, a little ditzy at times, but she loved to experiment. That was how they'd gotten together and ended up in the club, and yes, it had been awkward at first since Josh ran the club on campus, but he didn't own her. They had been together during sophomore and junior years, but that was a couple of years back, and she assumed Josh had gotten over her once she connected with Kevin. Now that they were all in their first year of grad school, she hoped he would have forgotten all about her.

"You don't look very excited," she said.

"Sorry. My head is still in the philosophy exam. Look, meet me back at the apartment, and we'll grab some dinner in town before we need to be there."

He leaned across the table and kissed her passionately. "I am going to rock your world, but I need to finish studying."

He opened his book back to the page he'd been on before she sat down and started reading. Melanie finished her lunch, kissed him on the forehead and headed off to her next class. Tonight was going to be special, and she wanted to be ready.

As she left the cafeteria, she didn't see Josh sitting in the corner amongst a group of his friends, but he saw her. He tried to hide the scowl on his face by stuffing his mouth full of pizza. There was no doubt he would win Melanie back, but first . . . He looked across the room at Kevin, with his head buried in a book. He had formulated the plan in his head and had all the details worked out when one of his friends slapped him on the back and told him it was time to head for class. The group waited until

Josh stood up before they headed out. Everyone on campus knew their place, and that place was always behind Josh DiNardo.

Josh was the "big man" about campus. He knew everyone and everything that happened on campus, since most everything that happened revolved around him. When Carly had come to him with the request to let Melanie use the gallows, he knew that the perfect opportunity had just landed in his lap, and he intended to take full advantage of it. Josh wasn't worried because he always got his way, and that included getting Melanie back. He looked once more at Kevin as he left the room and smiled.

Chapter Two

Melanie had showered, dabbed on a little perfume, and worn her shortest skirt and her highest heels. Kevin couldn't stop staring at her when she appeared at his apartment door just before nine. She had called him earlier and told him to forget about dinner, that they would eat afterward. She wanted to take the time to get ready, and now that she stood in his doorway, she knew she had made the right decision. She looked stunning. If his roommate weren't in the front room playing a video game, he would have taken her right there in the hall. He was aroused, and she knew it.

"Slow down. We have all night," she said with that sexy voice.

Kevin grabbed his jacket and closed the door. They headed outside and started the short walk to the old hospital wing along the edge of the campus. It was a chilly night, with a little fall in the air, which helped Kevin because he was sweating like a pig under his jacket.

Melanie checked her phone and led him around to the back of the old building that housed classrooms and the campus hospital. She found the back door and entered the code she had been given into the electronic lock. She breathed a sigh of relief when the light turned green, and she heard the lock click. They both looked around the area to make sure no one was watching, and they stepped inside.

She studied the map and the instructions on her phone carefully. Carly had warned her that there was no cell service in the subbasement where they were headed, so she needed to memorize the route so they wouldn't get lost in the old maintenance and steam tunnels. She put her phone away, took Kevin's hand, and they headed down the stairs to the basement. After a couple of wrong turns, they finally found the second set of stairs and headed down to the subbasement. They both shivered as they walked down the stairs.

The room they were heading for was in the oldest part of the building, and there were all kinds of creepy noises as they walked. Kevin had no idea what to expect, but he felt nervous and a little afraid the deeper they traveled into the bowels of the building.

At the end of a long corridor, they found the door to the maintenance area. There was a shiny electronic lock on the door. It appeared new compared to the old, dirty walls and exposed pipes that dripped god knows what onto the floor. Melanie entered the code in the door and waited. Nothing happened, and she tried again. The second time was the charm, and the latch clicked. She pushed open the door.

The space they walked into was a huge two-story space full of cabinets and toolboxes. Several long shelves, full of spare parts, lined the walls.

Stepping into the room, they just stared for a minute until the door behind them closed and latched with a thud. They both jumped at the sound. Kevin was having second thoughts when Melanie called him over to the center of the room. There were candles of all shapes and sizes surrounding a blanket that lay on the floor. Next to the blanket was an open bottle of wine and two plastic cups. In this dark, dank basement, it looked romantic. And very out of place. Kevin wondered if the maintenance guys knew what their space was being used for after hours.

They picked up an envelope that was propped against the wine bottle and read the card inside.

WELCOME TO THE GALLOWS.

THE LIFT IS DESIGNED FOR ONE PERSON, USE YOUR IMAGINATION. THE SPACE IS YOURS UNTIL 5 AM. PUSHING THE UP BUTTON WILL CAUSE THE LIFT TO RISE SLOWLY. RELEASE THE BUTTON AT THE PERFECT HEIGHT FOR YOUR ENJOYMENT. THE DOWN BUTTON WORKS THE SAME WAY.

IN AN EMERGENCY, JUST PULL ON THE LOOSE END OF THE ROPE AND THE KNOT WILL UNTIE. ENJOY YOURSELVES, BUT TELL NO ONE ABOUT THIS PLACE.

Melanie placed the card back in the envelope and set it on the floor next to the bottle. She turned and walked to where Kevin was standing. He was looking at the noose that was tied to the hook on the electric lift. The lift, attached to a track, was used to bring heavy equipment from the loading dock elevator to the maintenance shop. Melanie looked at the noose and was impressed. It looked perfect, and someone had put a soft terry cloth wrap around it to keep it from bruising the neck.

Melanie noticed that Kevin was quiet, and she could see the concern in his eyes. "Why don't we sit down for a bit and have some wine," she said. "That will help you calm down. This is going to be fun."

She poured two cups of wine and handed him one. He drank slowly, never taking his eyes off the noose.

She touched his hand. "It's okay. We can go slowly until you get a feel for it. Carly told me that the record for someone in the noose is five minutes. Can you imagine?"

They sat on the blanket, drank their wine, and just held each other until Kevin calmed down. "I think I'm ready," he said. They stood up and walked to the noose. He stood under the lift and put the noose over his head. He pulled the noose until it was comfortable and told Melanie he was ready. She undid his belt and let his jeans drop down to the tops of his shoes, then pulled his underpants down to his ankles, stepped back and admired his manhood. He was very excited.

She grabbed the controller hanging from the lift and pushed the up button, and the lift slowly, soundlessly started to rise. Kevin grabbed at the noose with both hands as it pulled tighter against his chin. She released the button.

"Are you okay?"

Kevin nodded. "Let's do this."

She pushed the up button again and waited until he was at what she felt was the perfect height. Kevin struggled until he got his breathing under control. This was a new experience for both of them, and Kevin started to settle in.

Melanie walked over to him and wrapped her lips around his manhood. He started to get into the groove and was enjoying the experience.

She had no idea how long they had been at it, but suddenly Kevin started to shake and twist the rope. She looked up and he was frantically pulling on the loose end of the rope. His face showed panic, and his lips started turning blue. She reached up and grabbed the end of the rope with him and pulled, but the knot didn't loosen. It looked like it was getting tighter the more they pulled.

Kevin was now in a full-blown panic and was twisting and turning and pulling at the noose. Melanie grabbed the controller and pushed the down button, but nothing happened. She pushed it again and looked back at Kevin, who was struggling to breathe. She didn't know what to do. She pulled out her cell phone but saw no bars.

"I need to get help." She grabbed her blouse off the blanket and ran for the door as Kevin continued to twist and turn, his face showing the fear that had now overcome him.

Melanie ran through the subbasement, up the stairs and through the basement until she spotted the door they had entered earlier in the evening. She pushed open the door, pulled off her spike heels and ran across the campus towards the grad student apartments.

She crashed through the front door, ran up the stairs and started banging on Josh's door. Josh opened the door, looking half-asleep, but before he could say anything, she screamed, "Kevin is in trouble. I can't get him down!"

"Mel, where is Kevin?"

"He's in the gallows. I can't get him down. He can't breathe." He could see the tears in her eyes.

Josh ran into the second bedroom and woke his roommate, Billy. They both threw on sweatpants and T-shirts and raced out the door, followed by Melanie. They raced across the campus and stopped at the basement door. Josh entered the code and told Melanie to wait outside while he and Billy ran into the building.

Chapter Three

Josh entered the code in the maintenance room door, pushed it open, and stopped in the doorway. Kevin was hanging from the noose, not moving. His face was ashen, and his eyes were wide open in fear.

Billy pushed past Josh and ran for the controller for the lift. He pushed the down button, but nothing happened.

"We need to get a knife and cut him down!" said Billy.

He started looking around for something to use to cut Kevin down while Josh stood there and stared at Kevin. Billy had found a box cutter and approached the body when Josh told him to stop. Billy looked at Josh; the question in his eyes was obvious.

"He's dead. There's nothing we can do for him. Give me a minute to think."

Billy wasn't sure what to do, so he stood there and waited for Josh to gather his thoughts.

"Gather up the wine, the candles and the blanket and get it out of here," said Josh. "We need to protect the club, so none of this can be here. It looks to me like Kevin had an accident. Let's get out of here."

Billy gathered up the wine and the cups. He

grabbed the blanket and rolled it up. He took everything and headed out the door. Josh reached for the controller, unscrewed the back, reconnected the wire to the down button and closed it back up. He wiped off the controller with the bottom of his shirt. He opened the door, wiped off the lock, turned off the lights and headed down the hall. He never noticed the little red flashing light on the shelf in the corner.

He needed to figure out how to tell Melanie but decided that it would not be a problem. Melanie came from a very devout family, and they would never understand her involvement in the club. She was also not the brightest bulb in the room. Sexy as hell, but not real smart. He smiled as he walked up the stairs.

He opened the outside door, and Melanie was standing there in tears. She shook uncontrollably, and he walked over and put his arms around her. She smelled good, and he held her tighter.

"He's gone, Mel. There's nothing we can do for him, but we need to protect you."

She pushed back and looked at him. "What are you talking about?"

"When the cops get here, they're going to find an accidental hanging."

"What are you talking about?" she asked again. She pulled away and headed for the door. Josh grabbed her arm. She turned and glared at him, wiping the tears from her eyes.

"He's our friend, and you left him there, hanging?"

"We had to, Mel. It's gonna be a crime scene. They might think you killed him. How do you think your family will react to that?"

She stared at him in disbelief. "I loved him. I didn't kill him. We can't just leave him there. I came to you for help, and . . ."

"That's what I'm doing. I'm trying to help you."

"Bullshit. You're just trying to protect the club. How could you? He was your friend too."

"Look, Mel. This is the way it is. A dead black man is hanging from a noose in the basement with his pants down around his shoes. Do you want to try to explain that to anyone who asks? You wanted the excitement; you also have to take what comes along. You played a dangerous game, and Kevin paid the price. We made it as safe as possible, but somehow he died, and you were the only one there. Now you need to deal with it."

"I told you the lift didn't work, and we couldn't loosen the rope. It's not my fault."

"Mel. We used the lift earlier tonight. It worked fine." He let his words hang in the air for a minute until the realization of what he was saying crossed Melanie's face.

She stopped him with a wave of her hand. "You think I killed him?" She glared at him in disbelief.

"That's not for me to decide. I don't know what happened, but I know how it looks. And it looks bad for you. If you do what I tell you, we can make this all go away, but you have to trust me."

She calmed down, and he could see the wheels

spinning in her brain. She looked at him. "What do we tell the police?"

"Nothing. We'll let the maintenance guys find him. They'll call the police and tell them they found a hanging victim in their space. Let the cops draw their own conclusion. As long as you stick to the story that you were home all night, they can't touch you. If the cops ask, you hadn't seen him since lunch and he seemed preoccupied with something, but he wouldn't tell you what it was. Now head back to your apartment and go to sleep. Billy and I will take care of everything."

She looked uncertain, but she wiped the tears from her eyes and nodded. She trusted Josh, and she knew he wouldn't do anything to hurt her. She turned and walked away, just as Billy came around the corner. He stopped as she walked by and nodded his head. Melanie didn't acknowledge his presence and continued walking.

"What are we going to do?" he asked Josh.

Josh was quiet for a minute. "Nothing. I need to make a call. As long as Melanie can keep it together, we will be fine."

"Do you think she can hold up if the cops question her, or is she going to be a problem?" asked Billy.

Josh thought for a minute. "I hope she can. If not, we'll cross that bridge when we come to it."

Billy smiled. "Did you have anything to do with this?"

Josh smacked him on the arm and laughed. "Of

course not, man. What kind of monster do you think I am?"

They both laughed, and Billy headed back towards their apartment. Josh was one step closer to getting Melanie back, and that pleased him, but despite his comment to Billy, he was worried that she wouldn't be able to keep it together when the cops came to talk with her. He decided he would talk to Chief Anderson and make sure there was no blowback on him. Josh pulled out his phone, pressed a speed dial button and listened to it ring.

"Sir," said Josh. "We have a problem." He explained the situation, listened for a minute and disconnected the call. This was going to be an interesting weekend.

Chapter Four

Buck Taylor walked through the Denver federal courthouse's door and found a place along the plaza wall to sit for a minute. There was a fall chill in the air, but the sun felt great after spending two days cooped up in the courtroom. He pulled a warm Coke from his backpack and took a long sip. He spotted Jess Gonzales walking out the door and waved her over.

"Jesus, Buck, that defense attorney is a real motherfucker," she said as she walked up and sat on the low wall next to Buck.

That was one of the things Buck liked so much about Jess Gonzales. She was not afraid to tell it as she saw it, and you never knew what to expect. He was also constantly surprised by her appearance. For the most part, Jess wore black tactical boots, black jeans and a black T-shirt that was tight enough to show off some impressive curves. The last time Buck had seen her, her hair was gray, short and spiked.

Today, her appearance was more in keeping with her position. Jess Gonzales was deputy director of the Drug Enforcement Administration (DEA) and was the special agent in charge of a seven-state area. She was based out of Grand Junction, and she and Buck had been friends for more years than either one wanted to remember. Jess wore a black pantsuit with high heels and a burgundy blouse. Her hair was combed back in a cut that made her look like the executive she was.

Jess was only about five foot five, but her body was tight. She prided herself on her less than fifteen percent body fat, and even in her new position, she still managed to work out at the gym for two or three hours a day. She was also an expert in several martial arts disciplines. Jess was one tough woman, and she wasn't someone you would want to mess with.

Jess had been the special agent in charge of the DEA's Grand Junction office a couple of years back when Buck called. She had joined Buck and several other local and federal law enforcement teams on a raid on a Mexican drug cartel warehouse and trucking operation in the small mountain town of Durango, Colorado. The raid resulted in one of the largest drug busts in history and put a serious dent in the cartel's operation. During that investigation, she also saved Buck's life during a shoot-out in his hotel parking lot.

Before heading to Durango, Buck had been involved in a triple murder investigation in Teller County. During a lull in the investigation, he had been sent to Durango while waiting on DNA and ballistics results. The two prime suspects in the triple murder followed Buck to Durango and attempted to ambush him as he walked through his hotel parking lot. Jess had just arrived on the scene as the shooting started, and she killed one of the suspects after Buck killed the other. For her heroism during the shoot-out and her exemplary work on the drug investigation, she was promoted to deputy director. She now oversaw drug-related investigations all over the western United States and Mexico.

Buck considered Jess to be one of his closest friends, and she had been instrumental in helping him get through those terrible days following his wife's death. Lucy had passed away after a five-year battle with metastatic breast cancer, and even though it was something his family had expected, it still hit Buck hard.

If you asked Buck, he would tell you that he fell in love with Lucinda Torres the first day of their senior year in high school. On the other hand, Lucy always told people that Buck stalked her the entire senior year before she gave in, mostly to shut her friends up, and agreed to go to the movies with him. She had always considered him just another jock, another football player who was too full of himself. What she found on that first date was a shy, unassuming gentleman, for lack of a better word, who, it seemed, cared more about pleasing her than bragging about his prowess on the football field. She would tell people it was love at first sight that had taken a year to accomplish. From that day forward, they were inseparable.

During senior year Buck had been approached by several college football scouts who wanted to sign him to play for their schools. Gunnison High School was a small school back in 1978, and Buck and his family were amazed at how many schools had recruited him, but for Buck, college just wasn't in the cards. Buck hated school and spent a lot of time getting himself out of trouble instead of getting an education. When he found something that interested him, he had no problem learning all he could about the subject, but regular schoolwork just bored him. After several long heartfelt discussions, first with Lucy and then with his parents, he had decided to join the army after graduation. Surprisingly, no one was surprised.

Buck spent four years after high school in the army, and by the time his enlistment was up, he had been promoted to First Sergeant. He spent three years of his enlistment in the military police and really took to police work. That was when he decided to apply for a position with the Gunnison County Sheriff's Office. Since he was already well known in the county, he had no trouble getting a job as a deputy. He proposed to Lucy on the night he received the call that he had gotten the position. His life and career were set. He made the most of his time with the Gunnison County Sheriff's Office, eventually becoming the undersheriff in charge of the Investigation Division and coming to the attention of the Colorado Bureau of Investigation.

Buck had worked with the Colorado Bureau of Investigation on several cases inside the county and had earned the respect of the investigators he had worked with. As twilight started to fall on Buck's career, he knew that unless he wanted to go into politics and run for sheriff, he had reached the highest position in the sheriff's office that he could obtain. He loved his job, but when the first offer came in from CBI, he sat down with Lucy and had a long heart-to-heart talk. He'd spent seventeen years in the sheriff's office and had always figured he would retire from that job. They had three children, two in high school and one not far behind, and he was a well-respected member of the community. Did he have the right to disrupt all their lives and pick up and move someplace else and start all over? The kids had friends, Lucy owned a small deli/ice cream parlor, and they had a good life. He could stick it out for another ten years and retire, and they could travel and see the world like they had always planned. Twice he turned down the offer from CBI, although more and more, he felt like he was trapped behind a desk instead of doing what he loved, which was investigating crime.

The final offer came directly from Tom Cole, then-director of the Colorado Bureau of Investigation. Buck always remembered that day. The Denver Broncos had just lost another game, the third one in a row, and his friends had all packed up and headed home, when there was a knock at the front door. Now, anyone who lives in a small community knows that no one ever uses the front door, and no one ever knocks. Who could this possibly be this late on a Sunday evening?

Buck answered the door and was surprised to see the director of the Colorado Bureau of Investigation standing on his front porch. The director smiled and said, "Before you close the door in my face, please listen to my offer."

Buck invited him in, and he and Lucy sat on the couch and listened as the director laid out his plan. He was opening a new branch office in Grand Junction, Colorado, that would house five agents and a small forensic unit. Buck could continue to live in Gunnison but would have to report to the office in Grand Junction twice a month. Otherwise, he would be free to work out of his house. There would be no disruption in his life other than having to spend some time on the road as his investigations warranted. He would work alone, but he would have all the branch office's resources at his disposal.

Before Buck could say a word, Lucy said, "Buck, this is what you have been waiting for, a chance to be a real investigator again. You have to take this." That was one of the things that made him love Lucy every day. She always knew what he was thinking, and she always understood what drove him. She had nailed it this time. Buck looked at the director and replied, "Well, I guess it's settled; looks like you have a new investigator on your team."

That was twenty-four years ago, and Buck had never looked back. He had made the most of those years and was one of the most respected and feared investigators in the state, but all that work couldn't make up for the loss he suffered.

Lucy was diagnosed with metastatic breast cancer following a routine mammogram, and they set off together on their next adventure: the quest to beat the dreaded disease. After a double mastectomy and five years of chemo, they knew their time was drawing to a close when the cancer returned several times to her brain and was no longer controlled by the radiation. They made the decision together to stop all treatments, even though they had always told the family that the decision was Lucy's alone to make. Lucy spent the last couple of months of her life taking care of her small business and spending as much time as she could with her children and grandchildren.

The end came quietly one spring night. Lucy had been sleeping on and off for twenty or so hours a day in the end. The night she died, Buck had been lying in bed next to her, reading a report, when she snuggled into his arms and rested her head on his shoulder. Sometime during the night, Buck had fallen asleep. When he woke up, Lucy was gone, and his world was shattered.

They say that time heals all wounds, but Buck wasn't sure that was the case when you lost your closest friend. And even now, all these years later, he missed her more and more each day.

Buck always thought back to that Sunday morning when the family had gathered for a private ceremony at the little dock along the Gunnison River to scatter Lucy's ashes. Each family member got to say a few words about Lucy, and when they finished and turned to go, they were stunned to see several hundred of their neighbors and friends standing silently behind them in the park. Word had gotten out about their private service, and everyone turned out to pay tribute to Lucy. The affair turned into a huge party, with plenty of food and drinks. Lucy never wanted any kind of service, but Buck figured she would have loved this spontaneous outpouring of love.

Chapter Five

Buck looked at Jess and nodded as he loosened his tie. He seldom wore anything but jeans and T-shirts, but today he wore his gray "court suit," as his granddaughter liked to call it. She always told him he looked "sharp like a pencil." Buck liked the way the suit fit even after all these years.

At six feet tall and one hundred eighty-five pounds, Buck was in the best shape of his life. He looked like he could still play football for the Gunnison High School Cowboys.

He wore his salt-and-pepper hair, which had a lot more salt than pepper in it, longer than the style of the day, and considerably longer than when his wife of thirty-four years, Lucy, had still been alive.

"I thought that lawyer was trying to trip you up," said Jess.

"Yeah," said Buck. "He almost pissed me off a couple of times."

Jess knew that that wasn't going to happen, no matter how hard the lawyer tried. Buck was one of the most level people she had ever met, and he had turned patience into an art form. She recalled hearing a story about Buck getting a murderer to confess just by sitting at the table opposite him and not saying a word for four or five hours. The time got longer or shorter depending on who told the story, but it was always told as a sign of respect.

Jess had decided to stay in the courtroom after her testimony to watch Buck testify. He was the last prosecution witness to testify and had spent the last day and a half being badgered by the defense attorney during cross-examination. Buck had held up fine, and in the end, it was the defense attorney who had lost his cool because he wasn't able to trip Buck up. If he had done his homework, the lawyer would have known that Buck had never lost a case in court because of a problem with his investigation details. Buck was meticulous, and he logged everything in minute detail in his investigation file.

"So, what do you think?" said Jess. "Will they vote to convict?"

Buck laughed. "Come on, Jess. You know juries as well as I do. We never know how they'll vote until it's all over."

They were both testifying in a complicated case from an investigation that had happened a couple of years back. Buck had been called in to investigate a mysterious fire at an exclusive fishing lodge that was under construction. The lodge fire had turned into one of the largest forest fires ever to hit the state of Colorado, and the destruction was massive. During the investigation, Buck had uncovered an illegal drug manufacturing facility in a small town near Meeker, Colorado, started by a fellow named Jack "Red" Muldoon.

Red Muldoon was a former U.S. Army colonel

and had built up a sizable town near the remains of an old town called Buford. Muldoon was a survivalist. He and many like-minded people set up an underground facility for the manufacture and distribution of several drugs, including many counterfeit drugs, most of which came in from China or Pakistan. The unique thing about Muldoon's enterprise was that he used several overnight shipping companies to deliver the drugs to his clients, all over the western United States. He never tried to hide what he was doing and worked right out in the open.

When Buck had first spoken with Jess to see what the DEA had on this guy, he found out that Muldoon wasn't even on their radar. During the investigation, Buck had also uncovered at least two murders committed by Red Muldoon. One was a member of his community, who had inadvertently brought an undercover DEA agent into the town. The other was the DEA agent, who it turned out was running a rogue operation for his own benefit. Jess got involved because another DEA office had asked her to locate their missing agent, supposedly vacationing in Colorado.

The raid on the town was a joint operation between local police, the DEA and CBI investigators and took place in the middle of a raging firestorm. Red Muldoon would have escaped during the firestorm that threatened the town had it not been for Buck, who chased him into the woods near the back of the property during a very welcome thunderstorm. After crashing the ATV he was driving on a rain-slick trail and killing his girlfriend in the accident, Muldoon attacked Buck, who was now pursuing him on foot. In a trench half-full of water, covered in mud, Buck and Muldoon fought, almost to the death. When Buck was finally pulled off Muldoon by Jess Gonzales, Muldoon was down for the count, and Buck spent the next several days recovering from a concussion and a lot of aches and pains.

Through the investigation, Buck was able to link Muldoon to the murders of both men. Thanks to the efforts and threats by the governor of Colorado, Richard J. Kennedy, the state got the first crack at Muldoon, and he was convicted and sentenced to life in prison, without parole, for murder, with special circumstances. Muldoon's lawyers had used every trick in the book to delay his trial in federal court for the murder of the DEA agent, but those delaying tactics had ended just over a week ago. They knew that if Muldoon were convicted of the DEA agent's death, even though the agent had gone rogue, he could face the death penalty. They hoped to avoid this by stringing the case out for as long as possible, but time and the judge's patience had run out.

Defense arguments had started immediately following Buck's testimony, and the judge was hoping to give the case to the jury by the end of the week.

Jess nodded in agreement and looked up at Buck, who appeared lost in another place. She saw the slight scowl on his lips as he panned his eyes around the courtyard. She called his name twice and got no response. She finally tapped on his shoulder.

"Earth to Buck. What's going on?" she asked.

Buck raised his finger to indicate for her to wait a minute as he continued to scan the area.

"Check out the guy next to the van by the curb, my three o'clock," he said.

Jess turned around and looked to where Buck was looking. She spotted the white cargo van parked in the no-parking zone and the guy Buck had seen. He was dressed in a workman's blue uniform and had a bald head and dark sunglasses.

"What about him?" she asked.

Buck was quiet for a minute as he scanned away from the delivery van and focused on another spot in the plaza. He looked at Jess.

"Notice anything odd about his clothes?"

Jess looked again. "Not really. What are you thinking?"

"Look at his neck. He has a skinny neck, yet a large body. He's out of proportion. I think he's wearing armor under his uniform."

Jess looked again and saw what Buck was talking about. "You think he's with the Marshals Service?" she asked. She knew the marshals were responsible for transporting federal prisoners between the courthouse and the federal jail. Maybe they were using an unmarked vehicle due to some threat.

Buck shook his head. "Check your six o'clock and nine o'clock." Jess looked around and spotted two more odd-sized men: one in a business suit and overcoat, and one in jeans and a huge baggy sweatshirt, holding a skateboard.

Buck checked his watch. Court had already closed for the day, and he knew that soon, they would be bringing Muldoon and several other prisoners out the side entrance to the building, which was in the parking garage and as secure as could be. Buck put his Coke in his backpack and placed the backpack in the bushes behind the plaza wall. Jess slid down off the wall. She did the same and reached under her jacket to check that her weapon was there. Force of habit.

"Jess, see if you can find a marshal or someone in charge and let them know that we think they're about to be ambushed."

"What are you going to do?"

In response, Buck unsnapped the thumb break on the holster hooked to his belt and made sure his badge was visible. He started to walk towards the man at the curb when the guy walked around to the driver's door and slid in. He started backing up towards the driveway that led to the garage's secure pickup area and then stomped on the gas and turned down the drive aisle. Buck glanced over and saw Jess running towards the front courthouse doors. He also spotted the other two odd-looking men making their way towards the garage. He picked up the pace.

Chapter Six

Buck reached the corner of the garage just as the gunfire from several automatic weapons started. He ran along the wall and slid between two parked cars. The barrage was relentless. He peeked over one of the cars and spotted two marshals lying on the ground, blood soaking the ground around them. He also noticed two other prisoners who appeared to have been hit. He didn't see Muldoon, and he hoped he wasn't in the transport van because the automatic weapons fire was shredding the van.

The driver of the cargo van slid out of the driver's seat wearing a ballistic covering over his head, as did his two partners who were working their way around some other cars and heading towards the transport van. Two more marshals were positioned behind the van, returning fire with not much luck. Buck could see the bullets hitting the men and staggering them, but the ballistic armor they wore was doing the job.

Buck knew his .45-caliber pistol was no match for the armor at a distance, but he needed to do something. He made his way around the parked cars and came up opposite the van driver. The noise in the garage was deafening as he made his way to the back end of a parked car. He could hear sirens in the distance and people screaming in the plaza, and he knew he needed to act fast. The driver, who was firing from behind the cargo van, ducked down to reload. He was facing away from Buck as he dropped the spent magazine and rammed another one home. He was about to charge the assault rifle when Buck stepped out from behind the parked car. It was just Buck's luck that at that moment, there was suddenly dead silence in the garage. Buck was exposed in the drive aisle when the driver turned and saw him coming up behind him. He raised the assault rifle and turned to face Buck. Buck fired once. The bullet hit the driver in the side of his head, just above his left ear. The bullet didn't penetrate the body armor hood, but at that range, the bullet's concussive force caused the driver to slam into the front fender of the van, where he lay motionless on the ground.

Buck grabbed the rifle off the ground and threw it in the van. He knew he needed to pick up the pace, so he pulled the driver out of the way, slid into the van, and hit the gas.

Shooter number two was stepping around a car that had stopped in the drive aisle and headed for the back corner of the transport van when Buck slammed into him and pinned him against the other car. His weapon flew out of his hands, and he slumped over the hood of the van. Buck dove over the passenger seat and pushed open the passenger door just as the third shooter opened up on the van. Buck scooted behind another parked car and crawled towards the back, away from the cargo van. Bullets were slamming into the cars around him. He crawled on his belly and moved between two parked cars, stood up and fired. The driver, who hadn't seen Buck move, was still firing at his original position. The distraction of Buck firing was enough, and the third shooter swung around to face Buck, who dropped to the ground and got as low as he could.

Buck knew the fight was over when he heard a loud crack from a high-powered rifle. He looked under the cars and saw the third shooter hit the ground, blood leaking from under the ballistic hood. He stood up and, with his gun leading the way, approached the body, just as Jess and two marshals approached. He kicked the automatic rifle away from the body and holstered his gun.

Buck walked back to the shooter he'd hit with the van and checked his pulse. He shook his head and moved on to the driver, who was still lying motionless on the ground. He checked for a pulse and then pulled his handcuffs from his belt and slapped them on the driver.

Sirens filled the garage as police cars and several ambulances arrived. Buck walked around the transport van and spotted Jess giving CPR to one of the marshals. It was obvious that the second marshal on the ground was dead, as were the two other prisoners. Buck looked around for Muldoon.

He spotted two marshals and an EMT in the transport van, and he stepped over to the door. The marshal next to the body looked up and told Buck that Muldoon was dead. Muldoon's body slumped across two seats, and his prison shirt was covered in blood. Buck stepped back to let the marshals out of the van.

Jess, who had been relieved by a paramedic, walked up to Buck and looked in the van. Her burgundy blouse was covered in blood. "Was this a hit or a rescue?" she asked.

"Not sure. Maybe both. They were prepared, whoever they were."

She was about to say something when a tall African American man walked up to them. He wore a ballistic vest that said marshal on the front pocket. He held out his hand. "Agent Taylor, Deputy Director Gonzales. U.S. Marshal Sam Keating." They shook hands all around.

"We're sorry about your men, Marshal," said Buck.

"Thank you. It might have been a lot worse if you two hadn't been here. Can you walk me through what happened?"

Chief Deputy Marshal Harvey Willets walked up and stood next to Marshal Keating. They both listened as Buck and Jess walked them through the attack.

When they finished with their debrief, Keating said, "So you spotted the van and the three attackers outside the courthouse before the attack?"

"It was just a hunch," said Buck. "Something didn't look right about those guys, which was why I asked Jess to find a marshal or a cop. It was just luck I arrived in the garage just as the attack took place. If it's any consolation, your guys went down with the first shots. I don't think they saw it coming."

Jess nodded her head in agreement. They all stepped aside as the EMTs rolled a gurney past and loaded the wounded marshal into the waiting ambulance.

Buck looked at Keating. "Did you guys have any idea that this attack was a possibility? These guys were well prepared, and . . ." Buck hesitated.

"What is it, Agent Taylor?" asked Keating.

"Well, I was thinking they had to have someone inside the building to alert them to Muldoon's movements; otherwise, how would they know when he was being brought out? Their timing was to the second. They moved off the plaza and into the garage moments before Muldoon came out. Had to be coordinated."

"The only people allowed in the holding area are marshals. If they had inside help, we will find out who that was and deal with them," said Keating.

Keating and Willets walked off to speak to the other marshals who had been involved. Jess looked at Buck. "You're gonna need a new suit, Buck," she said.

Buck looked down and noticed his suit pants were ripped to shreds from crawling around the cars. His jacket was stained, and his white shirt had blood and grease stains all over the front. He nodded his head. "Maybe I can get my granddaughter to go with me, and she can pick out my next 'court suit.'" They both laughed and walked towards the plaza. They had left their backpacks in the shrubs where they had been standing, and they hoped everything would still be there.

They had just reached the plaza wall when they spotted Kevin Jackson passing through the crime scene tape that had been set up around the front of the courthouse. He headed towards them.

Kevin Jackson was the director of the Colorado Bureau of Investigation and Buck's boss. He had been the youngest person ever appointed to head up the CBI when Governor Richard J. Kennedy tapped him to run the agency. He'd spent the early part of his career on the Colorado Springs Police Department's administrative side and was highly regarded by the law enforcement community. He was not only an effective manager but a seasoned investigator in his own right. Buck held the man in high regard.

"Buck, Jess, good to see you again. You guys okay?" he asked. He looked at Buck's torn suit and Jess's bloody blouse. "You look like you've been through a war."

Buck pulled his even warmer Coke out of his backpack, and Jess grabbed a bottle of water out of hers. They filled him in on what had happened. Director Jackson didn't say a word until they both stopped speaking.

"Good thing you guys were here. It could've been a lot worse. Are you certain they were after Muldoon and not one of the other prisoners?"

Buck thought for a minute. "These were survivalists or white supremacists. It's possible they were here for one of the other guys, but either way, all three prisoners are dead."

"I'll bet Keating wasn't happy when you suggested that this was an inside job. You let me know if you get any blowback, and I'll deal with it."

"It's just a shame," said Jess, "that we won't get to see Muldoon's face when the guilty verdict was read. I was looking forward to that."

They talked for a few more minutes until Director Jackson looked at his watch. "I need to head for a meeting. You guys need anything, let me know. I'm glad you're both okay."

Director Jackson walked off and stopped to have a few words with Marshal Keating, who was standing by the garage entrance. Buck and Jess grabbed their backpacks, and they hugged for a minute.

"You need to talk, I'm here for one more night," said Buck.

"Thanks, but I'm gonna head back to Grand Junction and hug my son. You need anything, let me know."

She started to walk off, stopped and turned towards Buck. "You know, I should stop hanging out with you. It seems like every time we're together, someone is shooting at us. You might be bad for my health." She laughed and headed towards the garage. Buck laughed and started walking towards his hotel. What he needed now were a shower and a good night's sleep.

Chapter Seven

The shower helped, but there wasn't going to be a good night's sleep. He had just laid on the bed when his phone rang. It was his son Jason. Earlier, Buck had called and left a message canceling dinner with Jason and his family at their home in Boulder. He hated to do it. He hadn't seen the family in a while and was looking forward to the time with his grandkids. But he was beat. He would make it up to them the next time he got to Denver. Jason was his youngest son and was a partner in an architectural firm. He was a devout Catholic, which he got from his mom. He was also the one member of the family that took everything to heart, and he worried about Buck and his job.

Buck told him about the shoot-out. He was sure it would make the local news programs, and he wanted to get ahead of it. Jason asked a few questions, told his dad he understood about dinner and told him he would call him tomorrow.

After Buck hung up, his phone rang again. Buck looked at the number on the phone and smiled. "Hey, kiddo. What's going on?"

"Dad, are you all right? The news said you were involved in a shoot-out at the federal courthouse in Denver."

"That's correct, Cass. Jess Gonzales and I helped

out some marshals." He told her about the trial and the shoot-out. He tried to avoid the fact that several people had died, but the news report was in-depth.

Cassandra, or Cassie to everyone she knew, was Buck's middle child, and she was every bit a middle child. In high school, she'd played soccer, ran track and played volleyball. She lettered in all three sports. She was also the one who got in trouble for violating curfew, drinking and getting into whatever other mischief she could find. Buck was surprised when she was accepted to the University of Arizona with a full volleyball scholarship. He was even more surprised when she was accepted into law school. Cassie had never been one for regimented education.

Several years ago, she'd suddenly dropped out of law school, and her career path took a different track. She joined the Forest Service and was now working as a wildland firefighter with the Helena Hotshots, one of the country's elite firefighting teams, based out of Helena, Montana.

Buck had not been surprised by any of this. He never saw her sitting behind a desk as a lawyer. She loved the outdoors, and she was as tough as they come. Lucy hadn't been pleased that she quit school without any discussion, and she always worried whenever Cassie was called out on a fire, but she also knew her daughter, and if this was where she was happy, then so was her mom.

Ever since Lucy died, Cassie had been Buck's sounding board, the way Lucy used to be. Another voice and another viewpoint to help him see a case more clearly.

"So, you and Jess again?" she said, more as a statement than a question. "Did it ever occur to you that maybe you guys are the problem?"

Buck laughed. "I'm glad in situations like today that Jess has my back and I have hers."

"Okay, Dad. You win." They talked for a few minutes about the latest wildland fire that Cassie and her team had been assigned to, and they promised to get together soon. Buck hung up and was about to set his phone down when it rang again. He looked at the number and laughed.

"Hey, Bax. What's up?"

"What the fuck, Buck? We let you out of sight for a couple of days, and you get into trouble." She laughed.

CBI Agent Ashley Baxter worked with Buck on many interesting cases, in between working on her own cases. At thirty years old, she was one of the youngest agents in the Grand Junction Field Office, and she valued the time she got to spend with Buck because she learned so much about running an investigation. Bax was also a whiz at doing deep background searches—a talent Buck did not share—so he relied on Bax to help him out. They worked well as a team and had found themselves collaborating more and more as the years rolled by.

"What can I tell you, Bax. My daughter thinks Jess Gonzales and I draw trouble."

"I heard Muldoon was killed in the fight."

"Yeah," said Buck. "Along with two other

prisoners and a deputy marshal. The other marshal is in the hospital in critical condition. These guys had this planned to the second."

"I spoke with the director earlier. He said you think they had inside help. Any thoughts?"

Buck thought for a minute. "No other way it could have gone down. At least we don't have to mess with it. It's in the marshals' hands."

"What are you gonna do?" she asked.

"Not a thing. Tomorrow I'm heading home and getting back to work."

They talked about a couple of open cases they were working on, and then Bax signed off. Buck took a sip from the bottle of Coke that was on the table and laid his head on the pillow. He was just about asleep when the phone rang again. He sat up, looked at his watch and then at the number.

"Yes, sir?"

"Buck, I hate to do this to you, but I need you to attend a meeting. Now," said Director Jackson.

"What's going on, sir?"

"This is a bit of a sticky situation, and I'd rather wait till you're here to discuss it." He gave Buck the address of another downtown Denver hotel and hung up.

Buck got dressed, clipped his badge and gun to his belt and grabbed his backpack and laptop off the table. He closed the door and headed for what, he had no idea.

Chapter Eight

The elevator opened on the tenth floor of a lovely boutique hotel a few blocks from the state capitol. Buck stepped through the door and was greeted by Director Jackson.

"Sorry about this, Buck. This couldn't wait."

"Can you tell me what this is about, sir?" asked Buck.

"I hate to sound cryptic, but this will all be revealed in a moment. Follow me."

The director knocked on a door at the end of the hallway, and Buck was surprised when Colorado Governor Richard J. Kennedy opened the door.

Governor Richard J. Kennedy—who was, in fact, one of "those" Kennedys—had won the election for governor three years before by one of the largest margins in the history of the Colorado governor's race. Despite the fact he was a multimillionaire businessman, regular people loved him. During those three years, Buck had been instrumental in closing several high-profile investigations that made the governor look good, and the governor relied on Buck for his competence and discretion. He also valued the fact that Buck was completely apolitical. He treated everyone the same, whether you were the governor or the janitor at the state capitol, and he knew Buck would never get involved in any kind of political maneuver.

"Buck, good to see you. Please come in." The governor stepped aside so Buck could enter one of the most lavish hotel living rooms he had ever seen. He gazed around the room as he shook the governor's hand and stepped inside, focusing on the tall African American man who was standing by the window overlooking the capitol.

"Nice to see you as well, Governor."

The governor could see the confusion and surprise on Buck's face. He rarely met with Buck face-to-face, choosing instead to work through Director Jackson. The man by the window turned and faced Buck and walked across the room, setting his glass of light brown liquid on the table as he passed.

"Buck Taylor," said the governor. "Please meet Marcus Ducette. Marcus, CBI Agent Buck Taylor."

Marcus Ducette held out his hand as he approached. "Agent Taylor pleased to meet you. The governor and Director Jackson speak very highly of you and your team. Please come in."

They all took seats—the governor and Marcus Ducette on the couch and Buck in one of the opposite chairs. Director Jackson stood with his back to a magnificent bar.

"Governor, I hate to be forward, but may I ask what this is all about?" asked Buck.

The governor looked at Buck, picked up a glass off the end table, took a sip and set the glass down.

"Buck. Mr. Ducette and his wife are in town to

pick up the remains of their son, Kevin," said the governor. "Their son was twenty-three years old, a student at Copper Canyon College, in Copper Creek, CO and the Ducettes are concerned that they are not getting the full picture of his death." The governor yielded to Marcus Ducette.

"Agent Taylor, we—my wife and I—believe our son was murdered. A week ago, we received a call from his college saying that Kevin had committed suicide. This was devastating for us. Kevin is our only child, and no parent ever wants to hear words like that. We didn't know what to think. In all the calls to his mother and myself, there was never a hint of depression or sadness. Just the opposite. He was excited to be graduating in the spring and marrying his high school sweetheart back home."

Marcus Ducette stopped for a minute and took a sip from his glass. Buck had learned over the years never to interrupt someone while they were speaking. He would hold his questions till the end.

"We were told his remains were being taken to a funeral parlor in Denver, and we made arrangements to fly out here this morning to pick him up and take him home. We have a private jet waiting at the airport."

"When we arrived this afternoon, we went straight to the funeral home. We were stunned when instead of a coffin containing my son's remains, we were handed a small urn containing his ashes. My wife was so distraught that she passed out on the floor in the mortuary. You need to understand, Agent Taylor, we are devout Catholics. We do not believe in cremation and were hoping to bury our son in the family cemetery, which is consecrated ground."

Marcus Ducette wiped the tears from his eyes and took another sip from his glass. "Once the doctor left, having given my wife a sedative, I called the college. I was told by the headmaster that Kevin was cremated per his wishes and that I would need to speak with the chief of police. I spoke with a man by the name of Anderson, who was surly and turned me over to a Detective Cummings. He said they found a last will and testament in his room that requested he be immediately cremated upon his death. He said they also found a suicide note on his laptop.

"There is no way that could be. Kevin already had a will back in Ducette, Texas, and he knew his mother would never accept cremation. The other odd thing is that we never received his cell phone or laptop in the box sent with the ashes. The police have been no help."

Marcus Ducette stopped talking and slumped back on the couch, exhausted. Director Jackson stepped forward and handed Buck a manila envelope. He undid the catch on the back and slid out the picture that was enclosed. He stared at it for a minute and then looked at the director and the governor.

"Mr. Ducette," said the governor, "received this on his private email account this afternoon after they had arrived in Colorado. After seeing the picture, he called me."

Buck looked at the picture again. It was dark around the edges but clearly showed a young black male hanging from what appeared to be some kind of lift. Buck slid the picture back into the envelope. He sat quietly for a minute before speaking.

"Mr. Ducette, your son was in college, which means you probably haven't seen him lately. How can you be certain that something hadn't changed in his life recently that might cause him to take his own life?"

The door to the bedroom behind them opened, and a tall, thin African American woman stepped out of the room. Unlike her husband, who was dressed in jeans and a flannel shirt, Mary Ducette wore a perfectly tailored gray dress. Her hair was done up with care, and she looked like she was dressed for an evening out. What she couldn't hide were the tearstains on her face. She held her head proudly as she stepped into the room.

The men all stood, and Marcus Ducette stepped over to his wife. "Mary, the doctor said you needed to rest."

She silenced him by placing her finger against his lips, then walked over and shook Buck's hand. She sat on the couch and dabbed away tears with a tiny white handkerchief.

"I needed to speak with Agent Taylor myself." She looked at Buck. "Agent Taylor. I know my son. We were closer than two people could ever be. He knew how we felt about suicide, and he most definitely would not have asked to be cremated. That goes against all we hold dear. He also would not have hanged himself. Our family grew and prospered after the Civil War and the freeing of the slaves, but we were not removed from that time when lynching was the way to deal with black people. Several family members had met their demise under those same circumstances, and Kevin found that portion of our history abominable. I believe my son was murdered. For what reason, I have no idea, but it is important to my husband and me to learn the truth."

The Ducettes stood, and Marcus led his wife back towards the bedroom. Buck looked first at the governor and then at Director Jackson.

"They are distraught," he said. "But what are they expecting from us?"

The governor spoke first. "Buck, I understand your hesitancy. They are distraught parents who do not want to believe that their son killed himself. I get that. I need to look at this from a political standpoint. We are in a climate of civil unrest in this country right now, and as you well know, Colorado is not immune from the violence. I fear that the picture you have in your hand will find its way to the internet, and all hell will break loose. Headlines about a young black man being lynched in Colorado will not do anyone any good. You are here, Buck, because as the governor of Colorado, I need to know if that young man took his own life, as the police and his school seem to think, or if he is the victim of a terrible hate crime."

Buck nodded just as Marcus Ducette entered the

room. Buck turned to face him. The governor and Director Jackson knew what was coming.

"Mr. Ducette, you and your wife have my deepest condolences for your loss. I know about the loss of a loved one, and it is never easy. We will look into your son's death to the best of our ability, but I need you to understand. When we investigate a crime, we leave no stone unturned. We will take this investigation in whatever direction the evidence leads us. My team and I will ask the hard questions, some of which may make you and your family and friends uncomfortable. We will be direct when required and discreet when we can be, but rest assured, we will have a better understanding of the events that led to your son's death when we are finished. You may not like what we find, but what we find will be the truth."

Marcus held out his hand, and Buck shook it. "Agent Taylor, based on what the governor and Director Jackson have told me about you and your team, I would expect nothing less. We are prepared for whatever you find. And thank you."

The governor and Director Jackson shook hands with Marcus Ducette, and they all left the room. They were silent during the ride down in the elevator. They stepped into the cool night air. Director Jackson told Buck he would send him everything they could find about this case so far, and he thanked him for his help. The governor remained behind after Director Jackson left.

"Buck. I heard about the shoot-out earlier today, and I am truly thankful that you survived unscathed. I am proud of the way you handled yourself." He walked towards his car, his state trooper escort standing by the open door. He turned before entering the car. "This one is important, Buck. We need to know the truth, and time is not on our side. You need anything, do not hesitate to call."

Buck watched as the governor's car drove away. He pulled out his phone and speed-dialed a number.

Chapter Nine

Buck spent most of the day telling and retelling his recollection of the events that had unfolded in the garage. The Denver Police Department bagged up his torn suit, and the forensic department test-fired his pistol several times, each time bagging up the bullet in an evidence bag. It was important to confirm his role in the shootings. He had fired several times, as had all the participants on the scene, and it was critical to determine where each bullet had stopped.

Buck was happy to cooperate, but he was in a hurry to get moving. He would not have time to return home to Gunnison, so he had called his oldest son, David, to let him know what was going on and that he would be away from the house a few more days. David and his wife, Judy, lived around the corner from Buck, and they kept an eye on the house while he was away.

David had heard the reports of the shoot-out on the news during his shift, and Buck was able to reach him just as he was heading home. David was a sergeant with the Gunnison Police Department and was the night shift supervisor, a shift he had spent many years on as a patrol officer.

David was a shade over six foot and a few pounds heavier than his father, but he looked exactly like Buck had when he was David's age. It was almost scary how much they resembled each other. He also moved with the ease of a young man, which made Buck jealous at times.

They talked for a few minutes, and Buck filled David in on the events of the day before. Buck described the shoot-out in precise detail, and when he was finished, he asked David not to reveal too much about the shoot-out to Judy or his kids. Buck told him that he would be heading to Copper Creek later that day and would call once he was settled. David wished him good luck, and they hung up.

Buck's phone rang just as he got back to his state-issued Jeep Grand Cherokee, so he slid into the driver's seat and answered.

"Hey, Bax. Whatcha got?"

"First, how are you doing?" she asked. He smiled. He wondered some days if Bax and his daughter, Cassie, ever spoke and discussed how best to take care of him in his "old age." Since Lucy had passed away, it seemed like he had a lot more people looking out for his well-being, and even though he never said anything, he appreciated Bax's concern. He knew she looked up to him, and he treated her like a daughter and not just a colleague. They worked well together, and they both knew that the other would have their back.

"I'm good. Spent the morning retelling my story, but I think everything is good. Marshals Service and the FBI are working jointly with Denver PD, and they have everything in hand."

"Any idea who those guys were?" she asked.

"If they know, they aren't sharing, but you know the FBI. That's the way they operate."

"Okay," she said. "I am sending a file to your email with everything I could find on the Ducette family. There is a lot of information. They appear to be a very public family back in Texas. The town they live in is named after them. I also included some information on the college their son was attending. That was a little tougher to do, but I got what I could. I'm still working through some stuff, and I will send you what I have later tonight."

"Did you happen to do any background on Copper Creek? I didn't even know this town existed until last night."

"I will send you what I found. Where are you staying?" she asked.

"I spoke with Marty Womack earlier. He said he'd have a place for me when I get there later. Gonna meet him and his dad for dinner in Walden. I'll text you the name of the hotel when I get there."

"Okay. You need anything else, let me know. Paul is wrapping up the trial on his fraud case, so we are both available if you need us."

"Thanks, Bax. We'll talk later."

Buck hung up and placed his phone in the dashboard cradle. He pulled out of the parking garage and headed for I-70. He had a long drive ahead of him, and he wanted to avoid the afternoon traffic. That was the one thing he hated about Denver, and he was grateful that he very rarely had to come into the city for a meeting. He turned off I-25 and merged onto I-70, and he headed west.

He had decided to go over Berthoud Pass and go through Winter Park and Granby. He could catch Highway 125 and take that north to Jackson County. This would be his first case in Jackson County, but he was pleased he would be able to meet up with some old friends who lived up that way. He leaned back in his seat, turned on the radio and hit the gas.

Chapter Ten

Buck entered the small town of Walden, pulled off Highway 125 and pulled into the Nugget Saloon parking lot. He checked his watch. He had made good time. He pulled into the space next to the Jackson County Sheriff's Department SUV and shut off his Jeep. He slid out, stretched and took a deep breath. He was back in the mountains after spending four days breathing bad air in Denver, and he appreciated the clear air and the smell of pine trees. He pulled on his Carhartt ranch jacket against the chill that accompanied the setting sun and stepped up to the door.

The incredible variety of smells hit him as he opened the door, and he realized how hungry he was. He stepped inside, looked around and spotted his friends sitting at the round table in the corner. The rustic walls, long counter and vinyl-covered chairs made him feel right at home and reminded him of all the other little restaurants he had eaten at over the thirty-seven years he had been doing his job. When he eventually retired, this would be one of the things he would miss the most.

His thoughts were interrupted by the tiny woman in the red apron. "Grab a seat anywhere you want. I'll be right with ya," she said.

Buck nodded and headed towards the corner

table. Marty Womack stood up and waited for Buck to approach. Marty was in his early forties, stood about five foot ten and had dark curly hair. He stretched out his hand as Buck reached the table. "Buck, great to see ya," he said. Marty was dressed in his "class A" uniform: tan pants, dark brown shirt and tie.

Buck nodded. "Nice to see you, Marty, but you didn't have to dress up for the occasion." Marty laughed. Buck turned and faced the other man at the table and reached out his hand. Charlie Womack grabbed his hand. He still had a hell of a grip for someone in his eighties, and he looked at Buck through his shiny eyes and smiled.

"Charlie, you look good; how ya been?"

"Can't complain, Buck. No one would listen anyway." He laughed a hearty laugh. Charlie wore an old brown suit and tie and a brown Stetson. Buck assumed it was to cover his thinning hair. He had a small badge-shaped pin attached to the collar of his suit jacket. Charlie had been the sheriff in Jackson County for some forty years before retiring ten years ago and turning over the reins to his son, Marty.

Buck had first met Charlie Womack at a sheriff's conference twenty-four years before, when he was serving as the undersheriff in Gunnison County. They'd hit it off right away and spent the better part of the night swapping stories of their time in law enforcement. He'd met Marty while working with CBI, but not during an investigation. Marty had stopped by the Grand Junction CBI office to pick up some forensic evidence CBI had examined, and he mentioned to the forensic tech that he was looking for someplace near Grand Junction to do a little fly fishing.

Buck was an avid fly fisherman, and he always had his gear in the back of his Jeep, since you never know where you might be when a river or stream calls your name. The tech introduced Marty to Buck, who fortunately was in the office, which was rare. They spent several hours fishing some streams on the Grand Mesa that Buck knew about and then enjoyed a nice dinner before Marty needed to hit the road.

Buck grabbed a chair and sat down at the table. They spent a few minutes catching up, and the tiny woman in the red apron walked up to the table and handed them menus. Marty introduced Rose McGovern to Buck, and Buck commented about how much he felt at home in restaurants like hers. During the short conversation, he found out that Rose had owned the Nugget since 1957, when she and her husband had settled in the valley, looking for some peace and solitude.

Buck looked over the menu and ordered the meat loaf, as did Marty and Charlie. Rose stepped away to get their drinks and returned a minute later with a Coke for Buck and coffee for Marty and Charlie. When Rose left to get their food started, Buck asked, "So, why the dress uniform and suit?"

"Funeral," said Charlie. "Young deputy in Carbon County was killed last week. Not that far over the border. They held his funeral today, so we represented the county. Sad times, Buck. Kid left a young wife and two small kids. So tragic." Carbon County, Wyoming, sat just across the border from Jackson County, Colorado. Buck had spent some time over the years fishing the North Platte River in Carbon County. The fishing was always outstanding.

"Was it an accident?" Buck asked. He knew the roads in this part of the state were dangerous considering the size of the moose herd that inhabited the area. He'd heard too many reports over the years of car–moose collisions, which didn't end well for either party.

Marty looked up from the table. "Murdered. Took two days to find the car, which was in the river. He was recently assigned to that area. He was previously assigned farther north, up near Riverside."

"Any forensics?" Buck asked.

"No," said Marty. "Strange case though. His patrol radio had been pulled out of the car, his cell phone and laptop were missing, and whoever killed him had taken his body camera and the dash cam from the patrol car. Problem is, the cameras were old school, and they weren't connected to cloud storage, so no footage of the shooting. One shot, behind his left ear."

"Sounds like an execution," said Buck.

"Damn straight," said Charlie. "We find that sum bitch before they do, and he's gonna pay."

Marty looked cross-eyed at Charlie, and he slunk back into the seat. Rose brought their plates and set them on the table. Buck looked at the pile of food and wondered if this was the standard meal or if they were getting a little extra. He glanced around and saw several hunters grab a table near the door. An elderly couple had taken seats at the counter. Rose was getting busy, and she looked thrilled.

They dug into their meals and continued with small talk until they were finished, and Rose removed their plates and refilled their drinks.

"So, you're looking into that suicide up at the college, huh?" said Charlie. "You think it might be something more than a suicide?"

Buck leaned into the table to keep his voice from traveling to the other tables in the now-busy restaurant.

"Don't rightly know. There's some oddities about the case I need to look into."

"Your folks worried that it might be a hate crime?" asked Marty.

"Why would you think that?" asked Buck.

"Black kid, straight-A student, found hanging in a basement. That was my first thought when I heard about it."

"You have any involvement in the investigation, such as it was?" asked Buck.

"Nah. We stay out of Copper Creek," said Marty.

Buck looked at him sideways. "But your coroner was involved, right?"

Marty looked at his dad. Charlie picked up the conversation. "We're not allowed in Copper Creek. Never have been—some kind of arrangement from back in the eighteen hundreds. The city may be in

Jackson County, but they are autonomous. We don't get any taxes from them, and they have their own police and fire departments. Don't use any county services."

Buck looked stunned. He had never heard of such an arrangement. "So, you never go to their aid?"

Marty laughed, as did Charlie. "Shit, Buck," said Charlie. "We have three deputies in this county and a handful of reserve deputies. They have a twenty-five-man police department and a beautiful new state-of-the-art justice center. They don't need our help."

"Besides," said Marty. "We're not allowed. Orders from the county commissioners, two of whom live in Copper Creek. That city is rolling in money, and the chief of police, Anderson, keeps a tight lid on everything that happens there."

They talked for a few more minutes, then Marty handed Buck a piece of paper with the name of a small B and B in Copper Creek. Buck read the paper.

"Victoria James owns the place. She'll take good care of you while you're here. Good luck, and if you need anything, don't hesitate to ask."

They all stood and shook hands. Marty left first, and as Charlie walked past Buck, he leaned in. "Watch your ass. That's a strange town. I got your back. Marty may not be allowed in town, but they can't stop this old man." He winked his left eye and headed for the door.

Buck was confused by what he'd heard, and by

what Charlie said as he was leaving. He had been expecting a simple investigation. Now he wondered what he would find when he got to Copper Creek. He left a nice tip on the table, snugged into his coat and headed for his car.

Chapter Eleven

"Do you have any idea why he's here?"

"No, sir. All we know is that he had dinner in Walden with the sheriff and his old man. They spent a lot of time talking, but we didn't have time to get anyone inside to overhear the conversation."

There was silence around the table. No one dared to interfere. The man took a couple of bites of his dinner and took a sip of red wine. "Do you think someone knows?"

"Maybe we should postpone Saturday night until we know for sure?"

He looked up from his plate. "Are you out of your fucking mind? We are sold out. Canceling now will ruin my reputation, and that could cost us millions. Besides, Saturday night is only one part. What about the rest? We have a schedule to meet, and our friends are not interested in our problems, just results. No. You need to deal with this guy. Find out why he is here and get rid of him as fast as he arrived. The last thing we need is CBI crawling around town asking questions."

"If we get rid of him, it could bring a lot of heat down on us. He's a state cop, for Christ's sake."

The man put down his fork and looked over the top of his glasses. "You can't possibly be that fuckin' stupid? I don't want him dead, you idiot.

I want him gone. I want you to get him to leave town."

The others around the table looked at the Chief of Police like he had two heads. He stood up and pushed the chair back from the table. "Sorry, sir. I'm just concerned. CBI usually shows up when they're requested. We did not request they send someone, especially him. I'll make sure he gets whatever he needs and leaves town as quick as I can."

He left the table, passed through the huge double doors, and was let out of the entrance by one of the servers. The others at the table looked at the man. The concern on their faces was evident.

A tall, thin man with a full head of white hair and white mustache was the first to speak. "He's right, you know. We knew this day would come eventually. CBI showing up on our doorstep uninvited can only mean trouble."

The man took his glasses off and looked around the table. He tented his fingers as if in quiet contemplation. "You are correct. But. We have been doing this a long time, and no one has gotten close. Before we panic, let's see what this is all about. Who knows. It could be something in the county that doesn't affect us at all. In the meantime, it's business as usual, and if we find we need to deal with the cop, I will make sure that gets taken care of."

He had spoken, and there was nothing left to be said. They finished their dinners and drinks, shook hands all around and left. All but one. The man poured them both a brandy, and they stepped into his private study. The fire in the massive fireplace gave the room a warm glow, the deep rich tones of the wood wall paneling highlighted by the flames. The deep cushions of the leather high-back chairs engulfed them as they sat by the fire, and for a minute, neither spoke.

The man looked at his guest. "You have something on your mind. Out with it."

"I'm as concerned as the others about this state cop showing up. This guy has a reputation, and I'm concerned that Chief Anderson is not up to the task. Do you think this could be about the deputy? That was stupid and sloppy."

The man thought for a minute, sipping his brandy. "You're right. It was stupid and sloppy, but it happened, and there's already a plan in place to deal with it. You worry about production. I'll deal with Chief Anderson if the time comes. In the meantime, let's keep a close eye on the state cop. I don't want this getting out of hand."

The man's guest swallowed the last of his brandy and left him sitting in the study. He hated when his people started to worry. He would need to think through all of the most recent events and make sure he had a clean way out.

Chapter Twelve

Buck parked his Jeep in one of the numerous visitor's parking spaces and looked up at the justice center. He was impressed. The building was a modern and rustic mix with large wood columns and beams and flat boxlike structures. It looked like something that could have been designed by Frank Lloyd Wright. He slid out of the Jeep and grabbed his backpack. He took a moment to look down the main street. It was a pretty town, clean and neat, almost picture-postcard perfect. He also noticed the CCTV cameras that seemed to be on every light pole. Unusual for a small mountain town.

Buck recalled the information Bax had emailed him. Copper Creek, Colorado, was founded in the late 1880s by the Martelli family, who still owned significant real estate holdings in the area. At that time, the biggest asset of the town, other than the mining and forestry industries, was the Elizabeth Martelli School for Girls. An interesting name. It made it sound like a great educational opportunity for young women of the time, which couldn't be further from the truth. The slang term used in the early 1900s would have been a school for wayward girls.

The Martelli School was where single or underage pregnant girls were sent by their wealthy families so as not to be an embarrassment. The girls would spend several months during their pregnancy at the school, continuing their education and working full time to cover the costs. Once the baby was delivered, the girls would return to their families, and the baby would be put up for adoption by the school. The cost for this discreet service would have been considered outrageous by the standards of the time. Still, it eliminated those embarrassing questions that might arise from friends, neighbors, clergy or, most importantly, business partners.

As the town grew up, it turned from mining and forestry to tourism. The newly founded Rocky Mountain National Park sat up against the town's southern border. The town had been unsuccessful at getting a primary entrance into the park, despite huge amounts of money donated to various political campaigns, but there were several trails and backcountry camping areas that were accessible from the town.

Through this period, the Martelli School continued to prosper and in the early thirties became the Martelli Normal School and started offering college classes to those same wealthy families it had helped through the years. It still took care of those wayward young women, but now in a college environment. By the 1970s, Copper Canyon College was one of the premier private colleges in the United States, with a price tag to match. If there were a step above Ivy League, Copper Canyon would fall into that category. The college was focused on education and medical research, having built an incredible and highly regarded research hospital, offering various medical degrees. Still, most of the students were placed there by their parents to earn business degrees, so they would one day take over the family business.

The alumni were an impressive and generous group, and it was rumored that it cost upwards of a quarter million dollars a semester to live and study at the college. A small college by every standard, but with only twenty-five hundred students, it was considered very exclusive and difficult to get into, which was why these alumni families donated vast amounts of money every year to ensure a place for their children. The town of forty-five hundred grew up around the college and, for the most part, survived due to the college. Mining still went on in the area, but tourism and the college were the big players in town.

Buck walked up to the massive bronze doors at the entrance to the justice center and entered a marble lobby befitting a luxury hotel rather than a police department. He stepped up to the woman seated at the reception counter, presented his ID and asked to speak with the chief of police. She picked up the phone, spoke for a moment and pointed him towards a seating area consisting of several leather couches. Buck took a seat and waited. And waited.

Buck was patient and spent the time reviewing the sparse information he had received on the case. He checked his watch several times and wondered if this was how the entire investigation would go.

He was about to approach the reception counter, to remind the woman that he was still waiting, when a door to the side of the lobby opened, and a policewoman stepped into the lobby and called his name.

The young woman introduced herself as Officer Tracy Terrell and apologized for the wait. She told him that Chief Anderson had been tied up on a phone call. Buck noticed the spit-shined shoes, utility belt and holster, and the sharp creases in her uniform pants and shirt. She appeared to be one well put-together police officer. He followed her down a long hall, past several small offices and through an open bullpen area with conference rooms along the outside walls. She stepped up to a beautiful wooden door, knocked sharply and opened the door.

"Agent Taylor, sir." She stepped aside to allow Buck to pass and closed the door after he entered.

In the thirty-seven years Buck had been in law enforcement, he had seen the inside of more offices than he cared to remember, from offices the size of closets to offices that were old and had seen better days, but he was not prepared for what he saw as he looked around this office.

The office was huge, by any standard. More befitting a corporate CEO than a chief of police. The walls were covered in dark wood paneling, and there was a huge window that looked straight down the main street through town. Chief Paul Anderson sat behind a massive wood desk that was devoid of the typical police department clutter. The only things on the desk were a computer monitor and keyboard.

Buck couldn't see much of Chief Anderson, with the paper he was reading blocking his face, but he knew from Bax's research that Chief Anderson was five foot ten, was slightly overweight at two hundred pounds and had been the police chief in Copper Creek for about eight years. Buck noticed the two high-backed leather guest chairs opposite the desk, but Chief Anderson never indicated for him to take a seat, so he stood near the door and waited.

Without looking up from the paper he was reading, Chief Anderson said, "CBI Agent Buck Taylor. Is it customary at the Colorado Bureau of Investigation to present yourself to local law enforcement at your earliest convenience?"

Buck was caught a little off guard. "Yes, it is, which is why I am here now."

Chief Anderson lowered the paper and placed it at the center of his desk. He studied Buck for a minute. "You had no problem checking in with Sheriff Womack last night, but you waited until today to introduce yourself to me. Why is that, Agent Taylor?"

Buck was surprised by the comment. He wondered how Chief Anderson knew he had met with the sheriff.

"I had dinner last night with two old friends. By the time I checked in to the B and B, it was late, so I arrived here first thing this morning. Is that a problem, Chief?"

Chief Anderson picked up the paper off his desk and put his reading glasses back on.

"You have a very impressive resume and have been involved in some big cases during your career." He looked up from the paper and removed his reading glasses again.

"Why are you here, Agent Taylor?"

Buck stayed near the door since there had still been no invitation to venture farther into the room.

"I have been asked to look into the death of one of the students at the college, a possible suicide victim. He was a young man named Kevin Ducette, and his family is not convinced his death was a suicide."

Chief Anderson lowered the paper. His mind was racing. He had never even considered that this was about the black kid found dead in the gallows. He almost let out a sigh of relief, but he needed to maintain his composure. Buck noticed the signs of relief that passed quickly across Chief Anderson's face, and he wondered to himself what that was all about.

"Do you often take on investigations from grieving parents? If I remember correctly, the young man was found hanged, and a suicide note was found on his computer. What is there to investigate?"

"Chief Anderson, I go where I'm told to go and investigate what I'm told to investigate. I don't make those decisions. I was told the family is concerned. Who they voiced that concern to, I have no idea. I was told to be here, and here I am." Buck decided to continue. "What I would like to do is take a look at the young man's personal effects, speak with some of his classmates and review any evidence you have. If I could use a desk or a conference room for a couple of days, I will be out of your hair as fast as possible."

Chief Anderson smiled. "I'm sorry, Agent Taylor. You've caught us at a bad time. We are about to begin a major remodeling project, and all the desks have been assigned to my officers. Had I known you were coming; I could have made some arrangements. Unfortunately, the conference rooms are part of that renovation. Since I am certain you won't be here more than a day at the most, I am certain we can find a chair for you someplace."

He picked up his phone and punched two buttons. "Can you come in here for a minute?" He hung up and looked at Buck. There was a knock at the door, and a young man wearing a suit jacket and tie stepped into the office. "Yes, sir?"

"Agent Taylor here would like to look at the evidence and personal effects of the young man who we found hanged at the school. Please show him what he needs."

He looked at Buck. "Detective Cummings investigated the suicide. He will show you what you need to see." He hesitated a moment. "Agent Taylor. Any materials you might like to remove from the premises will need to be cleared through me, personally, understood? And I expect to be the first to know if you find anything that might cause you to believe this is not a suicide."

He smiled. "Anything the Copper Creek Police Department can do to help you with your investigation, please don't hesitate to ask, and have a nice day."

Buck turned and walked out of the office. This day had undoubtedly started strangely, and he wondered if it was going to get any better.

Chapter Thirteen

Chief Anderson sat back in his chair. He felt good. He figured he'd put that CBI agent in his place and let him know who was in charge in Copper Creek. He pulled out his cell phone and dialed a number from memory.

"Yeah, it's me. CBI is here to look into that black kid's suicide. Something about his parents concerned that it wasn't a suicide." He listened for a minute.

"No. I'm sure. With any luck, he'll be gone by the morning."

The voice on the other end of the call said, "Are you certain he's not blowing smoke up your skirt? Can this kid's death lead back to us?"

"No, sir. When he finishes looking at the evidence, he'll conclude that it was nothing more than an unhappy kid who lost his girlfriend and decided to take his own life. Suicide. Pure and simple."

"Okay. Keep an eye on him anyway. I don't want this to get out of hand."

"Nothing to worry about," said Chief Anderson. "I have Cummings showing him around. He'll make sure he sees only what we want him to see."

"Don't fuck this up, Chief. We have too much riding on this." Chief Anderson was about to respond, but the line was dead. He put his phone away and picked up the paper he had been reading when Buck Taylor had first walked into his office.

"Thirty-seven years as a cop. Broke up a huge cartel thing in Durango, which was great for us. Lots of big investigations and a serious closure rate," he said to himself.

He got to the bottom of the page. "Killed seven people during his career, including two just yesterday in a shoot-out in Denver. Must be some kind of cowboy."

His mind started to go places he hadn't intended it to go. His smile disappeared along with his confidence. He hoped he hadn't given his assurances too soon. This wasn't the kind of cop you sent to investigate a suicide. This was the guy you sent in to mount a serious investigation. Was he really here to look into the suicide? He would need to keep a careful eye on Buck Taylor. He picked up the office phone and pushed two buttons.

"I've got a job for you."

Chapter Fourteen

Buck stood outside the cage in the evidence room while Detective Cummings unlocked the gate and walked to the second row of shelves. He came back with a banker's box, checked the side of the box and entered the case number and victim's name on the sign-out sheet. He turned the sheet towards Buck and handed him a pen. Buck signed and picked up the box.

"Any place I can open this and spread out a little?" asked Buck.

"Sure. Follow me," said Cummings. He walked out the door, and Buck followed. He led him to a small counter in the back corner of the bullpen. There was no stool.

"You need anything else, let me know." He walked away before Buck could respond, and Buck placed the box on the narrow counter and looked around. He spotted several officers watching him and turning away when he looked towards them. He felt like he was under a microscope, but that was okay. If this was the game they wanted to play, he was happy to play along. For now.

Buck opened his backpack and pulled out his laptop and a pad of paper. He opened the laptop, pulled up the CBI internal website and entered the information he had so far into the investigation file information page.

CBI had gone digital a couple of years back, so instead of having a blue binder for each case, Buck just had to open a program on his laptop. The new case was automatically assigned a case number, and Buck would list everyone who needed access to the file and send them email invites. All evidence, lab reports, photos, etc., that were part of the case would be uploaded into the file, and anyone who needed access just had to open the file. That was a lot better than the old system, where everything had been placed in the binder by hand, and Buck would spend half his time trying to track down who had the binder.

For a tech dinosaur like Buck, this made his life so much easier, and he had ready access to anything he needed. He opened the chronology page, which was the first page in the file. Nothing was ever entered into the file without a note being entered in the chronology first. The chronology kept track of everything that happened in the investigation. Buck was meticulous about his case files and had never lost a case in court in all his years in law enforcement because something was missing from his files. He entered the email addresses of everyone he wanted to have access to the file and hit send.

Buck photographed the sealed banker's box, then turned on the video recorder on his phone, positioned it on the counter so it could see the entire box, pulled the knife off his belt and slit the evidence tape that wrapped around the box. He noted the date and time on the chronology sheet in the file and then lifted the box's cover.

There wasn't much in the box. He was removing the first evidence bag from the box when Cummings walked by and dropped a manila file folder on the counter. Buck left the file where it was and continued with the box. The first evidence bag contained jeans, black underpants, white socks, Adidas running shoes and a green T-shirt. Buck set the bag on the counter and took a picture of the seal showing the date and Cummings's signature across the flap.

The next bag contained the rope. Buck followed the same process and set that bag aside. He made a note on the pad: Where are the rest of his clothes, etc.?

The last bag in the box contained items that must have been removed from his pockets—comb, wallet, keys, condom and pocket change. Buck took pictures of everything and set the bag aside. He compared what was on the counter to what was listed on the inventory sheet attached to the box. He made another note on the pad: Cell phone and laptop?

Buck logged all the evidence into the investigation file's evidence section and then pulled a pair of black nitrile gloves from his backpack. Keeping the video recorder on, he slit the first bag and removed each piece of clothing, one at a time. He ran his hands over each piece to make sure nothing was hidden in the lining. There was nothing unusual in any of the garments until he got to the underpants. He pulled out his reading glasses and got closer. There were a couple of small stains on the inside of the fly. He removed a sterile swab and plastic tube from his backpack, looked around the room and then swabbed the fly. He made a note on the label on the tube, replaced the swab and placed the sealed tube in his backpack's front pocket. He wasn't sure if he would share this with the police chief.

He replaced everything in the bag, placed a new seal on the bag, dated and signed the seal and placed it back in the box. He followed the same procedure with the bag containing the rope. He was pleased to see that Cummings had left the noose intact. Unfortunately, the other end of the rope was loose, where it had been untied after the body was discovered. Buck looked carefully at the noose and noted there was no abrasion on the inside of the noose. Buck had investigated several hangings, and even in suicides, the victim usually struggled at the end, which would cause some of the rope fibers to break or shred. This rope looked pristine.

He looked around the office again to make sure no one was watching, and he opened two new tubes and swabbed the noose and the other end of the rope. Those went back into his backpack. He was about to put the rope back in the evidence bag when something caught his eye. He pulled a magnifying glass from his backpack and took a closer look at the noose. Stuck in between the rope strands were a couple of small white threads. He pulled a small evidence bag from his backpack, and, using a pair of tweezers he kept handy, he pulled a couple of strands loose and put them in the bag. He then photographed the bag and sealed and signed it. That went into the front pocket as well.

He opened the last bag and removed the wallet. Inside was forty dollars in fives and singles, a platinum credit card in Kevin Ducette's name and several pictures. The first one showed a young black woman taken by a portrait study in Austin, Texas. Buck assumed this was the fiancée Mary Ducette had mentioned. Two others contained him and some male friends that looked like they had been taken while hiking in the area. The last picture was intriguing. It showed Kevin Ducette and a beautiful white girl in a passionate embrace. This one appeared to be taken on the shore of a lake, and the mountain visible in the background was not something you would find in Texas. Buck made a note on his pad to check for a local girlfriend. He took out both sets of keys: one included house keys, and one was the key fob for a BMW. Buck sealed the bag, placed everything back in the banker's box and resealed the box.

He placed the keys in his pocket and carried the box over to Cummings's desk.

"Find anything interesting?" Cummings asked, looking up from his computer screen.

"Not really. I would like to send the clothes and the rope to the state lab in Pueblo. Can you see if Chief Anderson will allow me to do that?"

Cummings looked at Buck and smiled. "Sure. I'll ask him. You looking for anything important?"

"Won't know until the lab gets a chance to look at them." Buck walked back to his little counter and opened the investigation file Cummings had dropped on the counter.

He checked his watch and realized why he felt hungry. It was now early afternoon, and he hadn't had any lunch yet. He put the investigation file and his laptop in his backpack, grabbed his jacket and headed for the door to the lobby. He was just about to the door when Cummings called after him.

"I'm gonna need that file back before you leave the building." Buck stopped and turned. He removed the file from his backpack and dropped it on Cummings's desk.

"Sorry, Detective. Force of habit. I'm just going to grab a bite to eat, and I'll be back to finish looking at the file."

Buck walked through the lobby and out into the sunshine. He stood for a minute until he spotted what he was looking for. He started walking towards the main street and spotted his tail before making it across the parking lot.

Chapter Fifteen

The cafe was larger inside than it had looked from the outside, and even though it was crowded, Buck was able to find a table for two near the back. He sat with his back to the wall and looked at the menu. His waitress was an older woman with a blueish tint to her hair. She had her pencil stuck in her hair above her ear. Buck ordered a Coke and a cheeseburger. She thanked him and moved on to the next table. Buck liked places like this. He was lucky to work in many small mountain communities and had managed, through the years, to find some great mom-and-pop restaurants. He just sat for a minute and watched the crowd. His tail was sitting at the counter near the front of the cafe, trying to look nonchalant while watching Buck with his peripheral vision.

He also noticed that several other people in the cafe seemed to be more focused on him than would have been normal. He recognized two of the men sitting two tables down from him. Their pictures were in the justice center's lobby, one on a wall showing the current city government and the other one on a wall showing the founding fathers and their families through the years.

The waitress placed his burger, fries and Coke on the table and set a bill next to the food, upside down. She told him to enjoy and call if he needed anything else. Buck dug in while continuing to watch the people around him. The burger was good but not as good as his friend Jimmy Palumbo made at La Bon Cafe in Durango, Colorado. Jimmy was one of Buck's closest friends and the owner, along with his longtime girlfriend, Loraine, of the tiny cafe. Buck had no idea what Jimmy's secret was to making great burgers, but he had never found another burger like it in all his years traveling the state. He thought fondly of Jimmy as he polished off his lunch.

He finished his Coke and picked up the check. He dropped a twenty on the table and placed the check in his pocket. He nodded to the waitress as he walked by, but she was busy filling a couple of coffee cups, and he walked back out onto the street. He looked back towards the justice center and then turned in the opposite direction. He wanted to take a quick walk around town. He pulled the bill from the cafe out of his pocket and unfolded it. The waitress had handwritten thanks, followed by her name, Cherie, with a little heart over the I, but it was what was written under her name that Buck found interesting. "Old Martelli School, 8 PM, watch." He put the note back in his pocket and headed off down the street.

Copper Creek was laid out on the square, like many small towns. The main street contained most of the commercial district. The justice center was the first or last building you passed as you entered or left the town. From that vantage point and with all the CCTV cameras visible, it would be easy to keep an eye on anyone entering or leaving the town. He stopped when he reached the end of the main street. At this point, it entered into a parking lot that was part of the national park. He saw several trail signs, and even this late in the season, the lot was full of cars with people carrying various types of backpacks and cameras. The gold color of the aspen trees was something that drew folks from all over to take pictures. Lucy had always liked this time of year the best.

Buck stopped and leaned against a rustic wood fence. He had checked several times during his walk to make sure his tail was still with him. He was about to start back on the other side of the street when a thought occurred to him. "How did Chief Anderson know about my dinner with Marty and Charlie?" He wondered if Chief Anderson had someone watching the sheriff's office, which led to the question: why?

Buck continued his stroll down the west side of the street and eventually ended up back at the justice center. This time, when he presented himself to the woman at the reception desk, he was buzzed right through to the back hall. He stopped at Cummings's desk, grabbed the file, which sat where he had left it earlier, and walked back to his counter. Once again, he pulled out his laptop and his pad, leaned against the counter and opened the file.

The file was thin, with just a few pieces of paper in it. He pulled up the page listed as the initial incident report and started reading. A maintenance man from the college, one Arturo Ruiz, had found the victim when he reported to work on Saturday morning. He wasn't supposed to be working that day, but his boss had authorized some overtime to fix a critical freezer in the hospital lab. He had gone down to the maintenance office to pick up a part he needed. He used the landline to call 911 and waited for the police and EMTs to arrive. Detective Cummings had indicated that he had confirmed the man's story by speaking with his boss and checking his timecard and the time code on the door. Buck made a note to do the same.

The detective had noted several photos that were taken, and those Buck found at the back of the file. He laid them out on the counter. He used his cell phone to take pictures of the pictures and the report.

The report noted no eyewitnesses to the death. The detective had also noted that he spoke to Kevin's roommate and that the roommate had offered to gather up all of Kevin's belongings and hold them until someone came for them. He did note that there was a cell phone on the body, and that a laptop was found in his room.

The report ended with a note that the body had been taken to the campus hospital for autopsy. Buck looked at the pictures on the counter. The first picture showed Kevin as he had been found by the maintenance man. The second photo showed the body after it had been lowered by the EMTs. There was a close-up of the noose around his neck and a close-up of the rope as it hung from what looked like a winch of some kind. Buck made a note to check out the site.

Buck pulled out his magnifying glass and looked more closely at the picture, concentrating on the neck area. Kevin was a lighter shade of black than his mom, more similar to his father, and he appeared even lighter in death. He noticed something odd in the picture. The noose was still tight around his neck, but there was a discoloration next to the noose. It looked to Buck like the noose was not in its original position. He made a note to check the autopsy report. There were several more pictures of the body after the noose had been removed, and the last picture showed the noose as it had been attached to the winch. Buck looked carefully at the knot that was tied to the hook on the winch.

The knot was unlike any knot Buck had ever seen. It seemed to be very intricate and looked like a series of loops. Buck leaned back from the counter. "Why would someone who was going to kill himself spend that much time creating a series of interconnecting loops in the knot, and to what end? A couple of half hitches would have been enough to hold the body."

He found the autopsy report deeper in the folder. Buck was surprised to see that they had not taken the body to the Larimer County coroner's office for the autopsy. It had been done at the campus hospital. Buck made a note on his pad to ask why and added the doctor's name to his notes. The autopsy was lacking a lot of information. Buck looked at the photos that were attached to the report.

The doctor hadn't done any internal investigation, which would have been standard procedure in any unattended death investigation. He'd noted the ligature marks on the neck, the petechial hemorrhaging in the eyes, and declared this death a suicide. Buck was amazed. This was the sloppiest autopsy he had ever seen. He took photos of all the documents and put them back in the file folder.

He looked at his watch. He looked around the office and saw that most of the desks were empty. He walked to Chief Anderson's office and knocked on the door. There was no answer.

"Can I help you, sir?" said a voice behind him.

"I was hoping Chief Anderson was still here, but he doesn't seem to be in."

The officer scrutinized Buck. "Chief left for the day. You'll have to catch him tomorrow. Have a nice evening, sir."

He saw the file in Buck's hand. "I'll take that, sir, and make sure Detective Cummings gets it." He held out his hand, and Buck handed him the file.

"Have a nice evening, Officer." Buck walked back to the counter, grabbed his backpack and coat and left the office. Out in the parking lot, he noticed a different tail, and he laughed. "No one is this inept," he thought to himself. He laughed, slid into his Jeep and headed for the B and B. It had been a strange day.

Chapter Sixteen

Buck would never be considered paranoid. He had spent his entire life dealing in facts and evidence, not supposition and speculation, but he had an odd feeling about this little town. He knew it wasn't his imagination that led to the thoughts he was having while he sat at the small desk in his room and looked out the window into the backyard. He needed to make some calls, but first, he needed to know he wasn't being bugged. He didn't know anything about Victoria James, and she'd seemed nice enough when he checked in last night, but he needed to be sure.

He removed an electronic scanner from his backpack, turned it on and walked around the room. It wasn't a large space, but it was beautifully decorated with a queen-sized bed along one wall. The furnishings were either antiques and had been here since the house was built, or they were excellent fakes. Victoria James had mentioned that the house was originally a brothel and was built by her great-grandfather. She told him that the house had been in the family since the town was first founded. Buck had an appreciation for old things, since it seemed that everyone he met anymore was younger than him.

Buck finished scanning the room and put the

scanner back in his backpack. He pulled out his phone, pulled up the contact list and dialed a number. Dr. Kate Milligan answered almost immediately.

"Hi, Kate, it's Buck Taylor. Did I catch you at a bad time?"

"Well, Buck Taylor. Twice in the same year. To what do I owe the pleasure?" Kate laughed and told Buck that she was just sitting in the office doing paperwork.

"Kate, I need a favor, and this might be tough. I'd like to send you the death certificate, autopsy report and a couple of pictures of a young man who supposedly hanged himself. There's not a lot to go on, but I need an opinion I can trust."

Dr. Kate Milligan was the El Paso County Coroner and someone Buck had worked with before. Besides being the coroner, Kate was also a licensed medical examiner.

Colorado was one of about a dozen states that still used the coroner system instead of the medical examiner system. The coroner for each jurisdiction was an elected official, and that person did not have to have any experience or even be a medical professional. Anyone could run for coroner. The system was gradually evolving so that the coroner was required to complete a formal training program in death investigations, but it was a slow legislative process. Unlike in the medical examiner system, and since the coroner did not have to be a doctor, coroners would contract with a licensed forensic pathologist to handle any investigations that required an autopsy. These forensic pathologists were highly trained doctors who split their time among several jurisdictions to keep costs down. Many of the forensic pathologists were current or former medical examiners, and several were retired, working part time to keep their hands in the game. In this case, Buck was lucky. Dr. Kate Milligan was one of the best pathologists he knew.

"I appreciate the confidence, Buck. Who performed the autopsy?"

"That's part of the problem. I'm in Copper Creek in Jackson County. They should have used the pathologist in Fort Collins, but that wasn't done for some reason. There was no autopsy to speak of, and the death certificate was signed by a local doctor, guy who runs the hospital on the campus of Copper Canyon College."

"Do you want me to make arrangements to have the body picked up and brought here?" she asked.

"That's one of the problems." He told her about the body being cremated against the wishes of the parents.

"You don't think this was a suicide?" she said.

"Not sure, Kate. I'm not getting a lot of cooperation from the locals. I think the investigation into this suicide skipped a couple of steps. Just want to make sure I have a clear picture of what happened."

"No problem, Buck. Send me the link to your investigation file, and I'll take a look. Hey, I saw the news last night. Sounds like you were in a hell of a fight. You doing okay?"

Buck spent a few minutes giving her the *Reader's Digest* version of the events at the courthouse. She told him she was glad he hadn't been hurt and if he needed anything to give her a call. They said their goodbyes, and Buck hung up. He opened the investigation file on his laptop and sent the link to Kate.

His next call was to Bax. "Hey, Buck. How are things in Copper Creek?"

Buck told her about his encounter with the police chief, about the tail and the investigation file that Detective Cummings had given him. There was silence on the other end of the phone.

"The police chief told you that you couldn't borrow an office and that you wouldn't be there more than a day? You have to be kidding. What's going on up there?"

"Not sure." He told her about the note the waitress had given him. "Maybe I'll have a better feel for the place after I see what happens tonight. In the meantime, can you run background on the police chief and the detective who handled the investigation, and see what you can find on the doctor who signed the death certificate? Their names are all in the file. Also, see if Kevin Ducette had a social media presence and let's see who his friends were. There's a picture of Kevin that I found in his wallet. I'd like to see if we can find out who the young lady is in the picture. She's not his fiancée, but the picture is very intimate. Last thing, let's get a warrant for his cell phone. It wasn't with his personal effects, and it's not in the evidence box."

"What are you gonna do?" she asked.

"I'm gonna take a little walk around the campus and see who visits the old Martelli School. There must be a reason she passed me that note."

"Okay. Be careful. Call if you need anything else."

Buck hung up and called Director Jackson. They had the same conversation he'd just had with Bax, and the director had the same questions and maybe a little bit more concern for what was going on in town. He told Buck to be careful and to stay in touch. Buck hung up. He had one more call to make. He opened his contact list and hit a couple of buttons.

Hardy Braxton answered on the second ring. "Hey, Buck. Saw you on the news last night. You doin' okay?"

Hardy Braxton and Buck had been on-again, off-again friends since kindergarten. They'd played football together for the Gunnison High School Cowboys. They were the team's defensive backfield and were called the "Wrecking Crew" during senior year. Between them, they broke every defensive high school football record in the state, many of which stood to this day.

Buck had passed up several full-ride scholarships and instead joined the army and later the Gunnison County Sheriff's Department. On the other hand, Hardy had accepted a full-ride scholarship to Stanford and spent the next four years as an all-American football player. He then went on to play in the National Football League until a knee injury sidelined him for good.

Hardy left the NFL and took over the reins of his father's small livestock company. Over the years, he turned that small company, based out of Gunnison County, into the world's premier bucking stock and livestock company. A rodeo didn't happen anywhere in the country that didn't have numerous animals from Braxton Bucking Stock in its corrals. He also invested heavily in energy exploration companies and owned the largest private fracking company in the country. By all measures, Hardy Braxton was hugely successful. He was also Buck's brother-in-law.

Hardy had married Lucy's younger sister, Rachel, the year after Lucy and Buck got married. Their marriage was blessed with four children, all of whom were now involved in the numerous family businesses. Businesses that now numbered at least a dozen and stretched from Gunnison to California and even dipped down into South America. Hardy was the big dog in Gunnison County, and he was not afraid to use that power to his family's advantage.

Buck gave him a quick rundown of the events from the courthouse. When he finished, Hardy said, "Fuck, Buck. You always manage to find yourself in the damnedest situations. Well, I'm glad you're okay. Now, what can I do for you?"

"I'd like to send you a picture of a rope. Ignore the noose. What I'm interested in is what kind of knot is on the other end. Looks like something that might be used on a farm or a ranch, and I thought I'd start with you."

Buck texted the picture to Hardy and waited while Hardy opened his text and took a look.

"That's easy, Buck. That's a quick-release knot. We use them on the ranch."

"A quick-release knot. What would you use something like that for?"

"Mostly for tying livestock to a fence. It's a popular knot amongst horse people. You wrap it around a fence rail and make a series of loops with the loose end of the rope. The horse can pull all day, and all the rope does is tighten, but all you have to do is pull on the loose end, and the knot unravels. Why you askin'?"

Buck filled Hardy in on what he knew so far and about the knot being found at the scene of a hanging. There was silence on the other end of the call.

"Hardy, you still there?"

"Yeah, hold on a minute, I'm getting my glasses."

Buck waited a minute until Hardy came back on the line. "This is an elaborate knot for someone to tie if they were going to kill themselves. Lots of easier knots to tie, but you may have another problem."

"What's that?" asked Buck.

"You still got the picture pulled up?" asked Hardy.

Buck replied that he did. "Take a look at the loose end of the rope," said Hardy.

"Okay," said Buck. "What am I looking at?"

"Whoever tied this knot secured the loose end so it couldn't be released. The loose end was run through the last loop instead of hanging free. Riders do that when they don't want the horse to accidentally pull on the loose end. It stops the knot from being able to release. You could pull on that end all day, and nothing would happen."

Buck looked at the picture of the rope. "I'll be damned. Anyone who knew how to tie this knot would know how to do that?"

"Of course," said Hardy. "I have to tell you, Buck, based on where you found this knot and what it was used for, this makes no sense. I could see someone contemplating suicide wouldn't want the knot to release, but then, why tie this particular knot in the first place?"

"Yeah," said Buck. "Just what I was thinking, but I'm gonna find out."

Buck thanked Hardy for his help and disconnected the call. He sat back and thought about what he had just learned, and a picture started to form in his mind. He wasn't sure if what he was thinking made sense, but the little bug that bounced around in his brain during a case suddenly started dancing. He was starting to believe this was not a suicide or a hate crime. This was something else. He wasn't sure what, just yet, but that would come. He pulled out his phone and speed-dialed a number. This case had just taken an interesting turn.

Chapter Seventeen

Max Clinton answered the phone the way she always did when Buck called. "Buck Taylor. How's my favorite cop?"

Dr. Maxine Clinton, Max to her friends, was the director of the State Crime Lab in Pueblo. She was a matronly woman in her early sixties, about five foot five with short gray hair. She probably thought she carried around an extra fifteen pounds she didn't need, but she was still a handsome woman.

Married for forty years, Max had four children, eleven grandchildren and six great-grandchildren. She lived in a 150-year-old farmhouse in Pueblo, where she liked to tend her garden and sit on her porch and drink iced tea. She was also a bourbon girl and could easily drink most people under the table. She was loud and outspoken, but she knew her job.

Max had received her PhD in biology from the University of Colorado and worked as a biology professor for twenty years before joining CBI and accepting the challenge of running the lab. Under her leadership, it had become one of the top crime labs in the country. She was a hard taskmaster, but she had a belief system that didn't allow for defeat. Her goal was to give the crime investigator, no matter which department or municipality they worked for, all the information they would need to solve any crime. She held that as a sacred obligation to the victims. She was incredibly dedicated, and her team at the lab practically worshipped her.

Buck would be included in that group. Many times, during a complicated investigation, it had been Max and her team that lit the spark that led to a breakthrough. Max was one of Buck's favorite people, and she felt the same way about him.

"Doin' great, Max. You got a couple of minutes?" They talked for a few minutes about the events at the courthouse, and she told Buck that she was pleased he had not been injured, or worse.

"So, I'm guessing you didn't call old Max just to shoot the shit. What's up?"

Buck told her about the noose found with the suicide victim and some nagging questions he had after talking to Hardy Braxton. Max listened without interrupting until Buck took a pause.

"How can we help?" she asked.

"Since you know everyone in the world, I was hoping you might know someone who is an expert with knots."

Max laughed. "Well, I don't know quite everyone in the world, but I do know a lot of people."

Max was Buck's first stop whenever he needed an expert opinion on some odd thing that might come up during an investigation. During one of his odder cases, Buck had been looking for information on sonic weapons—more to the point, infrasound weapons. Within a couple of hours of discussing this with Max, he'd found himself on the phone with a former government scientist that Max had gone to school with, who was able to give him the information he needed.

He always knew he could count on Max when he was stuck. She was also a great sounding board, and he knew if he discussed anything about a case with her, it would stay right there.

Max opened the investigation file on her laptop and pulled up the pictures of the noose and the rope Buck had taken and took a close look.

"I agree with your assessment, Buck. If you intended to kill yourself, there are much simpler knots to tie than this one. I recognize the knot from when my daughter was younger. She was into horses, and this is how they would tie the horse up to a hitching post or fence rail. What do you need to know?"

"I know what the knot is typically used for. What I would like to know is what else it could be used for that might be a little unconventional?"

"No problem, Buck. Let me make some calls and see what I can come up with. It's late, so it might not be until tomorrow, but we'll figure it out."

She ended the call the way she always did. "You're a good man, Buck Taylor. God will watch over you. Stay safe."

Buck hadn't been to church since he'd received his confirmation, but he always appreciated Max's little blessing. It wasn't that he didn't believe in God. He wasn't sure what he really believed in. He didn't like organized religion, but he never held that against anyone. A lot of people had prayed for his wife during the five years she fought metastatic breast cancer, but in the end, Lucy still died. Although he had been mad at first, he soon realized that to be angry at God, he first had to believe in God, and he could never get there. He always felt there were forces in the world that he couldn't explain, and he always thanked the river spirits whenever he had a chance to do some fly-fishing. He didn't have a place for one God in his life. He never held Max's beliefs against her. He always figured that it couldn't hurt if she believed he was worthy.

Buck checked the time and decided to head for the campus. He had no idea what he was walking into, but he wanted a few minutes to get the lay of the land. He grabbed his coat and backpack and headed out the door.

Chapter Eighteen

Buck found a spot behind a couple of dumpsters that gave him a good view of the old Martelli School. It took a little searching on his phone to locate the old building. He'd assumed it was on the campus, but he found no reference for it in his Google searches. He found it when he pulled up a map of the campus. The old Martelli School was the original building for the School for Girls.

According to the information he read on the sign outside the building, it had originally housed the school, the dormitory and the hospital. It was larger than he'd expected. He also wondered why he was here, since the place looked like it hadn't been used in years.

He zipped up his jacket to ward off the chill in the air and settled in. He didn't have long to wait. A few minutes before eight, he spotted several people arrive and greet each other on the steps leading to the front door. He pulled his SLR camera out of his backpack and looked through the 300mm lens. He snapped a couple of pictures of the individuals and waited. He wondered what Chief Anderson was doing when he walked up the stairs and unlocked the doors.

Buck watched as lights came on in many of the rooms on the second floor. There seemed to be some kind of blackout shades on the windows, but he could see little shafts of light along each side. He wished he could get closer to the building, but it sat in the middle of a large grassy area, and there were few places to hide near the building.

As more and more people arrived, Buck tried to capture as many faces as he could. The two lights on either side of the entry stairs didn't help him, and he hoped that some of the pictures would turn out to be useable.

Two hours passed, and Buck had counted forty people, men and women, entering the building. They varied in age from what appeared to be college students to older men and women. Buck's curiosity was piqued. During those first two hours, no one left the building, just entered. There was no music to be heard, so it didn't seem like a party, and little light came through when the doors were opened. If he hadn't been there since the first people arrived, he would not have been able to tell that anything was going on in the building.

He put the camera back in his backpack, sipped from the Coke bottle he had stashed in the outside pocket and waited. He checked his watch when people started leaving. Midnight. Soon after, he saw all the slivers of light go dark at the windows and then Chief Anderson and a young man exited the building and locked the doors. Buck was trying to make sense of what he had and hadn't seen when he heard a noise that sounded like a breaking bottle. He stashed his backpack under one of the dumpsters and made his way in the shadows towards the sound.

Buck stopped alongside a short fence and could hear breathing on the other side. He worked his way to the end of the fence, just as a person in a dark hoodie rounded the fence post. Buck grabbed the person as he passed and pushed him against the fence. He pulled the hoodie back and was surprised to see a young blond girl staring at him with fear in her eyes. She struggled but relaxed when Buck told her he wasn't going to hurt her. Buck released the grip on her arms.

"Who are you, and what are you doing here?" he asked the young girl.

"Please don't send me back to them," she said, her voice trembling.

"Calm down a minute. I'm not sending you anywhere. Now, let's start with your name?"

"Nadia," was all she said. Buck picked up on the accent. He thought it might have been Russian or eastern European.

"Okay, Nadia, my name is Buck. What are you doing here?"

"I can't go back in there. I won't go back."

"Nadia, were you in that building over there?" He pointed to the old Martelli School. Nadia started to shake. Buck loosened his grip on her arms even more. Nadia kneed him in the groin and broke loose from his grip. She ran behind the maintenance building they were standing next to and disappeared down a trail leading to the national park.

Buck was lying on the ground, barely able to move. He felt like his nuts were in his stomach, and he felt like he wanted to vomit. After a few minutes, the pain began to subside, and he could stand on wobbly legs. He made his way back to the dumpster where he had stashed his backpack. He was able to stand upright, and then the embarrassment set in. He had lost focus for a minute and let the girl get the better of him. That pissed him off.

He looked back towards the maintenance building and the trail behind it. "What the hell is going on here?" he wondered out loud.

He picked up his backpack. Took a long drink from his bottle of Coke and threw the bottle in the dumpster. He felt foolish, and he wondered if he was starting to lose his edge. Maybe he was getting too old to do this work anymore. He thought for a minute about what Lucy would say if she heard him talking like this. He knew she would kick him in the ass and tell him to get his head back in the game. People needed him to have his head on straight.

He walked back to where he had encountered the girl and looked around. There was no broken glass on the ground around the fence, so he wondered what he had heard.

He walked towards the building and looked around. He was looking at the windows when he crunched on something underfoot. Broken glass. He looked up at the window just above his head and saw that the bottom pane was missing, or at least most of it was missing. There were some broken shards stuck to the window frame. He noticed something else too. A red stain on one of the shards. He pulled a pair of nitrile gloves out of his pocket, reached up and wiggled the piece until it came out in his hand. It looked like blood.

Buck put the piece in an evidence bag he took from his backpack and sealed it. He stood for a minute listening but didn't hear any noise coming from the building. "Why didn't she just come out the door with the rest of the people when they left?" he said to himself. "And what was she afraid of?"

Buck finished circling the building and then headed back towards the B and B. Something was definitely wrong in this town, and the little bug in his brain agreed with Lucy. He needed to get his head in the game.

Chapter Nineteen

The man threw his glass of bourbon against the stone fireplace, sending the liquid and shattered glass in all directions.

"How the fuck did she get away?"

Chief Anderson looked nervous, as did the two young men standing next to him. What made them more uncomfortable were the two huge guys standing behind them. They had seen the man mad before, but this was a new level.

One of the young men, Josh, spoke first. "We don't know. We fed them and doped them up. She should have been out for the night. She must have palmed the pills. We found the broken window when I went back to check on them earlier this morning. I called Chief Anderson right away."

The man walked over and looked out the window. "This is becoming a pattern. First the deputy, then the black kid who committed suicide and now one of my girls is gone."

Chief Anderson started to speak, but the man held up his hand. He turned from the window and walked back to his huge desk.

"We have been doing this stuff since the eighteen hundreds and never had a problem. Now we've had three screwups in one week, and to top it all off, we have a state cop here investigating the suicide. What are you not telling me?"

Chief Anderson looked at Josh and then back to the man at the desk.

"Nothing, sir. It's just a bad week. We have everything under control."

The man cut him off. "From where I'm sitting, it doesn't look like you have anything under control. And that's a problem."

He looked at the second young man, who, to this point, had remained quiet. "You were there to watch them, correct?"

The young man looked around the room. He felt sick to his stomach, but he knew better than to let anything happen in front of the boss. "Yes, sir." The quiver in his voice was noticeable.

"Did you try to find her when you saw she was missing?"

"No, sir. I didn't know she was gone until Josh came this morning to check on things. We called you right away."

"So, on top of losing her, she is now out there, free as a bird, to tell anyone she can find about our arrangement. Do you think that is wise?"

The young man hesitated for a bit too long. The boss pulled a pistol out of his desk drawer and shot him in the chest. The young man flew backward and landed hard on the floor. Chief Anderson and Josh almost jumped out of their skins. The noise was deafening.

The boss put the gun back in the desk drawer and closed the drawer. Chief Anderson and Josh were speechless. They just stood there shaking. Both of them looked like they had seen a ghost. Josh started to wobble and looked like he might fall. One of the guys came over and held him up by his collar.

"Now, maybe we can restore a little order to our enterprise." He walked around the desk and looked them both in the eyes. "I would like you to tighten up security on the rest of the girls." He looked at the body on the floor. "Find someone who can do the job better, or I will find someone to replace you. Understood? And find that fucking girl."

They both nodded, turned and raced to the door. The boss looked at the two big guys. "Please get that shit off my floor." He walked out of the room and spotted his son coming down the stairs. He held up his hands.

"What the hell was that? Sounded like a gunshot."

"Personnel issue. Nothing for you to worry about."

"You didn't . . . ?"

"No. DiNardo's kid is still alive, but I'm getting tired of dealing with his screwups. We need to get out from under his father. Where are we at with those connections in Canada?"

"They've got an efficient organization with a lot of sharp people. Would fit in well with us. I just need to work out the details on the split."

"Good." He stood aside as the two guys carried the plastic-wrapped bundle out of the office and turned down the hall.

"Any place in particular?" asked the first guy.

"Take him to the mine and have Jenson put him someplace where he won't be found." The guy nodded, and they moved down the hall.

The boss looked at his son. "DiNardo is bringing a guest this weekend. Let them enjoy the evening and then arrange a special reception for him. I'm done dealing with that bastard."

"What about his guest?"

"I heard it's one of the family guys from New York. Take care of that fat fuck as well. Then we'll decide what to do with the son. It's time to clean house and get some new blood around here."

He walked out the front door and headed for the barn. He did his best thinking in the barn. "Could be a fun weekend," he said out loud to himself. "A fun weekend indeed."

Chapter Twenty

Buck was buzzed through the security door, walked down the hall and stopped in front of Chief Anderson's open door. He knocked on the doorframe. Chief Anderson looked up from his computer, and Buck could see visual signs of discomfort in his face.

"Agent Taylor. I see you are still here. What do you want?"

"I asked Detective Cummings to see if you would let me send the rope and clothes to the State Crime Lab. Did he discuss that with you?"

Chief Anderson set his glasses on the desk. "We discussed it, and I don't see the point. There was no crime. Request denied."

He picked up his glasses and looked back at his computer screen.

"Where's Kevin Ducette's phone and laptop?" asked Buck. Chief Anderson's expression grew angrier by the second.

"What the hell are you talking about?"

Buck looked at Chief Anderson. "The report says you found the suicide note on his laptop, but his laptop and phone are not on the evidence list. Where are they?"

Chief Anderson stood up and almost knocked his chair over. "What the fuck are you implying?

That my people screwed up this investigation? It was a fucking suicide." His face turned red, and he looked like he was going to have a heart attack.

Several of the officers in the bullpen started walking towards his office. He looked up, saw them and waved his hand, indicating they should back off. They stopped but stayed where they were.

He sat back down in his chair and gripped the sides of the desk. He looked up at Buck, some of the anger starting to disappear. He spoke slowly. "We probably sent them to his parents along with his personal effects." He looked like he considered that a rational answer.

"They weren't," said Buck. "And they're not in the file as having been retrieved. I also don't see anything that might have come out of his dorm room or apartment."

Chief Anderson glared at Buck. He picked up the desk phone and hit two buttons. "In my office, now." He hung up and took a deep breath.

Detective Cummings walked up to the door. "Yes, sir?"

"Agent Taylor here is questioning how you do your job. He says we are missing evidence from the kid that hanged himself. Perhaps you would care to explain?"

Detective Cummings looked hurt. He looked at Buck. "What's missing?"

"Cell phone, laptop, personal belongings from his apartment. None of that is in the evidence box," said Buck. He stood there and waited for an explanation. He could see the wheels turning in Cummings's head.

"There must be some mistake. I boxed up the phone and laptop along with the kid's ashes and asked his roommate to box up everything else and send the stuff to his parents. Are you sure they didn't get them?"

"Yes, I'm sure," said Buck.

Cummings looked at Chief Anderson. "Honest to God, Chief. We did everything by the book. Let me look into it and see what happened. If they didn't get to the parents, they must be around here someplace. I'll find them." He turned and headed back to his desk.

Chief Anderson smiled at Buck. "See, Agent Taylor. Nothing nefarious. Probably just a simple clerical error. To show there's no hard feelings, go ahead and sign out the clothes and the rope and do with them what you will."

"Thanks, Chief. I'd also like to see the space where Kevin was found. Can you have someone show me?"

"Of course. Stop by the dispatcher on the way out and have them call Officer Terrell. She was the first officer on the scene. She'll be happy to take you over there."

Buck nodded his head and walked towards Cummings's desk. Without saying a word, he opened the evidence box sitting on the floor, pulled out the bags with the rope and the clothes and signed the form on the top of the box. He headed for his car, first stopping at the dispatch center.

Officer Terrell was available, and she would meet him at the building. The dispatcher wrote down the directions Officer Terrell dictated and handed them to Buck. He left the building with a smile on his face.

Chapter Twenty-One

Officer Terrell was good to her word, and Buck found the parking lot for the maintenance workers with ease. She was standing next to a locked door with a heavyset Hispanic man with curly brown hair and a large mustache.

She introduced him to Buck as Pedro Olivario, the school's maintenance director. Buck and Pedro shook hands, and Pedro asked them to follow him. He entered a code in the lockset on the back of the building and opened the door. Buck stopped for a moment.

"Is this the only way into the basement area?" he asked Pedro.

"You can reach the basement from inside as well, but all the doors are coded."

Buck thought for a second. "Who has the codes for this area?"

"Just the maintenance team," said Pedro. "We change the code about once a year unless there is some kind of incident."

"When was the code changed last?" asked Buck.

Pedro pulled out his phone and started scrolling through an app. He stopped and handed Buck his phone, which was open to a diary page. He flipped through several entries, and about halfway down the page was a note assigning one of his maintenance guys, a Steven Castro, with the task of changing all the codes. Buck handed him back his phone and pulled a small notebook from his inside jacket pocket. He made a note of the name. "How long has Steven Castro worked here?" he asked.

Pedro put his phone away and searched his memory. "Must be ten or fifteen years. I've been the director here for nine years, and he was on staff when I started. Why do you ask?"

Buck nodded. "Just covering all my bases. We can go now."

Buck, Pedro, and Officer Terrell descended into the basement and then down another set of stairs into the subbasement. They walked down a long corridor and stopped at another door with an electronic lock. Pedro entered the code and opened the door.

Buck stopped him for a minute. "Do all the doors have the same code number?"

"Yes," said Pedro. "Since only my people have access to the maintenance spaces, it is easier having one code. There are over a hundred doors on campus that have the same code."

Officer Terrell took over the tour at this point. "Arturo Ruiz called nine-one-one on Saturday at six thirty-seven a.m. and reported the hanging." She opened an app on her notebook computer and read down the notes.

"I received the call at six thirty-nine, and dispatch told me that paramedics were en route. They arrived right after I did. Arturo was waiting at the same door we entered earlier. He appeared to be shaken up and had to enter the code twice to get the door unlocked. I asked Arturo to unlock the door to this room and asked him to wait in the hall. I entered with the two paramedics. We found Kevin Ducette hanging here." She pointed to the metal I-beam track that ran the length of the room. She walked Buck over to the sidewall and pointed towards the winch.

"The winch was in the location I just showed you, and Kevin was hanging from a rope attached to the hook at the end of the chain."

Buck took a couple of pictures of the track and the winch. He looked around for a wall switch on the control panel, but all he saw was a wire with two buttons hanging below the winch. Pedro saw his interest and walked over and reached for the controller, but Buck reached out his hand and stopped him. Pedro backed up a step.

"Officer Terrell, did you take a picture before the body was lowered?"

"Yes, sir. It was obvious when we entered that Kevin was deceased. The body was cold and waxy, and there was a puddle of liquid under the body." She opened another page on her notebook and handed it to Buck. He flipped through the pictures, none of which were in the investigation file, and held the notebook up to the winch to get a feel for how the body had been found.

The body was about two feet off the ground. Buck observed the controller hanging next to Kevin's right arm. "Has anyone touched this controller since the body was lowered?"

Pedro said, "Just the paramedics when they lowered the body. None of my guys have needed to use the winch this week."

Buck pulled a small fingerprint kit out of his backpack. "Officer Terrell did anyone dust the controller for prints?" he asked.

"Not while I was here, sir. They might have done it after I left."

"Were the paramedics wearing gloves when they lowered the body?" he asked.

"Yes, sir," said Officer Terrell.

Buck put on a pair of black nitrile gloves and pulled the controller closer. There were no signs of fingerprint powder anywhere that he could see. He sprayed the controller and the buttons with black powder, shook off the loose powder and looked closely at the controller. Officer Terrell took a step closer and looked past his shoulder. There were no visible prints on the controller.

Buck noted her interest. "Odd that the only way to activate the winch is with the buttons, yet our suicide victim didn't leave any prints on the controller. Why do you think that is, Officer Terrell?"

Officer Terrell looked confused. She looked at the winch, the track and the controller and then back to Buck. "I don't know, sir."

Buck pulled out his phone and took pictures of the controller. He put his phone back in his pocket and put the print kit back in his backpack. He walked around the rest of the space, matching up pictures from Officer Terrell's notebook with the area around where the body had been found. He found her email app and emailed her notes and pictures to himself, then handed her back her notebook; she started to object, but he just looked at her, and she stepped back. He pulled out his flashlight and walked around the space. Even with the lights on, the flashlight beam focused his vision on just that area. He stopped a few feet from where the body had been found. He kneeled and ran his finger over a spot on the floor. He looked around the space and noticed that the entire area was clean enough to eat off the floors. Pedro and his team took pride in their workspace, and it showed. Getting fingerprints from anywhere else in the space might be difficult.

Buck called Pedro and Officer Terrell over and showed them the spots. He pulled out his camera and took some close-ups, using his pen tip for reference. He stood and noticed the bewildered look on both Pedro's and Officer Terrell's faces. He pulled a small evidence bag out of his backpack and scraped up some of the wax using his pocketknife. He sealed the bag and placed it in his backpack.

He shouldered his backpack. "Officer Terrell, do you have time to take me to his apartment or dorm room?"

Buck thanked Pedro for his time and told him he was impressed with the cleanliness of the space. They shook hands, and Buck and Officer Terrell left the subbasement. Officer Terrell didn't say a word as they walked across campus to the student housing area. She called dispatch and told them where she was headed.

Chapter Twenty-Two

The student apartments were luxurious. Buck hadn't gone to college, but he had visited his daughter at the University of Arizona, and these rooms looked nothing like what he remembered. There was no laundry hanging in the halls, no notices taped to the walls and no old couches sitting on balconies.

Each apartment contained two bedrooms, a living room and study space and a compact but well-equipped kitchen. Kevin's roommate, Alex Goodrich, from Santa Rosa, California, greeted them wearing sweatpants and a T-shirt drenched with sweat. He apologized and told them he had been running. He asked them if he could get them a water or a soft drink, but they both refused.

Buck asked to see Kevin's room, and Alex pointed towards the room on the left. Buck walked over, opened the door and stood for a moment looking around. He entered the room, followed by Officer Terrell, and moved around the room from left to right. There was a double bed against the left wall with a large nightstand next to it, and a desk and study area on the right wall. In between was a sliding glass door with a small balcony.

Buck opened the closet door and looked around. He stepped into the private bath, opened the medicine cabinet and lifted the cover off the toilet bowl. He walked back out to talk to the roommate.

"Alex. Where are all of Kevin's belongings?"

"I boxed up everything," said Alex, "and gave the two boxes to Detective Cummings. He said he would see they got to Kev's parents. I was going to call them, but I didn't know what to say."

"Were you and Kevin close?" Buck asked.

"We liked each other, but we weren't like best friends or anything. We didn't hang out together, and when he wasn't in class, he was in his room studying."

"Do you know who his friends were?"

"Not really. As I said, he spent a lot of time studying." Alex paused.

"What?" asked Buck.

"I think he was dating a girl on campus, but he didn't want anyone to know because he was engaged to some girl in Texas."

"Why do you think he was dating?" asked Buck.

"Once a week, he would get out of class, shower and dress real nice. I asked him a couple of times where he was headed, but he just said around, so I let it go. Then one night, he came in looking ragged as hell. He smelled of perfume and sweat, and he had a scarf around his neck, like a bandana. I hadn't seen it when he left. Not sure what that was all about, but the next day he walked out of his room, saw me and ran back into his room and came out a couple of minutes later with this bandana around his neck."

"No idea where he went or who the girl was?"

"No, sir. I never asked him about it again."

Buck asked him about Kevin's laptop and phone. "His laptop was here when the cops came that next morning after they found him. They found his password under a calendar on his desk, looked through it and then put it in a bag the detective had. I didn't see his phone, but he probably had it with him. He never went anywhere without the phone."

Officer Terrell received a radio call and stepped into the hallway. She returned a minute later and told Buck that she had a call and needed to run. She left the room, and Buck looked at Alex.

"Why do you think he killed himself, Alex?"

Alex sat on the couch and was silent for a minute. "I don't know why he would have, sir. He showed me a picture one night of this girl in Texas. She was beautiful and is in medical school. He was a straight-A student, and he had a job already set up with his father's company as soon as he graduated. I never saw him look depressed or anything. He always seemed happy. I can't imagine why he would have offed himself. Didn't make sense when the cops told me, doesn't make sense now."

Buck thanked Alex for his time, stepped into the hall, pulled up the campus map on his phone, found the admin building and walked out of the apartment building.

He was almost to the admin building when a thought occurred to him. He changed direction and headed towards the main school building, which housed classrooms, the cafeteria and student union and the campus hospital. He walked into the hospital and walked up to the reception desk. An older woman with silver hair and a name tag that said marge, volunteer asked him how she could help. He asked for the hospital administrator's office, and she pointed him towards the elevators and told him to turn left on the second floor. He thanked her and walked to the elevators.

Chapter Twenty-Three

Buck stepped into the hospital administrator's office and told the receptionist he needed to see Dr. Edward Griffin. Griffin was the doctor who had signed the death certificate, and Buck had a couple of questions for the good doctor.

The receptionist smiled and said that the doctor was in surgery and was not to be disturbed, but she would be happy to take his card and pass it on to the doctor. She asked him what this was about, and he told her it was a private matter. He thanked her and left the office.

The hallway outside the office was lined with photos of past administrators going back to the beginning. Buck worked his way along the photos until he came to the last one. The sign under it noted that Dr. Edward Griffin, MD, had been the administrator since 1964. He was a distinguished-looking man with gray hair. He was clean-shaven and wore glasses. Buck figured he had probably been in his sixties when the picture was taken.

Buck walked back towards the stairs leading to the front entrance. The hospital was an older space but was clean and neat. Several students were sitting in various waiting areas as he passed. For the most part, there wasn't a lot of noise, which surprised him. He remembered the times he had been in various hospitals, as either a patient or an investigator, and they always seemed to have lots of movement and background noise from overhead speakers. There was none of that here.

He assumed it might have something to do with being on a college campus, since most of the patients were students. He knew as a kid he'd hated to go to the doctor, and as soon as he joined the army, he only went to the doctor when it was required. He'd had his fill of doctors and hospitals when Lucy was going through chemo and radiation treatments. He'd be happy never to set foot in another hospital as long as he lived, but here he was. His thoughts were broken by movement to his left, and he stopped on the stairs.

Dr. Edward Griffin had come off the elevator and seemed to be making a beeline for the front doors. Buck wondered what that was all about since the doctor was supposed to be in surgery, so he took the steps two at a time and raced out the front doors after him. By the time he got out the doors, the doctor was a good two hundred yards away, unlocking a black Audi. He looked up at Buck through the windshield and backed out of his space, almost clipping a student who was passing behind the car. He tore out of the parking lot.

Buck wasn't concerned. This was a small community, and he figured he would run into the doctor in due course. He looked at his watch and decided to head over to the student union. He still had the picture in his phone of Kevin and the pretty blond girl, so he thought he might do a little asking around.

The union was packed, so Buck found a place to stand against the back wall and just look around. All these bright shiny faces, full of enthusiasm and questions about the future. He laughed to himself. These kids were the cream of the crop—the children of the one percent. Most of them already had their futures mapped out for them, yet here they were laughing and giggling just like his own kids did when they were in college, only the future for his kids hadn't been so clear.

He spotted one group gathered around a dark-haired young man, and he stared for a minute. There was something familiar about the young man, but Buck couldn't figure out where he had seen this kid before. He finished the Coke he had bought out of the machine and threw it in the trash. He pulled out his phone, opened the picture of Kevin and the girl and started making his way from table to table.

He was feeling frustrated as he worked the room. Either this girl was not a student here, or something else was going on. He found it hard to believe that no one would acknowledge that they knew Kevin, let alone the girl. He approached the last table, where a sizable crowd was gathered.

It was clear that the center of attention at the table was the dark-haired young man. He introduced himself to the table and showed the picture around. Those who bothered to look at it didn't admit to knowing her, and those who didn't look too closely seemed to silently check with the dark-haired young man before saying they'd never seen her.

Buck walked around the table and stood looking at the young man. "Have we met before?" he asked.

The young man, showing total disinterest in the question, looked at Buck. "I doubt it, pops. I don't hang around with geezers. Now, why don't you piss off? We're talking here."

The group around the table erupted in laughter, but Buck had what he needed. He knew the face was familiar, but not from this period. He'd known that face when he was a younger man, and the voice confirmed it, since this young man sounded just like his father had years ago. He knew he was right.

Buck walked away from the table and understood why everyone was gathered around this young man. He was holding court, just like his father used to do.

Buck hadn't seen Frank DiNardo in almost twenty years, but he had files dating back that far, and DiNardo's name was all over them. He thought back to that first time he'd arrested Frank DiNardo.

Chapter Twenty-Four

Frank DiNardo was the "godfather" of western Colorado. He had his fingers in everything—drugs, prostitution, gambling, and protection—that went on in Colorado and a good chunk of Utah and Wyoming. He was a cousin of Vincent Scapelli, the mafia boss who controlled everything from Kansas City to Salt Lake City, a guy who ruled his kingdom with an iron fist.

When Buck had first joined CBI, he was assigned to a task force investigating the Scapelli crime family. It was a region-wide federal and local task force whose sole purpose was to break up the family. They never succeeded. Buck never got all the details, but one day they were running an investigation; the next, they were told to clear out their desks and leave all the evidence and documents with the FBI. He wasn't sure what changed, but he never heard another word about the investigation. As far as he knew, no one associated with the Scapelli family ever went to jail due to that investigation.

Over the years, he encountered Frank DiNardo during several investigations, but there was never enough evidence to make a case stick. Which, frustrating as it was, actually helped Buck. Frank DiNardo could be as charming as he was ruthless, but for some reason Buck never understood, Frank had taken a liking to him. He was never a confidential informant, but over the years, Frank had reached out to Buck with information about potential crimes that were occurring around Colorado. Buck had also reached out to Frank when he needed a piece of information he couldn't get from another source. They were never friends, more like adversaries with a vested interest. Frank DiNardo knew enough about Buck that he understood that if Buck ever found enough evidence, he would arrest him in an instant. Still, Frank also knew that it was good business to pass along information to Buck that might get one of his rivals arrested.

Buck would have liked nothing better than to put Frank DiNardo in jail and throw away the key, and he always vowed he would. As far as Buck was concerned, this guy was as dirty and ruthless as they come, but he was also careful.

Buck stepped out of the student union and sat on a bench. He pulled out his phone and called Bax.

"Hey, Buck. I loaded a bunch of information to the investigation file this morning."

"Hi, Bax. Don't you ever sleep?" They both laughed. It was an inside joke. "Can you give me the highlights?"

"I'm having trouble getting full background on Chief Anderson and Detective Cummings. What I've found so far is clean, but there's a lot missing. The town has an interesting past. Typical Wild West town, but I get the feeling that hasn't changed over the years. I'm running down some information on the Martelli family, the town's founders, which I should have later. I gotta tell ya, Buck. This is an odd little town. Read what I sent you, and then we can talk."

"How about the girl in the picture with Kevin? Any luck with her?"

"Yeah. Kevin was on all the social media platforms—Facebook, Twitter, etc. I found her pictures on his private page. She's a student at the college. Melanie Granville. She has her own social media presence, and I get the feeling she's into some interesting stuff. I think she was also in love with Kevin, and I doubt his fiancée knew."

"Bax, how did you get on his private page?" he asked.

"Not hard when you know how to look. Oh, Max posted some information on the rope pictures. Take a look. You're gonna love this."

"Great. Now for the big question. Would you like to do a little undercover work?"

"What did you have in mind?" she asked.

"I'd like to see if you can get a feel for this town and the people in it. I get some weird vibes around here, and I'd like to know more. You will need to be extra careful. The locals keep tabs on this town like they own it, so your background will need to be ironclad. Can you work something up?"

"No problem, Buck. I can be there in a couple of hours."

"Bax, make sure you're tight. The cops here have a knack for getting information."

"No worries, Buck. I'm all set to go."

"Okay, also tell Paul I'd like him to head this way. I will reserve a room for him at the B and B I'm staying in. Fill him in on the information you sent me, and we can discuss it over dinner. Bax. Be careful."

"Stop worrying, Dad. I have this covered." She laughed and hung up, and Buck wondered about what they had discussed. He also wondered why she would already have a background set up that she felt was iron-clad.

He opened the investigation file on his phone, read the information from Max Clinton and dialed her number.

Max answered the call as she always did, and Buck told her that he was sending her the rope and Kevin Ducette's clothes, and could she put a rush on them? He knew he didn't need to ask because she would have done it anyway, but he was raised to be polite and never assume. Then he got down to the reason for the call.

"Max, are you sure about this information?"

Max laughed. "You asked for unconventional uses for that knot. That's what I sent you."

"Yeah, but that's seriously unconventional," he said.

"Look, Buck. I don't ask my people about their private lives and what they do outside the office, so they can feel comfortable coming to me with information we need. One of my team identified that use for the knot, and I'm passing it along without passing judgment. What do you think?"

Buck thought for a minute. "I think it might make sense. It could explain some things I've found out today. Let me mull it over. In the meantime, keep an eye out for the evidence. And thanks."

Max ended the call as always. "You're a good man, Buck Taylor. God will watch over you."

Buck disconnected the call and sat for a minute. "Police interference, a runaway foreign girl who was scared to death, missing evidence, a questionable investigation and now autoerotic asphyxiation. What the hell is going on in this town?"

Buck shouldered his backpack and headed for the administration building. He needed to find Melanie Granville. She just might have all the answers.

Chapter Twenty-Five

James Martelli was pissed. "How the fuck did he find out about the girl? You told me she wouldn't be any trouble."

"I don't know, sir. There was nothing in the investigation report to indicate she was anywhere near the Ducette kid when he died. We cleaned up everything in the space and wiped everything down. There's no way Taylor could have known about her."

"I'm getting tired of all these screwups. I need you to get this under control before I lose my temper."

Chief Anderson thought back to the last time he stood in this room and how he'd felt when Martelli shot that college kid for losing the foreign girl. He felt his stomach churn at the thought.

"Where is the cop now?"

"He's still on the campus. He's probably looking for the girl. I had the DiNardo kid stash her away as soon as he called me. Thought we needed to get ahead of this thing and fast."

"Good thinking, Chief. Unfortunately, this kid's suicide is putting us in a bind. We've got a lot of powerful people showing up in a couple of days expecting to be entertained, and now we have to focus on fixing your fuckups. What can this girl tell him about the suicide that's not in your report?"

Chief Anderson stood for a minute, not sure what to do. All he had told Martelli was that this kid had committed suicide. He hadn't gone into too much detail about how it all came about. He was thinking long and hard about what to do next when Martelli stood up from behind his desk.

"What are you not telling me?" The scowl on his face matched his mood.

Chief Anderson swallowed hard. "Nothing, sir. It was a straight-up suicide. The kid was depressed, and he took his own life. That's it."

James Martelli had been dealing with criminals his entire life, and he had a great sense of when people were lying to him. Chief Anderson was lying, but he wasn't sure why. For now, he let it go. He had too much going on right now to worry about an unrelated event that he had no control over. He would deal with Chief Anderson once all this crap with the state cop blew over.

Martelli looked at him. "I want the girl gone. Do you understand what I'm saying? I've got too much on my plate right now to worry about this state cop. Make sure he doesn't find this girl and make sure he is gone before Friday."

"If we get rid of her, he might get suspicious."

"He's already suspicious, you idiot. The more he snoops around, the more things he can find. Now get this taken care of, and I don't want to hear another thing about this girl or this suicide. Do you understand?"

Chief Anderson left Martelli's office and raced to his car. He slid behind the wheel, pulled out his phone and dialed Josh DiNardo.

"We need to meet, now." He hung up. He didn't have to tell Josh DiNardo where to meet because Josh already knew. He pulled onto the main street and headed back into town. He felt like his whole world was unraveling, and he didn't like the way that felt.

Chapter Twenty-Six

Buck grabbed a table at a Mexican restaurant down the street from the justice center. He took a few minutes to look over the menu and ordered the large beef burrito platter. The waitress brought him a large plastic glass of Coke. He took a sip and sat back to think about the day.

He was more convinced than when he'd first arrived that Kevin Ducette had not killed himself. The question was, did he die by accident, performing a dangerous sexual act, or was he murdered? The knot made it clear that Kevin was involved in some interesting sexual games, but did he act alone, or was someone with him at the time of his death? The rope was the key, and he hoped that the crime lab would find DNA on the rope. If he knew who had tied the knots, he would be that much closer to finding the person who'd helped Kevin, if that person existed. Of course, Kevin could have tied his own knots.

After getting Melanie Granville's address from the administration office, he had gone to her apartment, but her roommate said she hadn't seen her since she left for class earlier that morning. Buck had also gotten her class schedule, and he headed over to the class she was supposed to be in, but it was the same story. No one had seen her.

Since Buck couldn't find Melanie, he spent a few minutes in the plaza looking up autoerotic asphyxiation on the internet. He was amazed at how much information was available related to the subject, and after reading some of the postings, he felt like he needed a shower to clean up.

Autoerotic asphyxiation is a method of gaining increased sexual gratification by strangling oneself. It is most commonly performed by an individual while masturbating, but two people can also use it during intercourse. A dangerous practice when performed by two people, it could be deadly when performed alone and could give the appearance of suicide if death should occur during the experience.

The strangulation can be performed in virtually any position, from lying in bed to sitting propped up against a door or a wall. The method that Max Clinton had relayed to him was the most extreme and was not commonly performed by practitioners. According to Max's source, being hanged intensified the sexual experience but was dangerous, which is why several different types of quick-release knots or nooses were used. This way, if the person panicked, they could pull a rope, and the noose or rope would release.

Buck wondered how someone would have the presence of mind in a panic to find and pull the end of the rope. In all his time in law enforcement, Buck had been exposed to many things, but this seemed like the strangest of all. You were taking your life in your hands and taking yourself to the brink of death to achieve sexual pleasure. Buck was amazed at how many ways people could come up with to kill themselves, whether on purpose or by accident.

Understanding the use for the noose was one thing, but several questions remained. Kevin Ducette had been fully clothed, according to the photos Officer Terrell had taken upon arriving on the scene. If he had hanged himself to masturbate, it would be a lot easier if his pants were off. Was it possible he had help? Buck thought about that for a minute. That would explain some things, but if it was an accident, why hadn't the person who was with him called for help or tried to get him down, even if the quick-release knot was tied wrong and didn't release? All someone had to do was push the down button on the controller, and he would have been lowered to the floor. Based on the pictures, he had only been about two feet off the floor at the most.

The other question nagging at him was how did Kevin access the space? He would have had to get the door code from someone, yet Pedro, the maintenance director, swore that only his team knew the code. Who else had access to the code?

He was thinking of the last question when he looked up and spotted Paul Webber walk through the front doors. Paul looked around, spotted Buck and headed to the table. They shook hands, and Paul sat down.

Paul was over six foot four with a muscular physique. He had joined CBI four years earlier after spending ten years with the Dallas, Texas, police department. His last post had been as a homicide detective. Paul may have seemed like a giant, but those who knew him knew he was a pussycat. He was one of the most soft-spoken guys Buck had ever met.

They had first worked together on an arson fire that had almost cost Buck his life when the case got bigger than just a fire. Paul had also been instrumental in helping Buck unmask a decades-old serial killer in Aspen a year ago. It had been Paul's diligence that led to the information that revealed that the old serial killer's granddaughter, Alicia Hawkins, had taken up her grandfather's cause. Paul was instrumental in tracking down Alicia Hawkins when she'd returned to Aspen a few months back to fulfill a sick promise she had made to her dying grandfather. A promise that would embolden her and secure both their sick legacies.

Paul looked at the burrito sitting on the table in front of Buck. "That looks good." He waved over the waitress and ordered a burrito platter and a draft beer. "So, what's going on, Buck? From what Bax was telling me, it doesn't sound like you have been welcomed with open arms."

Buck took a bite of his burrito. "First table to the left of the door."

Paul looked around the restaurant and spotted the two guys sitting at the front table. They looked to Paul like two local ranches, both wearing jeans, boots and Stetsons. Paul looked back at Buck. "Welcoming committee?"

"Been on me since about an hour after I left the

justice center yesterday. Must be a shift change. So far, it's been one at a time."

"What the hell are we into here, Buck?"

"I'm not sure. My gut is telling me that there is a cover-up at work surrounding the Ducette kid's death. I'm just not sure why."

Buck filled him in on his surveillance of the old school building and the partying that seemed to be going on. He told him about Nadia, the girl with the European accent, who'd seemed scared to death. He left out the part about being kneed in the balls.

"So, this Ducette kid. You figure he was into some kinky shit, which might have gotten him killed? Accident or deliberate?"

Buck gave him the highlights of the case so far. They eventually worked their way back around to the question Buck had been thinking about when Paul first walked in.

Chapter Twenty-Seven

Paul dug into the burrito the waitress set on the table and took a sip of beer. "So, we can explain some of it, but you're right. The fact that the controller had no prints on it is weird. If the kid was there alone, I don't see him taking the time to clean the controller, and he wasn't wearing gloves in the pictures, so who wiped down the controller? If someone was with him, either a sexual partner or someone to act as a spotter, why didn't they call for help?"

"Now you see the dilemma. We're missing something," said Buck.

Paul thought for a minute. "Either we're not getting the whole story, or the story we're getting is bogus. Someone is covering up this kid's death. Why?"

"Go through all the information on the Ducette family and see if there's something we're not being told. Have we gotten his cell phone records?"

"Bax thinks we'll have them tomorrow. You know the phone companies. No one's in a hurry."

"Also run a background check on Dr. Edward Griffin. We need to find him. I'd like to know why he skipped out on me earlier today."

"What are you gonna do?"

Buck slid his empty plate to the side. "I need to

have another chat with the first officer on the scene. She might be able to help me fill in some holes. Is Bax in town yet?"

"Yeah," said Paul. "She got here about an hour ago. She checked into the hotel, and after she got to her room, she looked out the window and spotted a cop running her license plate on his laptop."

"We need to keep an eye on her, Paul."

"No worries, Buck. You know as well as I do that she can handle herself. The locals mess with her, and she's gonna put a few of them in the hospital. She said she would be at the Mother Lode Saloon at nine to start to get a feel for the town. Maybe we should meet there later for a drink?"

"Okay," said Buck. "In the meantime, keep an eye out for a tail. My guess is they know you're here and they're gonna want to know why."

Buck shook Paul's hand and left the restaurant. He stood on the main street for a minute, watching the two guys at the front table in the reflection on a car window. They looked unsure of what to do, and the taller of the two was on the phone with someone.

Buck spotted Officer Terrell's patrol car down the street a couple of blocks and headed that way. He needed to lose the tail before he talked to her. He was taking a chance of either exposing her to whatever was going on or exposing himself to the police chief. He wasn't sure where she stood, but he needed to take a chance.

Buck decided to approach Officer Terrell discreetly, so he used the oldest trick in the book.

He walked past the car he had seen his tail driving when he headed to the college, kneeled next to the wheel to tie his shoe and jammed his knife into the sidewall of the tire. He stood, walked across the street to his Jeep, slid in and pulled away from the curb. He spotted his tail in the rearview mirror jump into his car, pull away from the curb and then pull back into the curb. He climbed out, ran around the car and stood looking at the flat tire.

Buck hung a quick left, drove through the neighborhood two blocks off the main street and parked his Jeep in a parking lot designated for college faculty. He killed the engine, slid out of the car and headed back towards where he had seen Officer Terrell.

Officer Terrell was working her way down the street, stopping at each store she passed to have a chat with someone in the store. She was also logging license plates on the cars she passed as she strolled. It had been a lot of years since Buck had seen neighborhood policing going on. Nowadays, most cops just drove around in their patrol cars looking for trouble or waiting for a call. It was refreshing to see proactive policing instead of reactive policing. He stood at the door of a bar and watched her as she walked. He also checked around to make sure his tail was nowhere to be seen.

As Buck watched, she stopped on the sidewalk to talk to a man sweeping the street in front of a little gift store. He pointed around the corner, and she nodded, thanked him and headed in the direction he had pointed.

Buck stepped out of the shadows and followed her. He spotted her at the end of a small parking lot that ran alongside the gift shop. She was standing behind a car, entering information into her handheld notebook. Buck turned down the drive aisle.

"Evening, Officer Terrell," he said as he approached. He had learned a long time ago never to approach a cop with a gun in the dark.

She turned, and Buck noticed that her hand was on her pistol grip. "Oh, Agent Taylor. Out for an evening stroll?" she asked. She removed her hand from her pistol.

"Actually, I was looking for you. I was hoping you might be able to spare me a couple of minutes. I am trying to fill some holes in my information and need some insight."

Buck could see the smile form on her face.

"Is there someplace we could sit and talk for a minute, maybe I can buy you a cup of coffee?"

She looked at her watch. "I'm due for my dinner break in ten minutes, but it's quiet tonight, so let me call in and let them know."

She keyed the mic that was hooked to a loop on her coat and told the dispatcher that she was taking her dinner break. She finished entering the license plate number in her handheld and said, "Follow me."

She walked out the back end of the parking lot, walked two blocks west and a block north and opened the front gate on a small white clapboard house. She led him up the walk and opened the front door.

"Hi, Nana. It's only me," she called out.

There was no response as she invited him in and closed the door behind them. She invited him to have a seat, and she excused herself for a minute. Buck sat on the couch in a tiny living room and looked around. The little house was neat as a pin, and he could hear Officer Terrell speaking with someone in the back of the house. He spotted a picture on one of the shelves that surrounded a small wood-burning fireplace, and he stood up and walked over to it.

The picture showed a smiling Officer Terrell standing between two people. She was holding a police academy graduation certificate in her hands. The two older people looked as excited as she was. He heard movement behind her and turned.

"That's my grandparents and me on the morning I graduated." She picked up the picture and smiled a sad smile. "Grandpa passed away a month after that picture was taken. That was three years ago."

"Did your grandparents raise you?" Buck asked.

"Mostly. My dad was a cop in Reno. He was killed during a casino robbery when I was five." She wiped a tear from her eye. "Mom disappeared right after that. I saw her once a few years ago. Almost didn't recognize her. Drugs had destroyed her. I heard she died not long ago."

"Do you live with your grandmother? I heard you talking to someone."

"Come into the kitchen. We can talk while I get Nana's food ready." She walked through a swinging door, and Buck followed her into an immaculate kitchen.

"Nana suffered a stroke right after we moved to town. She's completely bedridden. Mrs. Delany next door keeps an eye on her while I'm at work. She's a retired nurse. I'm not sure how I would be able to afford it if I didn't have her to help out."

She put some soup in a bowl and headed into a back bedroom. Buck sat at the kitchen table. Ten minutes later, she returned with the empty bowl. She poured a bowl of soup for herself and offered Buck a bowl. He refused.

"Okay, Agent Taylor," she said as she sat at the table and started eating. "I'm all yours."

"Officer, when you arrived at the scene of the hanging, was anyone else there?"

"No, the maintenance guy let me in, and it was just me and the body. It was horrible. Why do you ask?"

Buck thought about how far he wanted to take this. He decided to trust her. He hoped he hadn't made a mistake. "There are some things that don't make sense."

She stopped eating and looked at him. He told her about the two rope marks on the neck that suggested the body had been moved. He explained that there were no prints on the controller, and he asked her if she had any idea where Kevin Ducette would have gotten the code. He asked her if she had seen the knot that was hanging from the hook before, and she told him she hadn't. She listened carefully while she ate. Then she looked at her watch.

"I need to get back on the street. I wish I could've helped more."

"No problem, Officer Terrell. Thanks for taking the time." She put on her coat, checked to make sure her grandmother was asleep and they left the house. Buck thanked her again and headed back to where he had parked his car. Officer Terrell stood by the gate and watched him go. She wondered why he had asked her to go over the whole thing again. She was just a minor player once Detective Cummings and Chief Anderson showed up. She stopped short. She looked to where Buck had turned the corner and was now out of sight.

"Why did Chief Anderson show up?" she said to the air around her. In the year and a half since she was hired, she had never seen the police chief at a crime scene—not that there was much crime in the city—so why did he show up for a suicide?

She focused on that morning, and something flashed in her eyes. She concentrated on the inconsistencies Buck had mentioned, and things started to fall into place. She needed to confirm some information, but she was beginning to understand why Buck hadn't been warmly welcomed into town. She looked around to see if she was being watched. Confident she was alone, she headed back to the main street and checked in with dispatch. She walked along the street, but she wasn't as focused as she had been. Something about the discussion she'd just had with Buck was nagging at her brain. Something she didn't like at all.

Chapter Twenty-Eight

Paul Webber sat in his car across the street from Dr. Edward Griffin's residence and read through the report he had printed off. The house was dark, and there was no sign of the doctor's Audi, so Paul settled in to wait. He didn't have to wait long before he saw the Audi turn onto the street. Paul watched the car weave down the street until it pulled into the driveway and drove through the corner of a hedge.

The car pulled to a stop in front of the garage door. The doctor opened the driver's side door and fell out on the ground. He tried to stand on his own but kept falling over. Once he was standing on his own two feet, he stumbled to the door and attempted to unlock it.

Paul sat and watched this fiasco unfolding until he had had enough. He slid out of his Jeep, walked across the street and approached the doctor, who was now sitting on the top step of the front porch with his head resting against the wrought iron rail. He had also pissed in his pants.

"Dr. Griffin. You seem to be having a little trouble. Can I give you a hand?" he said as he approached.

The doctor looked up with bloodshot eyes, and a look of fear took over his face. He held up his hands as if trying to defend himself. "I didn't tell him anything," he screeched as he tried to stand, finally pulling himself across the porch and crashing against the wall. "Please don't hurt me."

"It's okay, Doc. I'm a cop. I'm not here to hurt you," said Paul, in a soft voice he hoped would help the doctor settle down. It had the opposite effect. The doctor's eyes got as big as saucers, and he tried to regain his balance. He looked terrified.

Paul stepped forward and grabbed the doctor by his arms. "Calm down, Doc. No one is going to hurt you."

The doctor looked into Paul's eyes and, still fearful, attempted to pull away. Paul held on until the doctor tired. He picked up the doctor's keys and unlocked the front door. He half led and half carried the doctor into the house. He sat him on the couch and went to get some water. When he came back in, the doctor was passed out on the couch. Paul set the water on the coffee table and headed for the door.

"I didn't mean to hurt her," he mumbled, his words slurred. "It was an accident."

Paul knew better than to question someone this drunk, so he sat in the chair next to the couch and listened. The doctor was mumbling and making no sense. He twisted and turned on the couch as if evil spirits were tormenting him. He kept screaming out, "Don't hurt me. Don't hurt me."

He was silent for a few minutes, and Paul was about to leave when he suddenly opened his eyes and sat bolt upright on the couch and screamed, "They were just babies. My god, what have I done!" He fell against the arm of the couch and remained still.

Paul had no idea what that was all about, but it fired up his investigative juices. He pulled up the background information he had run on the doctor and went through it while the doctor snored away.

Dr. Griffin was in his mid-eighties, and he'd been at the hospital on the campus since 1964. Paul hadn't been able to find any specialty certifications or any specialized training. It looked to Paul like he had spent his entire life as a general practitioner. He wondered how he had come to run the campus hospital only a year or two after he graduated from medical school. That was a little unusual. Of course, the school wasn't nearly as big as it was today, and in the fifties and sixties, it was still a girl's school. Paul stopped reading.

Could that be what the doctor was mumbling about? Paul thought back to some of the stories he had heard while growing up in Texas, about a girl's school outside Dallas. His parents told tales of botched operations and the ghosts of the girls who went there and were never seen again. He always figured they were just tales his parents and the other parents made up to keep them from exploring the old hospital's crumbling ruins. Now he started to wonder if maybe there was more to it than that.

He checked the time on his watch and speed-dialed a number. He hoped it wasn't too late, but George answered on the second ring.

"Hey, Paul. What's up?"

George Peterman had joined CBI after retiring

from the navy, where he'd spent his entire career working in cybersecurity. As far as Paul was concerned, George and his partner, Melanie Hart, were two of the best computer people he knew. Paul was good. Bax was better, but these two were world-class. They made up the CBI cybercrimes unit based out of the Grand Junction Field Office and couldn't be more different.

Melanie, who was about five foot two, with shoulder-length black hair, wore black jeans, dark gray hoodies and had several piercings. Anyone meeting her for the first time would think she was a high school kid, but she had received her doctorate in computer science from MIT about a dozen years before. She'd joined CBI right out of college. George Peterman, on the other hand, could have passed for her father. George was about the same height as Buck, a shade under six foot, but where Buck still weighed what he'd weighed when he played football in high school, George had added a few pounds over the years.

"Hey, George. I need some background."

Paul gave him the doctor's name and waited. He checked to make sure the doctor was still breathing and poured himself a glass of water from the kitchen sink.

"Okay, Paul. I got into his medical records. He graduated from medical school in nineteen sixty-two. He was licensed to practice medicine in Kentucky that same year. Two years later, he's in Colorado, working at the school. He lost his license for a couple of months in 1965 and again in 1972.

Those files are sealed. I'll apply for a court order to get them opened." He was silent for a minute. "Now, this is interesting. He lost his license in 2015, and it was never reinstated."

"How's he working as a doctor?" asked Paul, not expecting an answer. "Any idea why he lost it?"

"Hold on, Paul. Melanie's pulling it up now."

Melanie clicked on to the call. "Hey, Paul. He was arrested for performing surgery while intoxicated. The young woman died from complications due to an abortion. Parents sued the school and were paid an undisclosed amount."

"So, he got arrested, lost his license and is still allowed to work at the hospital?"

"You got it. I also think he lost his license those other times because he was performing illegal abortions," said Melanie.

Paul was about to say something when George cut him off. "Paul, I just checked his license status in Kentucky. His license was suspended a year after he got it. He was arrested during a failed illegal abortion. The girl in Kentucky also died. He was released on bond and disappeared. The warrant is still active, but here's the kicker. He applied for the license in Colorado using his middle name as his first name."

"Shit," said Paul. "Send me the Kentucky warrant."

"Paul," said Melanie. "Here's something else I just found. There have been four missing persons in Copper Creek in the last three years. The victims were all students at the college, and they all disappeared without a trace. The local police investigated, but nothing ever came of those investigations. Shit, Paul, hold on a minute."

Paul looked at the doctor, who was still lying on the couch, snoring. He wondered if the missing person reports had anything to do with the doctor.

"Paul, this is crazy," said Melanie. "There have been a lot more than four missing person cases in Copper Creek. We found eleven more, the first one dating back to the year Dr. Griffin started working at the hospital. How the hell did no one notice this?"

Paul wondered the same thing himself.

"Mel, gather everything you can on the missing person reports and start an investigation file."

"What are you gonna do?" she asked.

"As soon as he wakes up, I'm going to arrest Dr. Griffin based on the Kentucky warrant. After that, I'm gonna start looking for a bunch of missing persons."

Chapter Twenty-Nine

Paul pocketed the doctor's car keys and checked to make sure he was still asleep. He needed to meet Buck at the Mother Lode Saloon and figure out what their next move with Dr. Griffin was going to be. He used the doctor's house keys to lock the front door and started down the sidewalk towards his car.

Paul sensed the movement to his right before he saw it, and he ducked just as the baton glanced off his head behind his ear. Momentum carried the baton downward, and it bounced off his right shoulder. Paul spun to his right without looking and fired a staggering left jab that shot out from his shoulder like a missile. The impact was staggering, and he heard cartilage crunch under his fist.

He spotted the second ninja, clad in black with a full ski mask covering his face, attacking from the opposite side. Paul didn't hesitate and, using all his mass, he charged the attacker, slamming into the guy's chest with his shoulder and driving the attacker towards the brick column that held up the front entrance cover.

They hit the brick column at full speed, and Paul could feel the guy's ribs breaking as he drove him into the column. His attacker screamed and slid down the column, with his arms wrapped around his chest. His raspy breaths told Paul that the guy most likely had a punctured lung.

Paul reached behind his right ear, and his hand came away covered in blood. He checked behind him, and the first guy he'd hit was still lying on the ground, holding his face, moaning. He checked the guy with the broken ribs for weapons and removed a semiautomatic pistol from a holster on his belt. He let him sit there, since it was apparent he wasn't going anywhere under his own power and walked over to the first assailant.

He rolled the guy flat on his stomach and checked him for weapons. This guy also carried a pistol in a holster attached to his belt. Paul relieved him of the pistol, pulled off the face mask, so he might be able to breathe a little better, and handcuffed his hands behind his back.

With the scene secured, he dialed 911, identified himself and reported the assault, requesting paramedics and police backup. He disconnected and dialed Buck. Paul filled Buck in and disconnected. He walked over to his Jeep and pulled out a plastic box marked evidence kit. He slipped on a pair of blue nitrile gloves, grabbed a couple of evidence bags and walked back to the scene.

He pulled out his cell phone and started recording the scene, narrating as he went. He could hear sirens in the distance. He gathered up the two weapons, both police-issue expanding batons, and placed them in the evidence bags. He took a close-up of the first attacker's face, covered in blood, then walked over and removed the second attacker's hood. He photographed him too. Then he sat on the front step and waited for the cavalry to arrive.

The first officer to arrive was a tall, skinny kid. He slid his police department SUV to a stop at the curb, jumped out, drew his weapon and moved cautiously up the sidewalk.

"Don't move!" he yelled at Paul, even though Paul was sitting on the stoop and his CBI badge was visible hanging from a lanyard around his neck. He could also see blood dripping down the front of Paul's shirt. Paul remained seated on the step and held up his hands.

"I'm a cop. I called this in."

The officer didn't look like he cared, and he took a flashlight off his belt and shined it in the face of the first assailant while not taking his eyes off Paul. Even though the assailant's face was covered in blood, Paul noticed there was instant recognition. He looked at Paul and spotted the other guy propped up against the column.

"Throw down your weapon," he said to Paul.

Paul looked at him. "I don't think so, and I would appreciate it if you would take your finger off the trigger and point your gun away from me." The aggravation in Paul's voice should have been all the kid needed, but he was going to be a hero cop. He took a step sideways and repeated himself, this time with more force in his voice.

"I told you to drop your weapon, and I'm not going to tell you again."

Two more cops arrived, followed by the

ambulance, and the EMTs raced across the lawn and checked on each attacker. They ran back to the ambulance and pulled out the first gurney. While they worked on the attacker propped against the column, Paul, with his right hand holding his head, and the first officer had a stare-off.

The two other arriving officers, one a sergeant, took in the situation. "Officer Toole," said the sergeant. "What do we have here?"

Officer Toole, still with his gun on Paul, said, "He says he's a cop, but he assaulted Jenks and Randolph."

The sergeant looked at each attacker; then he looked at Paul. "You assaulted two police officers. I'm gonna need your weapon and some kind of ID."

Paul's right hand was covered in blood, so he lowered his left hand and flipped open his jacket. He slowly removed his ID from his pocket and flipped it across the lawn. The sergeant picked it up and read it. "Now your weapon."

"Not gonna happen. And what do you mean I assaulted two cops? Who the fuck are these guys?"

"These guys are Copper Creek police officers."

Paul looked at him and spotted Buck pulling in behind the ambulance. The sergeant turned to see what Paul was looking at and frowned. Buck walked past the sergeant, without saying a word, and walked over to the first attacker, who was still on the ground. He walked over to the other attacker, who was being placed on a backboard, then stepped over to Paul.

He looked behind Paul's ear and pushed the hair away.

"You okay?"

"I'll be better if that kid puts his gun away. He's making me nervous."

Buck turned and looked at the officer and then at the sergeant. The sergeant walked over to Officer Toole, placed his hand on the officer's hand, and pushed the gun into a low ready position.

"Why are you pointing a gun at the victim?" Buck asked.

"Those two guys on the ground are two of my officers, and your guy is just sitting there. See how it looks from my perspective."

"Since my guy has a chunk taken out of his head, you might want to change your perspective," said Buck.

Buck walked over to the officer on the gurney and felt his pockets and inside his shirt. He then did the same to the other attacker, who started to object. He picked up the black ski mask and walked over to the sergeant. He pushed the ski mask against the sergeant's chest.

"Your guys always wear ski masks and not carry ID?"

The sergeant looked puzzled and stepped over to the attacker on the ground. He whispered in the guy's ear, listened while the guy said something in return and then stepped back to the sidewalk. He told Officer Toole to holster his weapon, which he did reluctantly. He walked over and handed Buck Paul's ID.

"Looks like we have a he said, she said situation here. My guy says they were on a stakeout watching the doctor because he received some threats."

"That's not true, Robert." The voice came from an elderly woman standing on the sidewalk with the rest of the onlookers.

The sergeant turned and faced her. "I'm sorry, Mrs. Howard. What did you say?"

She stepped up to him and snugged her jacket. "I said that's not what happened. I was taking the trash out to the curb and saw the entire thing. That big man was coming out of Ed's house when these two, with their faces covered and holding some kind of sticks, came out from both sides of the front walk and swung at him. He punched the first guy and then slammed into the other guy before he could hit him."

The sergeant did not look happy. "Thanks, Mrs. Howard. I'll have one of my officers take your statement."

He turned back towards Buck. "We'll figure this out, but we will need a statement from your guy."

"Not a problem. I want those two arrested, and I will have someone here in the morning to transport them to the jail in Fort Collins."

"We have good holding cells, right here," said the sergeant. Buck shot him a look, and the sergeant backed off. He led his officers away, and they followed the ambulance as it pulled away from the house.

Chapter Thirty

Buck sat on the step next to Paul. "You've only been here three hours. They didn't waste any time."

"Buck, what's going on in this town?"

He filled Buck in on the conversation he'd had with George and Melanie and showed him the warrant for the doctor. Buck looked at the investigation file on Paul's phone that Melanie had created. Paul told him about what the doctor had said before he passed out. It sounded like the doctor had some guilt about something. Once the doctor woke up, they would get confirmation of what that was.

Buck looked around the yard. "You think those two were here for you or the doctor?"

Paul thought for a minute. "I was sitting on the house for a while before the doctor showed up, and I didn't see anyone. They could have arrived after I went inside. What are you thinking?"

Buck ignored the question for the moment because he wasn't sure what he was thinking.

"That chief of police is going to freak out if we arrest the town doctor," said Buck. "We can't arrest him while he's unconscious, so maybe you should run over to the hospital and get patched up."

"I'll be fine," said Paul. "I would like to

interrogate those two pricks and find out what's going on."

"I'll take care of those two. I'll head over to the hospital right now and place them under arrest. It'll be best if you stay here with the doctor. Since we don't know if they were here for you or him, I would hate to see any harm come to him overnight."

Buck started to walk away. He turned and said, "Once we arrest the doctor, I want a forensic team here, ready to go. Coordinate it with Grand Junction and have them stand by in Walden. I'll call the director and have him send two state troopers up here to pick those two idiots up. They can take the doctor along with them. He should be mostly sober by then."

Buck looked at his watch. "After I arrest those two, I'm gonna swing by that bar and keep an eye on Bax. Call if you need anything. Have the office get a search warrant for the doctor's house, car, electronics, everything. If he's involved in something, I don't want to leave any stones unturned."

Buck turned and headed for his car. Tomorrow was going to be another interesting day in this picturesque little town. He wondered what kinds of secrets this town was hiding.

Chapter Thirty-One

CBI Agent Ashley Baxter walked into the Mother Lode Saloon, and the same thing happened that happened anytime Bax walked into a place full of men. It seemed like everyone in the bar noticed.

Bax was about five foot six with blue eyes and blond hair she often kept tied in a ponytail, usually hanging through the hole in the back of her CBI cap. She had been with the Colorado Bureau of Investigation for seven years, and she had earned Buck's respect.

Tonight her hair hung loose, and the cap was hidden in her car. She was what some would describe as husky, or what used to be called a "mountain girl" figure. She wasn't gorgeous, but she was pretty enough to turn men's heads when she walked into a room, at least until they spotted the badge and gun clipped to her belt. Tonight, she was working without her badge and gun.

Bax found an empty seat at the bar and ordered a glass of red wine. She turned slightly in her seat and scanned the bar. The group of local cops was easy to spot, so she turned slightly and watched them as she sipped her wine. The cops were entertaining several women, locals from the look of it, and at first, they didn't notice her sitting alone. She was beginning to wonder if she'd lost her touch when one of the cops staggered over and stood next to her.

"Hey, gorgeous. I've never seen you around town," he said, slurring the words. "You got a name?"

Bax looked at him, feigning disinterest. "Of course, I have a name." She smiled at him and sipped her wine.

"Why don't you tell me what it is, and maybe I'll buy you a drink."

"How about I don't tell you my name, and I'll finish the drink I have."

The cop looked unsure how to proceed. He put his hand on her shoulder and leaned in. She could smell the beer on his breath.

"I'm the police, and I'm asking your name," he said.

She stared into his bloodshot eyes, reached over and removed his hand from her shoulder. When she let it go, he fell into the back of her chair. His nostrils flared, and he scowled. "Oh, so you like to play games, do you? Suppose I slap the cuffs on you and haul you off to jail." He stood up taller and smiled at the other cops, who were now watching him and Bax interact. They cheered him on, and he puffed up his chest.

Bax faced away from him and took another sip of her wine. She watched him in the mirror behind the bar. He reached for her shoulder and started to swing the chair around. "I said I'm gonna buy you a drink," he slurred. A stream of drool hung from his lower lip. He leaned past her to call the bartender, and Bax struck.

She reached down, grabbed his crotch and squeezed. Surprise took over his face, and he tried to move but couldn't. Tears rolled down his cheeks, and his eyes got huge. She smiled at his agony, and with her other hand pulled his shirt until his face was even with hers. She squeezed harder, and she could see him fighting back the vomit. "I told you I didn't want a drink. Maybe the next time a woman tells you she doesn't want a drink, you'll think back on this moment and show her a little respect."

Bax gave one more good squeeze and then let him go. He fell to the floor with both hands holding his crotch. The other cops at the table stumbled out of their chairs and approached Bax, who had turned back to the bar and taken another sip of her wine.

"Hey, lady," one of them yelled. "What the hell did you do to our friend?"

They approached together. Close enough together that Bax could have taken them all out without working up a sweat. She smiled as they approached, and that seemed to piss them off even more. They stood around her and looked down at their friend lying on the floor, still holding his crotch.

The guy who appeared to be the ringleader spun her seat, so she was facing him. "Who the fuck do you think you are, lady? He was just having fun."

Bax remained quiet. She had learned a long

time ago that you can't argue with drunks or crazy people. She sipped her wine, never taking her eyes off the ringleader. If he made a move against her, she was coiled and ready to strike. When he started to poke her with his finger, the bartender had had enough, and he told them all to go back to their seats and leave the lady alone. They started yelling and threatening him, and he pulled a baseball bat out from under the bar.

One of the drunk cops pulled a pistol from his belt and pointed it towards the bartender. He started to say something, but Buck, who had just walked into the bar, didn't wait around to hear what he said. He waded into the group, grabbed the barrel of the pistol and twisted it towards the floor, wrenching it from the drunk's shaking hand. The drunk screamed in pain and grabbed his fingers. He turned to the others.

In a calm voice, he said, "It looks like you owe this lady an apology, and then it's time for you all to go." He dropped the magazine from the pistol, emptied the chamber, placed the gun and the magazine on the bar and slid it towards the bartender.

One of the drunks started to draw back his fist when a voice came from the door. "Don't," was all he said.

Buck turned to see the sergeant he had just left at the doctor's house, standing in the doorway. He did not look happy. He walked up to the group and looked at each cop. "You guys are a disgrace. Get out of here before I arrest you myself." He looked at the cop on the floor. "And take him with you. Be in my office tomorrow morning at nine, and a hangover is not an acceptable excuse for being late."

The five cops helped pick up their friend from the floor, which was a comedy of errors all by itself, but they were finally able to coordinate their efforts and help him to stand. They moved towards the door and left the bar.

The sergeant stepped up to Bax. "Not sure what went on here tonight, but I want to apologize for my men."

Bax smiled. "No need to apologize, sir. They were drunk and a little out of hand, and I helped them to understand that women deserve respect. Had things escalated, it might have gotten a little worse for them."

The sergeant looked at her and smiled. "I have a feeling they might have learned a hard lesson if Agent Taylor hadn't intervened."

He looked at Buck. "Agent Taylor, seems my people have not put their best feet forward tonight."

He nodded to Bax. "Have a good evening, ma'am."

He turned and walked out of the bar.

Chapter Thirty-Two

"Can I buy you a drink, sir?" asked Bax. She held out her hand. "Amber Frasier."

Buck shook her hand, introduced himself and declined the drink.

"No thanks, ma'am. Everything's under control, so I'll bid you a good night."

"That police officer addressed you as agent. Do you work for the FBI?"

"No, ma'am. Colorado Bureau of Investigation."

"So, you're not from around here?"

"No, ma'am. Here for another day or two and then on to another case."

"Well, I'm glad you were here. I was afraid for my life."

Buck smiled. "Somehow, ma'am, I doubt that's true."

Bax thanked him for intervening and smiled as Buck left the bar. Several of the women who had been sitting with the cops came over and gathered around her. The bartender brought over another glass of wine and told her it was on the house. The women wanted to talk about how she had put those guys in their place. They were not annoyed at all that Bax had broken up their party. They seemed relieved.

Bax introduced herself. "I'm Amber Frasier."

The girls introduced themselves, and then a couple of older women came over and asked the group if they would like to join them at their table. They all moved to the table, and the bartender brought another round of drinks for everyone.

Bax thought it seemed like a floodgate opened: the more they drank, the more they talked. She sipped her wine without drinking any and listened to what they had to say, which put this picturesque little town in a whole new light.

Bax listened until well after midnight, bought a final round of drinks for the group and then excused herself, telling them she needed to sleep since she planned on hiking part of the Continental Divide Trail in the morning. She said good night and left the bar. The night had gotten cooler, so she zipped up her down vest and headed for her hotel. She spotted the tail almost immediately. She would need to be extra vigilant. She felt her side and was comforted by the small .380 caliber pistol in the T-shirt holster under her flannel shirt.

She pulled out her phone and sent Buck a text to let him know she was safe and that she had some interesting things to tell him. They had previously agreed to meet in the morning, a couple of hundred yards from the trailhead, but she had some digging to do before she met with Buck.

She stepped into the hotel lobby and headed for her room. It had been an interesting evening.

Chapter Thirty-Three

Buck slid into his car when his phone rang. He felt comfortable leaving the bar since it appeared that Bax had everything well in hand, so to speak. He looked at the number and smiled.

"Hey, Kate. What's up?"

"Hi, Buck. Hope it's not too late," said Dr. Kate Milligan. "I had a chance to review the pictures, and the autopsy report, such as it is, and I wanted to give you my thoughts, right away."

"No worries, Kate. Whatcha got?"

"Well, first of all, the autopsy was a joke. I've seen better work from first-year pathology students. There was no internal examination, no toxicology and I can't find anywhere where the body was examined and samples taken for DNA analysis. So, what you do have is a mess. Now, the pictures helped some."

She stopped to take a breath, and Buck heard her clicking keys on her laptop. "There were signs that the body was repositioned. The picture you sent that you thought showed two different rope marks on the victim's neck does appear to do just that. The lighter-colored mark was most likely caused after death, which is why it's not as pronounced as the other one. Also, the darker rope mark should have been deeper. Even if he was intent on killing himself, the instinct when you can't breathe is to struggle."

"Do you think there could have been a softer material between the neck and the rope? I found some white fibers stuck in the strands of the rope."

Kate Milligan thought for a minute. "That would make sense. Something like terry cloth would protect the neck from abrasion, but why would you want to protect your neck if you were trying to kill yourself?"

"Great question," said Buck.

"One other thing," said Kate. "It's not clear in any of the pictures, but in one picture, we get a partial view of his left hand, and it looks like there might be an abrasion on his palm and fingers. Without better pictures, we can't be sure."

"Could that have happened if he was trying to pull on the rope?" asked Buck.

Buck told her about the conversation he'd had with Hardy Braxton about the quick-release knot and about the information on other unconventional uses for the knot he'd received from Max Clinton.

There was silence for a minute or two. It sounded like Kate Milligan was having a conversation with someone not in the room with her. She came back on the line.

"Sorry, Buck. I just called one of my assistant pathologists, who looked at the pictures with me. He thinks you might be on to something. Autoerotic asphyxiation isn't something we see every day, but we do see it. Usually, the victim is alone and dies by accident, and they're found hanging from a closet rod, or a rope, or a towel hung over a door. John, my assistant, has only seen one where someone was found hanging from a noose completely off the floor. That is an extreme form of AEA."

"How would they be different?" asked Buck.

"If you are hanging from a closet rod, doorknob, even a bed headboard, you lose consciousness, but because you are sitting partially on the ground or in a bed, it kind of sneaks up on the victim. They're comfortable, they've reached sexual ecstasy, and they don't realize until it's too late, if they ever realize at all, that they are running out of air. They sort of drift off to sleep. Hanging like your victim, you are completely off the ground, you have no contact with the ground, so when you start to run out of air, you fight back."

"Kate, how long could someone hang like that, and how long to reach a heightened sense of sexual awareness?"

Kate laughed. "Buck, sometimes you can be a real prude. You want to know if he could get himself aroused and ejaculate? Unless he had done this before, I doubt it. As soon as his feet left the ground, the tension on his neck would increase dramatically. With a soft pad under his chin, he would probably be okay for a minute, but the strain on his neck would start to hurt almost immediately. If he were trying to arouse himself, his focus would be all wrong. Think about swimming underwater. For the first few seconds, you are euphoric, but you start to think about running out of air, which becomes your focus. I would think the distraction would ruin whatever pleasure you could gain from the act."

Buck was silent. His mind was trying to work around the little bug stomping inside his head.

"What if someone else was arousing him?" asked Buck.

Kate thought for a minute. "I don't think it would change much. If he was focused on the sexual act, he might hold out for a little longer, but the urge to breathe is one of our strongest instincts. I still think he would have panicked, and the more he fought, the more he'd panic."

"Okay, Kate. Bottom line it for me, unofficial."

"Based on what you have told me about the knot, how the body was found and based purely on bad pictures, this young man either tied the knot and screwed up badly, or someone murdered him."

"Thanks, Kate. I owe you big-time."

Kate hung up, and Buck stood for a minute, looking at his phone. He had more questions than answers, but he knew where to start. He checked his watch and walked back towards the campus. He needed to find Melanie Granville.

Chapter Thirty-Four

Buck rang the buzzer outside Melanie Granville's apartment building and waited for a response. When a woman's voice came on the line, he identified himself and said he was there to see Melanie. The electronic lock on the door buzzed, and he pulled it open and made his way to the third floor.

He stepped off the elevator, and a young woman wearing gray sweats was standing barefoot in the hall. She looked like she was about to cry. Buck approached the door, and she said, "I don't know what to do. Mel isn't answering her phone, and I haven't seen her all day." Her arms wrapped tighter around her chest.

Buck signaled for her to go back into her apartment, and he followed her in, leaving the door to the common hall open. Stephanie Moore, Melanie's roommate, sat on the couch and was fidgeting with her hair. She looked frantic.

"When was the last time you saw Melanie?" he asked.

Stephanie thought back for a minute and, in a shaky voice, said, "At breakfast. We don't have any classes together, so I didn't see her during the day, but we were supposed to meet for drinks at the student union at four and she never showed. I just know something has happened to her."

Buck told her to try to calm down, and he walked over to the small kitchen and poured her a glass of water. She gulped it down like she hadn't had a drink in days.

"Does Melanie often not come home?" he asked.

Stephanie hesitated. She shook her head no. "She always answers her phone, and it just goes to voice mail."

"Was Melanie seeing Kevin Ducette?"

Stephanie's eyes got huge. "Oh my god. Did the same thing happen to Mel that happened to Kevin?" She started to cry.

"We don't know anything yet," said Buck. "How long were they seeing each other?"

Stephanie got control of herself, mascara running down her face. "Started over the summer, after she broke up with Josh."

"Josh DiNardo," interrupted Buck.

Stephanie nodded her head. "She was never into Josh, and they were bad for each other, but he took it hard when they broke up."

"Stephanie, why were they bad for each other?"

"Josh got her involved in some kinky stuff. They made a couple of sex tapes, and she came home a couple of times with a red mark around her neck."

"Stephanie, do you know where the sex tapes are?"

Stephanie pointed towards the closed door just off the tiny living room. Buck pulled a pair of nitrile gloves out of his backpack and asked her to show him. She stood and walked him towards the bedroom and pushed open the door. She pointed towards the rack of DVDs sitting next to the television. Buck asked her to sit back down, and he walked over to the TV. Most of the CDs and discs were for romance movies and romantic comedies.

He found one unlabeled jewel case, removed the disc and inserted it into the player. The scene that came on the TV was hard to watch. Melanie was hanging from the headboard, naked, with a rope around her neck, and she was masturbating. At one point, she almost passed out, then Josh DiNardo came into the picture, and he removed the noose, climbed on top of her and wrapped a piece of red velvet material around her neck and started to tighten it. Melanie gasped for air.

Buck fast-forwarded, and the next scene showed the reverse: Josh hanging from a noose while Melanie performed oral sex on him. Buck watched and checked the time on his watch. Josh lasted a lot longer than Kate Milligan had told him someone would be expected to, and in the end, he pulled on the loose end of the rope and dropped to the floor.

Buck turned off the TV, pulled out the disc and placed it in an evidence bag that he pulled from the front pocket of his backpack. He labeled the bag and asked Stephanie to come into the room. He showed her the disc and told her he was taking it, and he wrote out a receipt for it and had her sign it.

He spent a few minutes checking the rest of the bedroom and the small, attached bathroom but found nothing out of the ordinary. Her laptop was open on her desk. He sat down, clicked the ENTER key, and a picture of Melanie and Kevin appeared on the screen. It was an intimate photo. "Melanie really likes Kevin," said Stephanie. "But she knew it was just a school thing. He was engaged to some girl back home, so they were just in it for fun."

"Stephanie, was Melanie home the night Kevin was found?"

Stephanie got quiet and looked at Buck. "She came in late. I was already in bed. I heard her crying in her room, and when I knocked on the door, she told me to go back to bed. The next morning, we heard about Kevin."

Buck started walking towards the front door. "Oh, did anyone from the police ever talk to Melanie about Kevin?"

She shook her head no, and Buck thanked her and promised he would be in touch. He told her to try not to worry, which he knew, once he said it, was pointless.

Once outside, he called Detective Cummings, and it sounded like he woke him up.

"What the hell do you want this late?"

"Melanie Granville was Kevin Ducette's girlfriend, and they were into autoerotic asphyxiation," Buck said. "She's missing." Buck hung up and called George Peterman and asked him to get a warrant for Melanie's phone and see if the phone company could do an emergency locate. He headed for the hospital. He had two cops to arrest.

Chapter Thirty-Five

Officer Terrell sat at her desk in the police department bullpen and completed her reports for the night. She ran all her license plate contacts and left the list on the sergeant's desk. She always felt like she was spying on people by taking down their license plates and the make and model of their cars and running them through the Department of Motor Vehicles website.

When she first became a cop, she'd questioned the practice, but Chief Anderson had assured her that it was just part of good community policing. They would know who was visiting their town, and they were helping keep out the criminal element. She had to admit that the crime rate was low, and now and then, they got a hit on a stolen car or someone wanted by law enforcement elsewhere.

She walked past Detective Cummings's cubicle and spotted the Kevin Ducette file sitting on his desk. She looked around the room and checked her watch. There shouldn't be anyone else in the building for the next hour, at least. She sat down at the desk and opened the file. She read through the entire file and sat back in the chair.

She wasn't a seasoned investigator like Detective Cummings, but after reading the file, she wondered about some of the things Agent Taylor had said or maybe just implied. She closed the file. It seemed to her that more could have been done during the investigation. She thought back to the conversation she had had with Agent Taylor when they were at the scene.

There was no DNA, no tox screen, no fingerprints and the autopsy report looked to her like it had been phoned in. There was nothing of any value. She looked in the evidence box sitting next to the desk, but it was mostly empty. She noticed that the cell phone was not listed on the evidence list. She thought that was odd since she could see it sticking out of his back pocket when she'd first arrived on the scene.

The label attached to the top indicated that Agent Taylor had removed several items. She wondered if he was sending evidence to the crime lab. "What does he know that our people missed?" she said to herself.

She also wondered again why the chief of police had been on the scene. Nothing in the file indicated this was anything more than a suicide. It seemed odd that Chief Anderson would be there. She made a mental note to talk to some of Kevin's friends the next time she patrolled on campus. She would have to do some digging since there was no mention of any friends being questioned in the file. Something else she wondered about.

She stepped out of Cummings's cubicle and headed for the door. She needed to get home to check on her nana. She never saw the two cops standing in one of the conference rooms, watching her through the crack in the door.

Chapter Thirty-Six

Buck walked into the hospital and asked the woman at the front desk where the two officers were being treated. She pointed towards the emergency room.

The officers were lying in beds next to each other. They were both quiet. One was on oxygen, and the other had large pieces of cotton gauze sticking out of his nose. Buck could see blood soaking into the gauze.

On the way over, Buck had called the director and filled him in on the night's events. He was concerned about Paul getting hit in the head, but Buck told him not to worry. Paul was hardheaded when he wanted to be, and the director laughed.

He asked the director to send a couple of troopers to the hospital to take the two cops to Fort Collins. He didn't want them locked up in the place where they worked. He also didn't feel inclined to let the police chief know his plan until it was underway.

"So," said the director. "Bax really grabbed the guy by the nuts and crushed him? What was she thinking?"

"Whatever she was thinking, the display had a good effect. She texted me that she had a great conversation with some women in the bar, and she had some interesting things to look into."

"Okay. Keep an eye on her. She pissed off a lot of local cops tonight. That's not going to play well when they all sober up."

There was silence for a minute. "Buck, I don't like the fact that this young girl associated with Kevin Ducette is missing. We need to find her and fast. I will have the troopers there in a couple of hours. You be careful. I don't like the things we're finding out about this town."

Buck told him he would check in later in the morning.

The two cops looked at Buck when he walked into the exam room. Buck looked at each cop and made a quick assessment. The cop with the broken nose was able to be moved; the other cop with the broken ribs might not be able to travel.

The emergency room doctor walked in and looked at Buck. "Can I help you?"

Buck pulled out his ID and showed it to the doctor. "When can they travel?" he asked.

The doctor didn't look amused. "They can't travel. Officer Weems has a possible concussion and broken nose, and Officer Broncotti has a punctured lung and several broken ribs. We are waiting for the surgeon."

Buck walked over to the bed, slapped a pair of handcuffs on Officer Weems and clamped the other end to the bed rail. He turned and did the same thing to Officer Broncotti.

"You are both under arrest for assaulting a law

enforcement officer." They both sat in stunned silence as Buck read their Miranda rights from a card he pulled out of his pocket. The doctor started to object, but Buck looked him square in the eye and told him to back off.

Buck turned back towards the two cops. "Here is your one opportunity. This won't happen again. First one who wants to talk and tell me why you were at the doctor's house tonight gets to work a deal with the prosecutor. The other one is going to prison, and not the jail in town. You will both be transported to the Larimer County Sheriff's Office in Fort Collins, where you will be processed and jailed."

Weems stared at him. "You can't do that."

Buck laughed. "Oh, but I can. My jurisdiction covers the entire state. You guys assaulted one of my people. Both of you are going to jail tonight, and that will give you time to figure out which one of you will talk first. Remember, cops don't fare well in prison."

General population was a cop's worst fear about going to jail. Cops placed in a cell block with other prisoners found themselves in a precarious situation. They both looked at each other. Broncotti, on oxygen, looked at Weems and said, "Don't you say a fuckin' word."

Weems looked down at the blanket covering his chest, his voice sounding like he was talking through a can because of the gauze stuck up his nose to stop the bleeding. "I have a wife and kids. I can't go to prison."

"Oh, you are going to jail, either way. But one of you will be treated well, the other, not so lucky."

"You keep your mouth shut," yelled Broncotti, and then he wrapped his arms around his chest to stop the pain, tears running down his cheeks.

"What's going on here?" said the surgeon as he entered the space. "This is . . ."

Buck cut him off with a look. He pointed to Broncotti. "Doctor, can you move one of these men to a different room?"

The doctor glared at Buck. "For your information, I was coming to take Officer Broncotti to the operating room."

Buck stepped out of the way so the two orderlies could disconnect the tubes and wires and roll the bed out of the emergency room. Buck walked over and pulled up a chair next to Weems.

"Okay, Officer. It's just you and me. Anything you want to get off your chest?"

Weems looked at Buck with fire in his eyes. "Fuck you. We were at the doctor's tonight to protect the doctor from you people. He was afraid of what you might do to him. Your guy was in the wrong place at the wrong time."

Buck laughed. "And look who ended up in the hospital. The protection detail was bullshit. You were wearing masks, you had no ID and you went after my guy with a baton and not a gun. Your job was to scare us off. So, how about you tell me why?"

Weems was struggling with his loyalty. He worked for the chief of police, but he also didn't want to go to jail. He had a wife and two young kids, and they had a good life in Copper Creek. He was also struggling with the idea of giving up all the money he was being paid.

"Tell me about hanging the black kid. Were you guys involved in that?"

"No way. That was a real suicide. You think the kid was murdered? Is that why you're snooping around? Shit. We weren't even at the scene. Chief Anderson and Cummings took the call."

Buck held up his hand. "Why would the chief of police handle a suicide call?"

"You got me. I'm just a patrol officer. Nothing's got nothing to do with me, so why don't you go pester someone else."

Buck turned at that moment and saw the chief of police coming through the emergency room. He pushed the curtain aside and stepped next to the bed.

"Agent Taylor. I want you to leave my officers alone."

Buck smiled. "No problem." He patted Weems's hand and said, "Thank you, Officer, you've been most helpful. Get some rest, and we'll talk more tomorrow."

Weems's black eyes opened wide. "Wait a minute. What the fuck? I didn't tell you anything." He looked at Chief Anderson, who had a scowl on his face. "Chief, come on. You know me, I wouldn't help this prick. He's lying."

Buck walked past Chief Anderson. "He's under arrest, as is his buddy. State troopers will be here in an hour or so to take him into custody. Have a good evening."

Buck could still hear Weems protesting his innocence to Chief Anderson as he walked out of the hospital's emergency entrance.

Chapter Thirty-Seven

Buck parked in front of the B and B and sat in the car for a minute. On his way over from the hospital, he'd received a call from the state trooper, who was about twenty minutes out of town, and Buck filled him in on the situation with Weems. He then called the Larimer County sheriff and found out that Director Jackson had already filled her in and that the jail personnel were aware he was a cop and would be placed into protective custody under an assumed name.

He looked at his watch and decided he needed to grab a couple of hours of sleep. He would start searching for Melanie Granville at first light. He checked in with Paul, and the doctor was still passed out on his couch. He decided he would get Bax to also start looking for Melanie after they met in the morning. He swallowed what was left of his warm Coke, grabbed his backpack and slid out of the car.

He was almost to the front steps when he heard rustling in the bushes on the side of the house. He set his backpack on the porch and unsnapped the thumb break on his holster. He didn't want to be surprised like Paul had been, so with his hand on his pistol, he walked towards the noise.

As he got closer, he heard what sounded like air escaping from a tire. "PSSSST."

He looked behind the bush on the corner of the house and spotted Charlie Womack.

"Charlie, what the hell? I might have shot you."

Charlie stepped around the bush but stayed in the shadows. He waved Buck closer.

"I need you to come with me. I have something to show you."

Buck looked at his watch. "Charlie, it's late, I've got a lot to do tomorrow and I'm not gonna get much sleep as it is. Is this important?"

The old sheriff looked at him like he had two heads. "If it wasn't important, do you think I'd be standing here waiting for you all night, freezing my ass off?"

"Okay, Charlie, I'm in." Buck had no idea what was going on, so he decided to follow Charlie. After all, what else did he have to do but sleep.

Buck grabbed his backpack and started towards his car. "Not your car. They've been watching you since you got here. Follow me."

Charlie stuck to the side of the house and led Buck to the street behind the B and B. Buck was surprised at how easily Charlie moved through the yard. Buck knew Charlie was in his eighties, but he moved like a young kid. A young kid with a purpose.

Charlie stopped at an old pickup truck, opened the door and slid into the driver's seat. He set a large revolver on the seat next to him. Buck set his backpack on the floor, and Charlie pulled away from the curb. They rode in silence for the first couple minutes until Charlie took a turn just past the entrance into town. He started up a steep hill.

"Charlie, what's this all about, and where are we going?"

Charlie downshifted on the steep grade and then pulled off the road, if you could call it a road, and slipped the car into a group of trees. He stopped the engine and looked at Buck.

"Been lookin' into the death of that Carbon County deputy, from our side, and I found something suspicious. I need you to take a look."

"Charlie, you're retired, shouldn't Marty be doing this?"

"Let's just say that I'm helping him out. I'm still a certified lawman, so what the hell."

Charlie opened the door and slid out. Buck hadn't noticed earlier that the cab's overhead light didn't come on when Charlie opened the door. Buck smiled. Once a lawman, always a lawman. He grabbed his backpack and joined Charlie at what looked like an old game trail. Charlie headed off into the darkness, and Buck followed.

Charlie stopped just before the top of a rise and kneeled between two boulders. Buck was curious about where they were because he had seen the glow of the lights for the last quarter mile. Buck kneeled next to Charlie, and Charlie handed him a pair of binoculars. He got down on his belly and slid around the one boulder and looked through the binoculars.

The scene in the little valley below was full of

activity, and Buck scanned the area. There was a large metal building and a good-sized parking area next to the mine entrance. He recognized a lot of the mining equipment, but what caught his eye was the number of cars parked in the area. He watched for a few minutes and then slid back around to Charlie.

"Okay, Charlie, it looks like a mine of some sort. What's so suspicious?"

"That mining equipment never moves. I've been up here several times this week, and it's always the same scene. Lots of people, but nothing moving."

"That's not a lot to go on. What do you think you know?" Buck asked.

Charlie leaned back against the rock. "I started poking around after that young deputy got killed—just something to do to keep my mind busy. The gas station on Highway 125 had some trouble a while back, so Margaret—she's the owner—put in a couple of really good cameras and pays extra to store the video. She let me look at the videos, and on the night that young deputy died, there wasn't much traffic, but one car caught my eye. It went by the gas station about a half hour before they think the deputy was killed."

"I went back sixty days and worked my way up to yesterday. Twice a week, the same nights and same times each week, that same car runs by the station. The last time was last night. I was waiting for it and followed it here. They loaded a bunch of boxes in the trunk, and it headed back out to the highway and headed towards Wyoming."

Buck looked at Charlie. "You recognized the car, didn't you?"

"Car belongs to the Copper Creek Police Department. It's a black Camaro they got from Homeland Security a couple of years back. One of those government giveaway plans. Homeland picked it up in a drug raid. The police use it for undercover work, which they don't do much of."

Buck thought about what Charlie just said. He was starting to wonder if there was more to his being sent here than he initially thought. More than just a suicide investigation. It seemed like a lot of odd things were going on in this town.

"Charlie, who owns this mine?"

"The Martelli family. They own most of the mining claims in the valley."

"Any possibility you're reading this wrong, and they're running a legit mine?" asked Buck.

"Come with me. There's someone you need to meet."

Chapter Thirty-Eight

Charlie stood and headed back to his truck with Buck following. Buck looked at his watch. He figured he wasn't going to get much sleep with what was left of the night. They climbed into Charlie's truck and headed out the same way they came, but before reaching the highway, Charlie turned onto a road that Buck hadn't even seen. It wasn't much of a road at all, more like a cart path. They bounced for another mile or so and came to a stop in front of a ramshackle cabin.

Charlie slid out of the seat, told Buck to wait by the truck and walked towards the front door. There were no lights on, and Buck wondered who else they were waking up at that ungodly hour. Buck slid out of the truck and watched from behind the door. If there was some trigger-happy old geezer living here, he wanted some protection between himself and the cabin.

Charlie stepped onto the creaky porch and, instead of knocking on the door, sat down in one of the old cane back chairs Buck could see.

A voice came from nowhere. "You gonna have your friend join us?"

"Yeah. As soon as I was sure you wasn't gonna shoot us, ya old goat."

A tall, thin man stepped out of the woods on the

side of the cabin, walked past Charlie and opened the door. A light came on, and Buck could see the flickering yellow light through the window. Charlie waved for Buck to come forward.

When Buck entered the cabin, Charlie was already seated at a rustic wooden table and had a cup of coffee in front of him. Their host was standing next to the woodstove and holding up the coffeepot. Buck refused and sat opposite Charlie. The owner of the cabin sat down.

"Buck Taylor, Lars Gunderson, miner. Lars, Buck Taylor, CBI," said Charlie. They shook hands. Lars's hands were as big as dinner plates and rough enough that Buck had no problem seeing this guy as a miner. "Lars used to own the mine we were at tonight. Lars, go ahead and tell him."

Lars took a sip of coffee. He was at least as old as Charlie but was clean-shaven, and his hair was neatly trimmed. His face had the wrinkles to prove that he had spent a lot of time in the outdoors. He was rugged and fit. He looked around the cabin.

"This is my escape, this cabin. I live north of Walden. So that you understand that I know my stuff, I want to tell you a little about me. I was born right here in North Park. Granddad was a miner, and so was dad. At one time, we owned several mining claims in Jackson County. Besides being a miner and geologist, I have a master's degree from the Colorado School of Mines. The mine you were at tonight was the last mining claim I sold off. Sold it to the Martelli family some fifteen years ago. The Rose number two. Named after my late wife.

The mine was a good producer, but it played out long before I sold it. The Martelli family bought, or in some cases stole, every mining claim in the county."

Lars sipped his coffee. For a minute he had a far-away look in his eyes. Buck figured he was remembering some memorable moments.

"The Martellis ran every other mining operation out of the county, sometimes with money and sometimes with force. Couple of the old miners ended up missing and were never seen again—lots of accidents. My guess is they're down at the bottom of a shaft, somewhere. Anyway, I eventually sold him what we had left, except for the Rose. Sentimental maybe, or just plain stubborn. Just didn't want to part with her. The Martellis made good money over the years with their claims and still do. They now have mines all over Colorado and Wyoming, but they wanted the Rose.

"Fifteen years ago, James Martelli came to me with an offer that was too good to be true. At first, I refused him; then things started happening—brush fires at the house, break-ins, threats. I tried to talk him out of the deal, told him the mine was played out. He didn't care. I couldn't figure out what was so important about the mine. I watched him over the years make improvements and bring in equipment. On the outside, it looks like a thriving mining operation, but nothing ever comes out of it."

He took another sip of his coffee. Buck was now interested.

"When Charlie mentioned his suspicions to me,

it was like a light bulb going off. Martelli didn't want the mine for any gold or silver that was left. He wanted the mine for its location. You see, the Rose two is the only mining claim within the city limits of Copper Creek. The only one he can control without anyone looking over his shoulder."

Buck sat back in the old wooden chair and scratched his head. He looked at Charlie. "You think he's running drugs out of there?"

Charlie nodded his head. "You betcha, and I also think whoever drives that car killed that young deputy. It makes sense. The killer removed everything that could identify them—cameras, laptops, phone. They knew where all the cameras were located, and they got rid of them. Had to be two of them because someone had to drive the patrol car to the river overlook. Couldn't be done by one person."

Buck pulled out his phone and pulled up his mapping app. He pulled up a map of Walden and expanded it to cover Jackson and southern Wyoming. He set the phone on the table.

"Makes sense," he said. "From here, they can run up to Rawlins and send the drugs on I-80 West, all the way to California, or they could head to Laramie and send drugs on I-80 East, all the way to New York City, or a thousand places in between."

He looked at Charlie. "What does Marty think?"

"Haven't told him anything yet. Marty has to answer to the county commissioners, two of whom live in Copper Creek. That whole town is a crime hotbed, and there's nothing he can do about it."

"Okay," said Buck. "We are a little light on any physical evidence but let me work out some of the kinks. When is the next shipment?"

"Tomorrow night. They are at the mine around nine p.m. I can get set up where we were tonight and call you when they get there."

Buck smiled. "Charlie, let me handle this, okay?"

Charlie stood up fast and almost knocked over the chair. "No way. This is my case, and I'm on it until the end. You think I'm too old for this, shit. You sound just like Marty. I want to get the bastards that killed that deputy, and if you won't help me, I'll do it my own damn self."

Buck held up his hands in surrender. He felt like he had when his dad used to yell at him when he was a kid.

"You win, Charlie. Let me work a few things out, and then we'll go get them."

"That's better. You'll see I can still carry my own weight, and I can still shoot, a lot better than Marty."

Buck laughed. "Okay, let's keep Marty out of this until we have this figured out. And Charlie, stay away from the mine. You did good, so far. Let's not push our luck."

They thanked Lars Gunderson and climbed back into Charlie's truck. They didn't speak much on the way back to the B and B, and Charlie dropped Buck off on the block behind the B and B. Charlie drove off, and Buck looked around to make sure his tail wasn't around. He had a couple of hours until he needed to meet Bax, so he headed inside to grab some sleep.

Victoria James wasn't in her usual place behind the counter, which didn't surprise Buck, since he figured she had to sleep sometimes. He grabbed a cold bottle of Coke from the refrigerator in the lounge and headed upstairs. He unlocked the door to his room and pushed it open. The light from the hall revealed a brown envelope lying on the floor. He checked the hall, stepped into his room, turned on the light, closed and locked the door. Out of habit, he checked the bathroom and inside the closet; both were empty. He wondered how the envelope had gotten under his door since all the exterior doors were locked to all but guests and staff.

He sat at the small desk in the corner, put on a pair of nitrile gloves and opened the envelope. There were several eight-by-ten pictures and a thumb drive. Buck looked at the pictures. They were dark and grainy, but they were clear enough to get a good view of what was going on. Buck set them on the counter and picked up the thumb drive. He knew he wasn't going to get any sleep tonight.

Chapter Thirty-Nine

Buck opened his laptop and inserted the thumb drive. The video came to life as a door opened, and in walked Josh DiNardo and a friend, someone Buck hadn't met yet but recognized from their brief encounter in the campus cafeteria. The friend set up an area on the floor with a blanket, lit a bunch of candles and set a bottle of wine and a couple of plastic cups on the ground. While he did that, Josh lowered the hook on the winch and tied the noose to the hook.

Buck watched carefully as he tied the knot. The camera must have been a ways away from the winch, so it wasn't completely clear, but it looked to Buck that Josh placed the loose end of the rope through the last loop. He rewound it several times to try to see it better. Maybe George, at the office, could enlarge the picture or enhance it. When they were finished setting the stage, Josh raised the noose to about shoulder height, looked around and they left the space.

The time code said about ten minutes had elapsed when Josh entered the space for the second time, this time alone. He walked over to the noose, grabbed the controller and, using a small screwdriver, opened the back of the box. Buck couldn't see what he was doing, but whatever he did, he finished and closed the back of the box. He left the space, and the screen went dark.

According to the time stamp on the screen, Kevin Ducette and Melanie Granville entered the space an hour later. Melanie was a pretty blond woman who was slightly shorter than Kevin. She wore a very short skirt and very tall, spiked heels. They checked out the noose and the controller and then sat on the blanket and poured themselves a cup of wine. They spent time talking, laughing, kissing and groping each other. Buck wished the camera had volume, but he wasn't that lucky. He also felt like a voyeur, but he had no choice. This was all evidence, and as much as he hated it, he had to watch it.

A half hour passed, and they stood and approached the noose. By this point, Melanie had removed her blouse and bra. She was a very fit young woman. Kevin stood under the noose and placed it over his head. Buck could see that the noose was wrapped in some kind of fluffy fabric, which explained the white fibers he had found.

Melanie and Kevin kissed, then Melanie unbuckled his belt and slid his pants and underwear down to his shoes. She grabbed the controller, pushed the top button and Kevin was lifted off the ground. Kevin seemed to struggle a little as the noose tightened around his neck. Melanie raised the noose until his manhood was even with her face, and then she got closer and took him in her mouth.

Kevin seemed to enjoy what was going on, and Melanie was really into it because, at first, she didn't notice him struggling to breathe. He grabbed the noose to try to get some air, then he grabbed the loose end of the rope and pulled. Nothing happened.

Melanie, realizing that he was struggling for air, started pulling on the loose end of the rope along with him. She then grabbed the controller and pushed the down button, but nothing happened.

Melanie, looking around in a panic, grabbed her phone and said something to Kevin. Kevin was twisting and squirming, and the look of anguish on his face was heartbreaking. Melanie grabbed her blouse off the floor and ran out the door. Buck watched the time stamp.

After three minutes of struggling, Kevin's arms dropped to his sides, and he seemed to go limp. He didn't move again.

According to the time stamp, it was about fifteen minutes before Josh and his friend returned. They stopped in the doorway and just stared at the body hanging from the noose. Josh said something to his friend, and the friend gathered up the blanket, the candles, the wine and the glasses and what looked like Melanie's bra, folded everything in the blanket and left the space. Josh walked over and made sure the door was locked. He walked over to the controller and once again opened the back. He did something inside the controller and replaced the cover. He pushed the bottom button, and the body started to lower. He pulled out his phone, made a call and left the space.

Buck took a long drink from his bottle of Coke

and waited to see if anything else came on the screen. He was not disappointed.

The time stamp noted about an hour had passed when Josh walked into the space, followed by Chief Anderson. Chief Anderson looked at the scene and said some words to Josh. He did not look happy.

He walked over and pulled up Kevin's pants and underwear and tightened his belt; Josh lowered the noose until Kevin's feet just touched the floor, enough to take the weight off the noose. Chief Anderson removed the fabric around the noose, and Josh raised Kevin back off the floor. They both looked around the space and then left.

Buck uploaded the video to the investigation file and sent a note to George Peterman to see if he could enlarge or enhance it. He told George he needed a better view of what Josh was doing with the controller. He also asked George to see if there was any way to trace the video back to a person or location. Someone had set that camera up to record what went on in that space. The question was, how many other videos were out there? Then he sat back and stared at the blank screen.

Here were two young college students, engaging in consensual sex and expecting to enjoy an evening of what Buck considered to be dangerous behavior. It had ended in the death of a bright young man, and it was not an accident. It was clear that whatever Josh DiNardo had done to the controller led directly to Kevin Ducette's death. This was premeditated murder, and Chief Anderson was hip-deep in an attempt to make it look like a suicide.

Judging by the care Josh and his friend had spent setting up the scene with the blanket, candles and wine, it was also apparent that this was not the first time they had set this stage. The autoerotic asphyxiation was not, by itself, illegal, but it was certainly risky.

Buck finished his Coke and looked at his watch. He had time for a quick shower before he needed to meet Bax. He also needed to call the director and Paul.

Chapter Forty

Paul answered his phone as soon as it started ringing.

"Hey, Buck. Get any sleep?"

"No. It's been an interesting night."

He filled Paul in on the video he'd received and also about the time he'd spent at the mine with Charlie Womack.

"Do you think Charlie's onto something? He hasn't been a cop for a lot of years."

Buck thought for a minute. "I wasn't sure until I spoke with Lars Gunderson. There is a hell of a lot of activity going on at a played-out mine. I think Charlie is right, and I think he's right that the mine and the dead deputy in Wyoming are connected. I'm just not sure what we can do about it. We don't have any evidence that they're moving drugs, but the setup is perfect."

"How about a traffic stop?" said Paul.

"I was thinking the same thing. If we stop them right on the border, we can control the scene, but we can also get Carbon County to help us. Larimer County Sheriff's Office has a drug dog. We could let the dog walk around the car and see if he alerts. If he does, we move on them."

"What if he doesn't alert?" asked Paul. "Then

we've lost our opportunity, and we've blown the case."

"Yeah. Otherwise, we have no probable cause. I'll call Larimer and see what they think. How's the doctor?"

"He's up and around. What do you want to do?"

"Arrest him," said Buck. "Take him to Walden and put him in a cell. See what he's willing to tell us."

Paul hung up, and Buck called the director. They had the same conversation, and the director agreed that the traffic stop made the most sense.

"What about an accident?" asked the director. "Close the road, temporarily. Have Larimer County come in in civilian clothes. Let him get out of his car to walk his dog while they wait. If he doesn't alert, no one is the wiser."

Buck liked that idea. He asked the director to send him three or four state troopers and asked if he would call the Carbon County sheriff and set it up.

"What are you going to do about the chief of police? If the video is real, he covered up a crime?"

Buck hesitated for a minute before answering because there was a question on his mind, and he needed to get it out.

"Sir, I get the feeling I'm here for more than one reason. Is that true?"

"Let's just say that you have a way of making things happen, and if you should happen to find corruption or uncover other crimes while you're there, then that's a good thing."

The director told him to be careful and to call

if he needed anything. Buck hung up and circled the block once more to make sure he wasn't being followed. He headed for the trailhead for the Continental Divide Trail and parked under a tree. He slid out of the car, looked around and headed up the trail.

Bax was waiting in a small rock outcropping, just where she said she would be. Buck stepped behind the rocks and set down his backpack.

"You took a hell of a chance last night," said Buck.

Bax laughed. "I needed to win the respect of some of the women in the bar, and it worked. I also attracted the attention of the police. I spotted one of the cops from last night in the hotel parking lot early this morning. He was watching my car."

Buck looked concerned. "Will the Amber Frasier cover hold up? You didn't have a lot of time to backstop it."

"No problem, Buck. Amber Frasier is my twin. We've been swapping identities since we were little kids. Got us in some trouble growing up, and it has always been foolproof. The car is registered to Amber and her husband. Anything they find will hold up."

Buck was stunned. He had worked with Bax for over seven years and never knew she had a twin sister.

"A twin, huh," said Buck. "What else don't I know about you?"

"Someday, we'll sit down and have a long talk.

But right now, I have some interesting information," said Bax.

Buck grabbed the bottle of Coke out of his backpack and took a long drink. So far, this was a day full of surprises. He sat back against the rock and let Bax talk.

"This town is fucked up, Buck. The women I sat with last night don't like it much. According to them, the Martelli family, the folks who founded the town, control everything. Do you know that the family owns almost every commercial building in this town? The shopkeepers, restaurant and bar owners rent from them, and they receive a subsidy every month. The subsidy is more than they would probably make on their own, which is what keeps everyone silent."

She told him there had been talk around town of doing something about that, but they didn't know where to start. "The Martellis use the local cops to control everything and everyone who enters this town. It's almost like a lovely prison.

"The women said most of the town's economy comes from the college and the mining operations, but they all believe the Martellis are in the drug business, and there's even talk of sex trafficking."

"They told me that over the last ten years or so, at least ten people have disappeared. Some of those were college kids, and some disappeared in the national park. The cops do nothing about it. One woman suggested that crime was so low in town because the cops control all the crime. What the hell kind of town did we land in?"

Buck didn't say anything; he pulled out his laptop and opened the video he'd received earlier. He hit play and waited. Bax watched the video, and he could see an entire range of emotions run across her face. She hit the stop button and looked at him.

"Holy shit, Buck." She thought for a minute. "That might explain something I noticed walking around town. There are a lot of people, both men and women, wearing high collars, scarves, or bandanas around their necks. I felt like I was in a sixties sitcom, but the video makes sense. I think there's a bunch of people in this town who are into autoerotica."

Buck had seen the scarves on people, but he hadn't given it a second thought. Now, it became another piece of the puzzle. He closed the laptop and filled her in on everything that had happened since he hit town. She was worried about Paul, but Buck assured her he was okay.

"What do you want me to do?" she asked.

"First thing we need to do is find Melanie Granville and that girl Nadia. All their info is in the file. Stay in your Amber persona and see what else you can pick up around town while you look for them."

"What are you gonna do?" she asked.

"I'm gonna take on Josh DiNardo and see if I can shake him up a little. Stay in touch and be careful."

Buck put his laptop in his backpack and slung it over his shoulder; he nodded to Bax and headed back down the trail. He had a feeling this was going to be another long day.

Chapter Forty-One

Paul led the handcuffed doctor into the Jackson County Sheriff's Office in Walden and placed him in the only interrogation room they had. He removed the handcuffs and told him to sit tight.

He asked Deputy Haskins to keep an eye on him while he spoke with Sheriff Womack. Paul introduced himself and filled the sheriff in on the outstanding warrant from Kentucky and told him that the doctor was also being arrested for practicing medicine without a license.

"Wow," said Sheriff Womack. "A sixty-year-old arrest warrant. That's a new one on me. I can't believe his license was suspended here. He's the only doctor, other than the emergency room doctor at the hospital on campus, that we've had in this county for the past sixty years. People are gonna be shocked. What do you need me to do?"

"Keep an eye on him for a while, and don't let anyone except Buck or me talk to him. No calls to lawyers, nothing. Right now, no one knows he's here."

Paul told him about the two cops that had attacked him.

"You've got to be kidding. Cops. Always knew that town had some bad apples on the force. You think they were after the doc?" asked the sheriff.

"Right now, that's our working theory. So, he's here as much for his protection as he is for the crimes he's accused of committing."

Paul asked if the sheriff could print off the search warrant for the doctor's house that had come through that morning. He'd requested the warrant from the U.S. District Court in Denver since he didn't want to alert anyone in Copper Creek.

Paul took the warrant, thanked Sheriff Womack and headed back to the doctor's house. On the way out of town, he stopped at the Nugget Saloon, grabbed a coffee and breakfast and waited for the forensic team to arrive. He was finishing a platter of eggs when they walked in. They ordered breakfast while he filled them in on the warrant and what they might be looking for. They finished their breakfasts and followed him to the house.

The forensic team was getting into their Tyvek suits and donning face masks when the first police car pulled to the curb. Paul met the officer at the curb.

"Help you, Officer?" he asked.

"What are you doing here?" asked the officer as he tried to step around Paul to get a better look at what was going on.

Paul pulled the search warrant out of his back pocket and held it up so the officer could see it. He reached for it, but Paul pulled it back.

"We're searching the doctor's premises, pursuant to his arrest." He folded the warrant and placed it back in his pocket; the officer glared at him.

"You arrested the doc? On what charges?"

Paul decided to play it straight. "The doctor was arrested on a warrant out of Kentucky. He is wanted there for performing illegal abortions and possibly manslaughter as a result of some of the abortions. He is also under arrest for operating in Colorado without a valid medical license."

The cop looked bewildered. "You arrested the doctor for performing abortions? Abortions are legal in this country. What kind of bullshit charge is that? Where are you holding him?"

"The doctor was arrested during the night and was transported to a holding facility in another county," said Paul.

He started to walk away when the officer called out, "You're the guy who arrested two of my friends last night. You think you're some kind of badass?"

Paul stopped and walked back to the officer. The officer had his hand resting on the back strap of his pistol. Paul got right in his face, which caused the officer to back up a step. "Yeah. I arrested them. They broke the law. What concern is it of yours?"

The cop turned on his heels, slid into his patrol car and sped off—no doubt heading straight to the police chief. Paul headed back inside and joined the search.

Chapter Forty-Two

Bax caught up with Melanie Granville's roommate, Stephanie Moore, as she was entering the classroom.

"Hi," said Bax. "You're Melanie's roommate, Stephanie, right? I'm Amber. I was supposed to meet her to go over some class notes for my psychology class, but I haven't been able to get a hold of her. Have you seen her today?"

Stephanie looked at Bax with a suspicious look. What she saw in front of her was a blond girl wearing ripped jeans and a T-shirt and carrying a backpack. She lowered her guard.

"I haven't seen her since early yesterday, and I'm starting to worry. She's never stayed out of touch this long. I don't know what to do."

"Maybe I can help," said Bax. "I have an hour before class. Where was the last place you saw her? I can start there."

Stephanie told her that Melanie and her gang had all been together in the cafeteria during lunch. She wasn't part of the group but had passed them as she was heading to class.

Bax asked her who she had been sitting with, and Stephanie gave her the names of the students she knew. She said there were a couple of new faces she hadn't seen before. Bax jotted the names down in a small notebook and told Stephanie she would be in touch if she found out anything. She left the building and headed for the cafeteria.

She looked at the names she had written down and recognized the name Josh DiNardo. Buck had mentioned he was going to track down DiNardo, so she focused on the other names. She headed to the administration office to see if she could get their class schedules. The woman at the counter was helpful, and within minutes, she had the schedules for three of the names on her list.

She found Billy Wilson as he walked out of class, and she gave him the same speech she had given Stephanie. He told her he hadn't seen Melanie since yesterday, but she felt that he wasn't being truthful. He fidgeted a lot and kept looking around like he was making sure no one was watching him. He told her he had to go to class and headed down the stairs to the first floor. Bax decided to follow him.

Instead of heading to class, Billy Wilson headed out the main door and darted across campus. Bax had no trouble keeping up with him since running was her thing, and she participated in several marathons each year with her dad. She watched Billy enter a building that, according to the sign out front, contained the private offices of some of the professors and the on-campus branch of the police department.

Bax followed him into the building and spotted him entering the back door to the police department. She stopped outside the door, checked the hall to make sure no one was watching and placed her ear close to the door.

"I don't know what to do," said Billy. "Last night Melanie's roommate started asking questions about her, and then this morning, this Amber chick got in my face, outside of my class, and started asking. People are noticing that she's gone. I tried to call Josh, but his phone is off. What should I do?"

"First thing you can do is calm the fuck down," said the unknown male voice. "The second thing you can do is stop worrying."

"That's easy for you to say, but I'm the one getting questioned. What happens if her mom calls me? She knows we're friends. What if she calls me?"

"You tell her you've been off campus for a couple of days, and you haven't seen her," said the voice.

Billy was quiet for a minute. "Is she still alive?"

She heard a chair slide back on the hard floor surface. She had no way of knowing what was going on. Then the voice said, "Billy, let it go. You know where she is. As far as I know, she's still there. Keep your wits about you, and don't fuck this up. Once the state cop is gone, everything will get back to normal. Now get out of here."

Bax ducked into a nearby women's restroom and waited until Billy left the building. She walked by the office door and pushed it open, looking startled. "I'm so sorry. I was looking for a restroom."

Detective Cummings pointed her down the hall, and she closed the door. She went out the main door and spotted Billy heading towards the student apartments. She raced across the campus, slid into her car and headed around the back of the apartment buildings to the parking lot. She spotted Billy walking towards a Volkswagen Beetle in the back row. She pulled in front of it just as he started to pull out, and he hit the brake. Bax was out of the car in a flash. She held her badge up to the window and pointed her pistol.

"Out of the car," she said.

Billy froze, and for a minute, he wasn't sure what to do. He pulled out his phone, and Bax tapped the glass with the barrel of the pistol and shook her head no. He turned off the car and unlocked the door.

She put her badge back in her pocket and pulled him out of the seat, keeping her pistol on him the entire time. She pushed him against the car and, in two swift moves, had him handcuffed before he realized what was happening. She spun him around.

He started to say something, but Bax cut him off. "You are being questioned regarding the disappearance of Melanie Granville. Keep your mouth shut until we get to the sheriff's office."

She walked him around her car and placed him in the front seat, hooking the seat belt around him. She slid in and pulled out of the parking lot. She called Buck but got his voice mail, so she left him a message.

Chapter Forty-Three

Buck found Josh DiNardo sitting at the bar in the Mother Lode Saloon. He was nursing a beer and had three empty shot glasses sitting in front of him. The bartender spotted Buck as he came through the door and walked towards the other end of the bar.

Buck stood at the end of the bar and looked at Josh until Josh spotted him and sneered.

"What the fuck you lookin' at?" He slurred every other word.

Buck smiled. "Josh, I'd like to know what happened to Melanie Granville."

Josh took a drink of beer and waved for the bartender, who took his time walking the length of the bar. Josh pointed to the empty shot glasses. The bartender glanced up at Buck and walked back down to the end of the bar. Josh's anger grew. He glared at Buck.

"Fuck off, old man. You're not my keeper." He yelled towards the end of the bar, "Bring me another shot, you prick."

"You've had enough for now, Josh. Now, we can talk here, or I can drag your sorry ass to the sheriff's office, and we can talk there. Your choice."

"Do you know who I am?" asked Josh.

Buck smiled. "Usually, when someone asks me that question, they're not as important as they think they are. To me, you're just another prick who thinks he's more important than he is. Is that you?"

Josh's face turned bright red. Other people in the saloon looked towards the end of the bar and then looked back at their plates or drinks. It was clear to Buck that Josh was a problem.

Josh pulled out his phone. "One call to my old man, you fuck, and you're dead meat, you hear me?"

Buck pulled out his phone and held it up for Josh to see. "How about I call your old man? I have his number right here. He might like to hear about how stupid his son is. He'll also tell you that you don't want to mess with me." He looked into Josh's eyes. "Yeah, I know your daddy. You look just like him when I first busted him some twenty-odd years ago. So, let's give him a call, and while we have him on the phone, we can tell him about how you like being strangled during sex. We can even send him some of the videos you made with Melanie Granville."

By this point, everyone in the place was watching the two of them. Josh was getting madder by the minute, and Buck was standing at the end of the bar, showing no emotion, and talking in a steady voice, loud enough so everyone could hear the conversation.

Josh couldn't help but hear the snickers and the quiet laughter behind him, and he got furious. He grabbed the glass off the bar and threw it at Buck. His aim was terrible, and Buck just had to dip his head to one side to avoid it. The glass broke against the wall.

Buck didn't move. "What have you done with Melanie Granville?" he asked again, this time speaking slower than the first time he'd asked.

"Get out of my face," he slurred. "You don't know shit."

Josh pushed back from the bar, stumbled into the stool and fell back on his ass. He hit the floor with a thud, and more people laughed. He didn't look like such a big man, lying on the floor. He got to his knees, grabbed the top of the bar and stood up on shaky legs.

He reached into his back pocket and pulled out a knife, which he flicked open with one hand. "You think you're such a badass, Mr. Policeman. Let's see how you feel when I stick you." He waved the knife at Buck, who hadn't moved from his spot at the end of the bar.

"Josh, that's enough," said a voice from behind him. He looked around and lost his balance, again, and had to grab the stool to stay upright.

"Josh, put the knife away, now."

The guy who was speaking walked to the end of the bar and placed his hand on Josh's shoulder. "Josh, he's trying to provoke you. Put the knife down before someone gets hurt, most likely you."

Jimmy Martelli was shorter than Buck had expected, but there was no mistaking who he was. Everyone in the bar got quiet and stared into their plates. Several people at the bar got up and made their way to the door. He looked like a high school kid who was wearing his daddy's five-thousand-dollar suit and five-hundred-dollar shoes. He had dark wavy hair and didn't look like he needed to shave more than once a month, but he had evil eyes, which Buck noticed right away.

Buck watched him as he took the knife from Josh, folded it and stuck it into Josh's back pocket. He nodded to one of the two men standing behind him, who walked over and took Josh by the arm and led him out of the bar. Jimmy Martelli watched them leave.

"Drunk kids. It's a college town, what are you gonna do. I hope you don't mind, do you? You don't seem inclined to arrest him."

"Not yet," Buck said. He watched Jimmy Martelli. He could understand why some of the women Bax had talked to felt intimidated by the Martelli family. Buck had pegged him as a sociopath as soon as he stepped into the middle of the conversation. He glanced around the room and noticed everyone watching the exchange.

"You would be CBI Agent Buck Taylor?"

Buck nodded, never taking his eyes off Jimmy Martelli.

"I'm James Martelli, Jr. My family founded this town."

Buck smiled. He would have liked to grab this kid by his expensive suit and smash his face into the floor, but he held back. He was curious where this conversation was headed.

"Am I supposed to be impressed?" said Buck.

Buck's response caught Jimmy Martelli off guard, and he caught himself before he made another comment. He wasn't used to being spoken to like that, and he was unsure how to proceed. It was obvious to Buck that Jimmy Martelli liked to intimidate people. Buck was not intimidated in the slightest. Jimmy finally regained the composure he hoped Buck hadn't noticed he'd lost.

He took a step closer to Buck, followed by his henchman. "My understanding is that you are here to decide if that poor young man committed suicide. I'm sure that by now, you've had plenty of time to conclude your investigation and are ready to move on before the chief of police asks you to leave. That would be embarrassing. Don't let us keep you, Agent Taylor."

He turned and walked away from the bar and headed towards the door.

Buck waited until he was at the door. "Don't worry, Junior. As soon as Josh sobers up and I can finish my conversation with him, without your interruption, I'm sure I'll be getting close to wrapping things up. You know what the nice thing about my job is? I don't take orders from the local police. By the way, this is an interesting town you have here. Have a good evening."

Buck could see the back of Jimmy Martelli's neck turn bright red. He hesitated for a minute and then walked out of the bar. The bartender walked down to the end of the bar. He smiled at Buck, and Buck ordered a Coke. He sat on the same stool Josh had been sitting on and looked at his phone. A message from Bax had come in while he was talking to Josh and Jimmy. He played the message and drank the Coke that was now sitting in front of him. He left a five-dollar bill on the bar and walked out the door. He needed to get to Fort Collins to interview the cop who'd assaulted Paul and talk to the drug dog's handler.

Chapter Forty-Four

Paul walked into the sheriff's office in Walden and stopped to talk to Sheriff Womack. He asked if anyone had come by to talk to the doctor, and the sheriff told him there had been no interest so far. The office had one small interview room, and Paul asked if he could use it.

The sheriff led him to the room and told him he would get the doctor. Paul put the box he had been carrying on the desk and pulled his laptop out of his bag. He turned on the video recording function and pressed pause.

Sheriff Womack led the disheveled doctor into the interview room. He looked like he hadn't slept in a week. He was pale and drawn. He sat down at the table, and Paul walked around and removed the handcuffs.

He walked to the other side of the table and sat down. He pushed the resume button on the laptop and just sat and looked at the doctor without saying a word. He pulled the Miranda warning card out of his pocket and read the doctor his rights. He asked the doctor if he understood his rights, and the doctor said he did. He asked him if he wanted to waive his right to counsel, and he sat there still and thought for a minute. Paul sipped some of his water, offered the doctor a bottle, which he accepted, and opened the cover on the box.

The doctor said he was willing to talk without a lawyer present, and Paul pulled out a waiver form and had the doctor sign it.

Paul set a college diploma on the table. Next to it, he placed the sixty-year-old arrest warrant from Kentucky. He next placed a letter he had found from the Colorado Medical Board, suspending the doctor's medical license in Colorado for an indefinite period of time. The doctor looked on but said nothing. Sweat started to form under his nose.

Paul sat back in his chair and just looked at the doctor. He didn't say a word. The doctor fidgeted in the chair for fifteen minutes taking sips from the bottle of water, which poured onto his shirt because his hands were shaking.

"What do you think you know, Officer?" said the doctor, trying to control the nervousness in his voice.

Paul reached into the box and pulled out a stack of manila file folders, some old and some much newer. He fanned them out on the table like a dealer would spread a deck of playing cards.

"I have to admit," said Paul, "that was a good hiding spot. We had to take a lot of the furnace apart to get to your hidey-hole, but I give you a lot of credit for trying." He sat back for a minute to let the doctor look at the files.

Paul slid a file towards the doctor. "Why don't you tell me about baby girl Fletcher?" He paused and then slid another file forward. "How about baby boy Thompson?" He paused for another moment. "Or better yet, tell me about this young woman." He flipped open the file, removed a picture from under a paper clip and slid it forward. "Evelyn Perry, pretty girl, kind of sad."

The doctor looked at the picture on the table, and tears formed in his eyes. He reached for the picture, and Paul pulled it back. He stared at the doctor.

"There was so much blood," said the doctor, his voice barely above a whisper. "I tried to stop it, but I couldn't."

Paul slid the picture back towards him. "You told her parents that she ran away after miscarrying. What really happened, Doctor?"

The doctor pulled back from the table. Paul followed him with his eyes. "She died at your hands, didn't she? You aborted her pregnancy, and something went wrong, which is not an unfamiliar situation for you, is it, Doctor? What happened to the girl after she died on the table?"

Paul slid another file forward. "Veronica Westly was fifteen years old when her parents sent her to you. They had arranged a private adoption, which maybe you didn't know about. When her parents came to get her, you told them that the baby was stillborn, that their daughter couldn't deal with the pain and the horror and she checked herself out of the school and disappeared. Do you remember Veronica, Doctor?"

Paul reached into the box for another file. He opened it and slid a piece of paper towards the doctor. "You were very meticulous, Doctor." He tapped the paper. "You recorded the details of every baby you sold out of the school, including the names of the families you sold them to."

Paul grabbed for another file. "Enough!" yelled the doctor. He put his face in his hands and cried. Paul sat back and sipped his water.

The doctor looked up at Paul, with tearstains on his cheeks. "I wasn't a good enough doctor. I should have never been a doctor. I hated it. These people trusted me, and I took something precious from them. I'll never forgive myself."

Paul leaned forward. "Then help me give these families closure. Where are their daughters?"

The doctor got quiet for a minute; then he looked at the picture of Veronica. "She pleaded with me not to take her baby. Her father had arranged for the baby to go to a good, Christian family. The cesarean was successful, then, just like so many others, she started to hemorrhage. I couldn't find the bleeder. She died holding her baby in her arms."

"Tell me where she is, Doctor."

"I'm not a monster. The families came to the school to either let their daughters have the babies or to have me terminate the pregnancy. I wrote everything in the file. I hoped it would make me a better doctor, but I failed."

"Where are these girls, Doctor?"

"Under the patio behind the hospital." He started to cry again.

"Doctor, how long did this go on?"

The doctor looked up at Paul. "It's still going

on. The last girl died two years ago. We buried a stillborn female about six months later."

Paul sat back, stunned. "How were you able to bury bodies on a college campus and not get caught? I can understand when it was a school for girls, but two years ago it was a college. How?"

"How do you think? The police helped me. They made all the arrangements for the adoptions and took care of the young ladies."

The doctor wasn't finished. "When Martelli senior hired me, he knew about my past. He told me he would send me back to Kentucky if I ever said a word, and I never have. Over the years, I performed hundreds of abortions for huge money. These families didn't want the scandal. If they were too far along, I would do a cesarean before they were due, and the baby was adopted out. There is a lot of money in scandal and adoptions, especially overseas adoptions. A lot of my work now involves taking care of the unwanted pregnancies of the foreign girls."

"What foreign girls?"

"The ones who work for Mr. Martelli and his son."

"Doctor, does the chief of police know this has been going on?"

The doctor looked at him with a confused look on his face. "Nothing happens in this town that he and Martelli don't know about.

"What will happen to me now? I'm too old to stand trial."

Paul laughed. "Oh, you will stand trial, and you

will likely die in prison. You are a sick son of a bitch."

Paul reloaded the box, turned off his laptop and walked out of the room. Sheriff Womack met him at the door. "What a sick fuck. What do we do now?"

"Call Larimer County and see if they can send a transport up here to pick him up and take him to the jail in Fort Collins. I need him in protective custody, the sooner, the better."

"What then?" asked Sheriff Womack.

"I need to call Buck and fill him in; then I need to get ground-penetrating radar and a backhoe up here. We are going to have a lot of work to do. Is there a judge in town you trust? Someone not connected to Copper Creek?"

"Judge Fields is retired, worked in Denver for years, and now he fills in up here when he's not fishing. He's also my uncle. Family good enough?"

Paul smiled. "Let's go pay your uncle a visit."

Chapter Forty-Five

Buck turned off South Timberline Road onto Midpoint Drive and pulled into the Larimer County Jail complex. On the drive to Fort Collins, he called Larimer County Sheriff Loren Hatch and told her what he needed. She told him not to worry; it would all be set up by the time he got there. He left his backpack in the Jeep but grabbed his digital voice recorder and stuck it into his pants pocket. He slid out of the Jeep and headed to the main entrance of the jail. He presented his ID to the guards on duty, placed his pistol into the lockbox just outside the gate and was buzzed in.

Sheriff Loren Hatch met him on the other side of the gate. "Buck, nice to see you again. Been what, four or five years?"

Buck smiled. "Five since the law enforcement conference in Denver. How are you doing?"

"You know the job. Never enough time to get everything done."

Loren Hatch was dressed in a black pantsuit and light green blouse. She was almost as tall as Buck, with dark shoulder-length hair. She told Buck to follow her, and they were buzzed through several doors. She led him into a conference room and told him that Officer Weems was on his way. They chatted for a few more minutes until she got a page and excused herself.

Officer Trevor Weems entered the room wearing his bright orange prison clothes and a pair of Crocs on his feet. He sat opposite Buck and placed his cuffed hands on the table, looking for some compassion. He didn't get any from Buck.

Buck pulled out his voice recorder and set it on the table. Since it was voice-activated, he didn't need to turn it on. He pulled out his Miranda warning card and read Weems his rights again. He asked him if he understood his rights, and he said he did. He asked him if he wanted an attorney, and he said no. Buck handed him another small card and had him read his waiver of counsel into the recorder.

"It wasn't my idea to jump your man. That was all Broncotti. Chief told us to make sure he didn't talk to the doctor, but we got there too late. Your man was already inside, so we waited till he came out. Thought we'd thump him a little. I guess we thought wrong, huh? Feel like I ran into a truck." He touched his nose.

Weems's eyes were both black circles, and his nose under the bandage looked to be twice the size it had been before the encounter with Paul.

"Why didn't Chief Anderson want the doctor to talk to us?" asked Buck.

"Don't rightly know. Broncotti and me, we're just muscle. Chief says he wants somebody messed up, he sends us, and we mess them up."

"Give me an example."

Weems thought for a minute. "You know about the girls, right? One gets out of hand, or one of the guests gets out of hand; we make sure it doesn't happen again. Someone doesn't pay their fair share; we make sure they do."

"So, you want me to believe the police chief is running prostitutes and has a protection racket going. Come on. What do you take me for?"

Weems looked antsy. "That's gospel, and that's only part of it. You think the crime rate is low by accident? Not a chance. Chief Anderson knows everything that's going on. We got state-of-the-art surveillance equipment all over town. Nothing gets past him."

"Is the entire police department in on this?" asked Buck.

"Don't think so. You need to be around for a while before he trusts you. Then you get an assignment, and he evaluates how well you do. You do good, you're in."

"Where are the girls kept?"

"The basement of the old school building. Chief did it up real nice. We get a busload of guests on Friday nights. They stay for the weekend. They're big money people. Men and women. Pay a lot for the privilege. Get to gamble and then get their pick of a girl. He even has some of the college girls working for him."

"Did Kevin Ducette commit suicide?"

"Don't know. Chief said he did. He took care of everything. We weren't involved."

"How does Josh DiNardo fit into all this?"

"Josh is Chief Anderson's man on campus. Runs everything going on. His daddy is supposed to be some big mobster. Don't know much about that."

"What happened to the girl that escaped from the old school?" asked Buck.

Weems got quiet and looked around the room and at the floor. "Don't know about that."

Buck leaned across the table. "You're a liar. You take care of all the dirty work. I think you and your buddy were able to track her down. What did you do with her body?"

Weems looked horrified. "I'm being straight with you. We didn't kill her."

"Who did?" asked Buck.

"I'm not saying nuthin' else till I get a deal. I just gave you enough to hang Chief Anderson out to dry, and I want to see my kids grow up. You get me into witness protection, and I'll spill everything on Chief Anderson, the dirty cops and the Martellis."

Buck took out his phone and dialed Sheriff Hatch. "Did you get all that?" She told him she had.

"Is the DA here yet?"

She said he was and told him they would be right there. Buck sat back and saw relief come over Weems's face.

The door was unlocked, and in walked the sheriff, followed by Calvin Groves, the district attorney, four other folks in suits, who were not introduced, a court reporter and a deputy U.S. Marshal, who introduced himself to Buck and thanked him for helping his fellow marshals out during the shoot-out.

The DA took Buck aside. "Great job, Agent Taylor. We'll take it from here. I have a Colorado Superior Court judge on standby, and he'll issue whatever warrants we need for you. I will call you when we have what we need."

Everyone settled in around the table, and Buck and Sheriff Hatch left the room, picked up their weapons and headed for the sheriff's office across the parking lot. They entered through the back door, and she led Buck into a conference room. The only person in the room was a tall black deputy, who stood when they entered.

The sheriff introduced Buck to Deputy Everett Harcourt. Deputy Harcourt filled Buck in on his experience as a drug dog handler, and Buck filled him in on what they were looking for. They all took seats at the table, and Buck took the lead.

"We don't know what kind or if we're even dealing with drugs. Can your dog alert to everything, including fentanyl?"

"Yes, sir. Boomer is one of the best in the business. If these guys are carrying, she'll spot them."

Buck explained how they wanted to run the operation. The sheriff and Deputy Harcourt asked a lot of questions about the setup.

Buck stood up and shook hands all around. "If you guys are good, we'll see you, Deputy, in Walden by eight p.m." He handed Harcourt his card, with the address of the meeting location written on the back and thanked them for their help.

He left the building, slid into his Jeep and

checked his messages. He called Paul back and said he was on his way. He pulled out of the parking lot and headed back towards Copper Creek. He was running low on sleep, but the adrenaline was starting to kick in. Things were starting to break loose.

Chapter Forty-Six

Bax pulled into the sheriff's department parking lot just as Paul and Sheriff Womack were walking out of the building. She parked her car, slid out and walked around and unbuckled Billy Wilson. Paul and the sheriff walked over to the car.

"Hey, Bax," said Paul. "What have you got here?"

"Hey, Paul, Sheriff. Got a holding cell for one more?"

Sheriff Womack turned around and unlocked the office door. He walked Billy back, uncuffed him and placed him in the other holding cell, next to the doctor.

"What's his story?" asked Sheriff Womack.

Bax told them about the conversation she'd overheard at the campus police office between Billy Wilson and Detective Cummings. She was confident she could get Billy to tell her where Melanie was.

"I never liked that prick, Cummings. Let's get Billy into the interrogation room and see what we can get. We were heading over to see the judge; maybe we'll have more to tell him," said Sheriff Womack.

Bax went back to the car, grabbed her backpack and placed it on the interview room table. She pulled out her laptop, and, just like Paul, she opened the video recording app and hit pause. She would start recording once Billy Wilson stepped into the room.

The sheriff led Billy into the room, sat him in the chair and hooked the loose end of his handcuffs to a bolt that was welded to the table. He left the room to join Paul outside the observation window.

Bax hit the pause button and sat opposite Billy. She read him his Miranda rights and asked if he would talk to her without a lawyer present.

"Sure," said Billy. "I didn't do anything wrong, so you got nothing to hold me on." She slid over the waiver, and Billy signed it. She could see his confidence growing.

"My name is Ashley Baxter. I'm an agent with the Colorado Bureau of Investigation, and you are Billy Wilson, a student at Copper Canyon College, is that correct?"

Billy looked at her with nervous eyes. "You told me your name was Amber. You work with that other state cop?"

"That's right. Do you know why you're here?"

"Yeah, because you kidnapped me from the parking lot of the school."

"Billy, no one kidnapped you. All I want to do is talk about where Melanie Granville is."

Billy smiled. "Who? I don't know anyone named Melanie. What was her last name?" His nervousness was replaced by smugness. He was going to have this bitch for lunch. He leaned back in the chair.

"You know who she is, Billy. Your friend Josh DiNardo's girlfriend. You helped them make a sex video, didn't you?"

"That wasn't me. Josh . . ." Billy paused as soon as he realized he'd stuck his foot in his mouth.

"So, Josh made the video without you, but you know all about it."

Billy leaned into the table and told Bax that he didn't know what she was talking about. He never said he knew about the video.

Bax smiled. Bax looked into his eyes, which caused him to back up a little. "So, when I send the forensic team over to your apartment this afternoon, they won't find a copy of that video on your hard drive?"

Billy didn't say a word. She could see the wheels turning. "So, what if I do have a copy. There's nothing illegal about owning porn. I'm a college kid; it's part of the deal."

"You're correct. Porn's not illegal unless it was made without the consent of both parties. I wonder if Melanie knows she's the star of a sex tape?"

Bax didn't wait for an answer; she clicked a couple of keys and turned the laptop screen to face him. Billy stared with disinterest until the black screen disappeared and was replaced with a video of him and Josh walking into the maintenance area and staring at the body of Kevin Ducette, hanging from the noose. She let it play, and he watched as they cleaned up the blanket and candles and wine and left the space. He wasn't disinterested any longer, and his eyes were fixed on the screen.

"That's not real," said Billy, but there wasn't a lot of conviction in his voice. "You made this up with some kind of app." He kept his eyes on the screen.

Bax leaned over the laptop and pushed a second button. She leaned back and waited. The second video was the one from earlier, where Billy and Josh had entered the space to set it up. She let it run, and Billy watched until they left the room, but the video continued as Josh walked back into the room and started doing something to the control box with a screwdriver.

Billy turned white as a sheet and started to breathe heavily. He looked up at Bax, fear replacing smugness.

Bax asked him to explain why Josh had come back into the room alone and what he had done to the control box. Billy didn't say a word. He was too dumbstruck to even ask for a lawyer. He just stared at the screen.

"Why did Josh go back into the room after you finished setting it up?"

Billy was focused on the still photo on the screen, so Bax slammed her hand down on the metal table. Billy jolted.

"Billy, what did Josh do to the controller so it wouldn't work when the down button was pushed?"

She played the final part of the video again, but this time she let it run. Billy watched as he left the maintenance space, and Josh remained behind. He watched as Josh grabbed a screwdriver off one of the desks, opened the control box, did something inside, replaced the cover and wiped the entire box down with his shirt.

"Here's what I think, Billy. Josh wasn't happy about Kevin and Melanie being together, and he wanted to get even, so when you went over to set up the room, you guys rigged the controller to not work when the down button was pushed, so there would be no way for Kevin to lower himself if he panicked. I am going to recommend to the DA to charge you with first-degree murder. You'll spend the rest of your life in jail."

Billy was stunned, and tears rolled down his face. "I had nothing to do with that. It wasn't me. Josh must have done it on his own. I had no idea."

"Good for you, then your lawyer can argue that in court after we show the jury the video. I don't think you'll get much sympathy. We'll also see if they can charge you with a hate crime. You'll never get out of jail."

Bax could smell the distinctive smell of urine; she looked over the table, and the front of Billy's pants were soaking wet.

Sheriff Womack took Billy back to the restroom and gave him a clean yellow jumpsuit to put on before bringing him back to the interview room. For the next hour, Billy told them about as much of what was going on in town as he knew.

He also told them that Josh had told him that James Martelli shot a guy right in his office, in front of him, and Chief Anderson did nothing. "He was mad about them losing one of the foreign girls from the old school building. He sent his guys to find her." He didn't know if they did, but he suggested they look at the old mine up near Gould Mountain.

He also told them where to find Melanie Granville if she was still alive.

Bax turned off the video and closed her laptop. Sheriff Womack took Billy back to the holding cell to wait for the transport from Larimer County. He walked up to Bax and Paul.

"Unbelievable," he said. "We always knew there was crap going on in that town, but I had no idea what it was. I should have done something about it."

Bax looked at him. "Yeah, Sheriff, you should have. This is your fucking county, and you turned your back on it. Now, what are you going to do about it?"

Bax was angry, and she hoped that Melanie was alive. She sat down at the sheriff's desk and got quiet. Paul suggested that he and the sheriff would head over to the judge's office and that she should join them when she was ready. They walked out and left Bax alone with her anger.

Buck had asked her to do two things: find Melanie and find Nadia. She may have found Melanie. Now she had to focus on Nadia. She knew what she had to do, and she needed to start at the county clerk's office. As soon as she finished with the judge, she would find out where that mine near Gould Mountain was. She pulled out her phone and called Buck.

Chapter Forty-Seven

Buck was almost to Cameron Pass on Highway 14 when his phone rang the first time. Buck hit the answer button on the entertainment console.

"Hi, Max. What's up?"

Max Clinton didn't call people to chitchat. When she called, it was something important. "I wanted to call you with the DNA results on Kevin Ducette's clothes and the rope. Most of this you already know, but this will confirm some things."

"There were traces of semen in his underpants. The DNA was his, but we also got a match for a female. The sample came back to one Melanie Granville. She has her DNA on file at one of those online registries. The rope was a little tougher. There were a lot of samples on the loose end of the rope, so it was most likely used a lot. There were three good samples that we found, indicating they are probably the most recent. We got a match for Kevin Ducette, Melanie Granville and we have an unknown Caucasian male. We ran it through CODIS, and we did get a familial match. The male is either the son, grandson or brother of Frank DiNardo. I thought you'd find that interesting. I already uploaded the reports to the investigation file."

"That's great, Max. That helps to confirm the

information we have so far. Thanks for the heads-up."

"You're a good man, Buck Taylor. God will watch over you."

Buck disconnected the call, then it rang again.

"Hey, any luck?"

"You bet," said Bax. "I arrested Billy Wilson, Josh DiNardo's roommate."

She told Buck about the conversation he'd had with Detective Cummings in the campus police office, and she filled him in on the lengthy conversation they'd had in the interview room.

Buck listened without saying a word until she sounded like she was finished. "Bax, this kid seems to know a lot about what's going on. Do you think he's reliable?"

She told Buck about him pissing his pants during the interview. "This kid is scared. I don't think he's lying."

"Let's see if we can get a warrant for the old school building. Based on what we know now, we may find a lot more than just Melanie. What about the information about Nadia?"

"As soon as we're done with the judge, I was going to head over to the clerk's office and try to get a location of the mine. I want to run out there and see what we can find."

"I've got a better idea. Call Charlie Womack. He has a friend who knows where all the mining claims are. He can run out there with you. See if Marty can go as well. I don't want you out there alone."

"I'd rather take Paul."

"No, have Paul wait at the sheriff's office for the transport; I have a job for him. I will meet him in Walden."

There was something in her hesitation. "Bax, what's going on?"

She didn't know how far she wanted to take this, but she trusted Buck, so she dumped it all out.

"The sheriff let this go on, as did his father and the sheriffs before them. They knew there were all kinds of crimes being committed in Copper Creek, and they did nothing. We're talking sexual abuse, rape, murder, gambling, drugs, illegal abortions and god knows what else, and nobody did a shittin' thing about it. The whole fucking town is corrupt, the people are treated like slaves and no one cares."

"You're right, Bax. Right about almost everything except no one caring. We're here, and we care, and now we can do something about it. Stay focused. The cavalry is on the way. Let me know what you find at the mine."

Buck hung up, dialed Paul, got his voice mail and figured he was in with the judge. He drove over Cameron Pass and headed into the valley. He was worried that once the Martellis and the police chief found out that they'd arrested Billy and the doctor, they might do something to the girls in the old school building, and he was worried about Melanie Granville.

Buck drove down the main street and spotted Officer Terrell's cruiser. She was checking license plates in the same parking lot he'd found her in last night. He parked a block away and walked back to the lot.

"Afternoon, Officer Terrell."

She turned and raised her hand to her eyes to block out the sun. "Oh, Agent Taylor. Something I can do for you?"

"I'd like to talk to you for a minute if you wouldn't mind."

"Sure thing," she said. "There's a couple of things I'd like to talk to you about as well."

Buck led her between two of the cars and closer to the building. He looked around and didn't see anyone watching them.

Before he could start, she spoke up. "Agent Taylor, is there something going on I should be aware of?"

She told him about going to the police department after they'd spoken and looking through the file and the evidence from the hanging victim. She agreed with his assessment that there was little evidence and it was a poorly run investigation.

"You don't think he committed suicide, do you?"

Buck needed to be careful. He didn't know anything about Tracy Terrell, except that she had a sick grandmother living with her, and he didn't know how far to trust her. If what he'd learned in his interview with Officer Weems earlier was true, then she hadn't been a cop long enough to have been corrupted. The problem was that he needed some allies in town and would have to trust someone. He might as well start with her.

"Officer Terrell, I'm gonna take a chance that you're not part of what's wrong with this town, so I'm going to trust you. There is so much crime going on here that it boggles the mind. The chief of police and Detective Cummings are involved up to their necks. My people have already arrested several of your cops for a variety of crimes, and we are going to arrest a bunch more, but right now, I need your help."

He told her about Melanie Granville and Kevin Ducette, their sexual escapades and the fact that he believed Kevin had been murdered, and the chief of police was covering it up.

"We think Melanie Granville is being held against her will, possibly in the old school building, and I need someone I can trust to keep an eye on the building and make sure she isn't moved until we can get our search warrants. Can I trust you, Officer Terrell?"

Officer Terrell didn't hesitate. "Yes, sir. I won't let you down, Agent Taylor."

"Okay. All I want you to do for now is watch the building. If you see anything that looks wrong, you call me." He handed her his card. "Do not engage anyone on your own. These people are dangerous. You wait for backup, got it?"

She told Buck she understood, and she headed off to continue her rounds. Buck was concerned that he might have just made a huge mistake, but he was shorthanded as it was, and he needed her. He headed for his Jeep. He needed to coordinate a drug stop, and he didn't have a lot of time.

Chapter Forty-Eight

The chief of police stood in front of James Martelli's desk feeling weak in the knees. The last time he'd stood there, he watched a college kid get blown away, and he did nothing about it. He was more than a little concerned. He had been an eyewitness to the shooting of the kid, and now, here he stood, summoned by Martelli.

Standing next to the desk was Jimmy Martelli, or James Martelli, Junior, as he preferred to be called. He'd always felt that Jimmy was a little kid's name. He was not a little kid, although he was short in stature. He kept his eyes on the chief of police, never wavering. He knew it unnerved Chief Anderson, and he enjoyed the feeling of power.

James Martelli looked up as he hung up the phone on his desk. "What the fuck is going on in my town? I pay you to keep the peace and make sure my operations run smoothly, and that's not happening. Two of your cops have been arrested, as has the doctor, and you've done nothing about it."

"What did you want me to do, Mr. Martelli? He arrested my officers at the hospital. He would have hauled both of them to jail if the one guy wasn't in surgery. I'm still trying to find out why they arrested the doctor."

He looked at Jimmy. "How bad can the doctor hurt us?"

"A lot," said Jimmy. "He knows about the girls because he takes care of them, and he knows about the adoption scam. He could be trouble."

"Can you get to him?"

"If he's still in the jail in Walden. If they already moved him, then no. We have no control in Fort Collins."

"What about DiNardo? Can he get to him?"

"Who, the kid?" said Jimmy.

James Martelli looked annoyed. "No, you fuckin' moron, not the kid, his father."

Jimmy's eyes flashed anger for just a second as he got control of his emotions. "I'll call and talk to him."

James Martelli returned his gaze to Chief Anderson. "Can that officer hurt us?"

Chief Anderson thought about his answer. "It's possible. Those two were mostly just muscle, but they know about the protection, and they know about the girls." He hesitated.

"What?" asked Martelli.

"Well, they know where some of the bodies are buried."

Jimmy Martelli exploded. "That's just fuckin' great! You put our entire operation at risk." He stepped towards Chief Anderson, who stood up a little straighter and glared at him.

James Martelli raised his hand, and his son stopped and stepped back. "That call I just hung up from was with the commissioners. They each called the governor to have this cop sent packing, and the governor refused to speak to either of them. I don't like this one bit. You told me he was here to investigate that black kid's suicide. It looks like his investigation has branched out a little."

He stood up and walked around the desk. He stopped toe to toe with Chief Anderson and looked him in the eyes. "I want that motherfucker gone today. I don't care how you do it, but I want him gone. And believe me, Chief, when I say this. I am not afraid to sacrifice you to save my town and my operations, and that includes your family as well. Do you get me, Chief?"

Chief Anderson was furious. Martelli had just threatened his family. He was angry with himself because he didn't have the balls to do anything about it. He turned and walked out of the room.

James Martelli walked back to his desk. "Have you made arrangements to take care of DiNardo and his guest?"

Jimmy came around the desk. "It's all set up. I offered two of the girls their freedom if they slit their throats. Of course, after that, those two girls will disappear."

"What about that black kid's girlfriend. What are we gonna do with her?"

"I had the DiNardo kid stash her away where the cops can't get to her. We're keeping her doped up. Thought I'd use her for some of our visitors tomorrow night and then get rid of her."

James Martelli stood up and walked into the hall, with Jimmy at his heels. He stopped and turned. "Get rid of her tonight. And I want that DiNardo kid to die with his father. Don't fuck this up."

"What about the state cop?"

James Martelli smiled. "I'll deal with him myself."

He walked down the hall and disappeared into a side room. Jimmy smiled at the thought of killing the girl, but first, he might just have a little fun with her.

Chapter Forty-Nine

Buck had one stop to make before heading to Walden. He had called the college and asked to have Pedro, the maintenance director, meet him at the scene of the hanging. He pulled into a space behind the building, grabbed his backpack and slid out of the Jeep. Pedro, good to his word, was waiting at the back door to the building.

Buck followed him through the maze of basements until they came to the door to the space. Pedro entered his code and pulled open the door. Buck asked him if he could find a screwdriver, and he walked off.

Buck pulled out one of the pictures that he'd found in his room and held it up, scanning around the room until he had the same view. He walked towards the back wall of shelving, and there, mounted to one of the rails on the shelf, and mostly hidden by boxes, was the camera.

Pedro walked back, and Buck walked over to the control box. He pulled a pair of nitrile gloves from his bag and used the screwdriver to open the back of the box.

There was not much to the inside of the box. Just the two switches and a couple of wires. He took his fingerprint kit out of his backpack and dusted the entire inside of the box. When he blew the powder away, he had two good prints inside the back cover and a partial print on one of the wires connected to the down button.

He scanned the prints using the camera on his phone and sent them off to AFIS. He knew it could take a while because, unlike in those cop shows on TV, the results don't come back in two minutes so that the good guys can solve the crime within the hour of allotted time. Sometimes it could take hours to get back a match, and sometimes you didn't get a match at all.

Buck walked over and followed the same procedure on the camera, which was a surprise to Pedro, who had never noticed it there. He got a couple of good prints and did the same thing with those. He handed Pedro back the screwdriver and asked him to close up the box. He had what he needed.

Buck thanked Pedro and followed him back to the door. He walked to his Jeep and slid his backpack onto the passenger seat. He walked around the Jeep and straight into Chief Anderson, standing next to his car. Buck looked around.

"Chief," said Buck.

"I see you're still nosing around, Agent Taylor. I hope you have what you need, because I want you and your associate out of my town, within the hour. Do I make myself clear?"

Buck chuckled, never taking his eyes off Chief Anderson. "What is clear is this isn't your town. You're just another flunky working for a rich guy who thinks laws don't apply to him. What is clear is you don't make a move without his say-so. What is clear is you are involved up to your beady little eyes in more crime than I can even count right now. And what is clear is that as soon as I can get a warrant, I will arrest you and a good portion of your department for a whole host of crimes. You might have broken some kind of record for how many crimes you are involved in."

Buck watched as Chief Anderson's face turned white as a ghost and then red with anger. "You have no idea who you are dealing with," he said. "I will make sure you never work in law enforcement ever again. How dare you . . ."

Buck had had enough. In a move Chief Anderson never saw coming; Buck swung him around, slammed him into the Jeep, pulled his pistol out of his holster and slapped on the cuffs. Chief Anderson looked astonished.

"Wha,-wha-what are you doing? You can't do this."

Buck pulled out his Miranda card and read Chief Anderson his rights. He asked him if he understood those rights, and he nodded, still objecting.

"I am going to put you in the Jeep and take you to the sheriff's office. We will interview you when we get there. In the meantime, if you open your mouth to say anything, I am going to slam you into next week. Do I make myself clear?"

Buck placed him in the passenger seat after he threw his backpack into the back. He used the seat belt to secure him. As he turned to walk around his car, he stopped and looked at the small group of people who were standing on the sidewalk watching. One of the guys in front, whom he recognized as the bartender from the other night when he'd had his confrontation with Jimmy Martelli, smiled and gave him the thumbs-up sign.

Buck nodded and slid into the Jeep. He pulled his pistol and placed it on the seat between his legs. All he had to do now was get out of town without being seen. He knew his backup was twenty minutes away at best, but he called Marty Womack and let him know what was going on. Marty said to give him five minutes, and he would have someone to help. Buck wasn't sure what Marty had in mind, but he sat for five minutes and waited. He got a text from Marty a minute or so later that told him to head for the B and B.

Buck pulled out of the parking lot and took the back street to the rear of the B and B. He turned down the side street and was surprised to see Victoria James standing next to a gray SUV. She was holding a shotgun in her hand. More surprising, parked in front of her were Charlie Womack and Lars Gunderson. Charlie had his retired sheriff's badge hanging from a lanyard around his neck and was wearing his big .44-caliber revolver on his hip, and Lars carried a semiautomatic shotgun.

Charlie and Lars climbed into Charlie's truck and pulled in front of Buck, and Victoria James pulled her SUV in behind him. The little caravan pulled onto the main street and headed out of town, past the police department building. Once clear of town, Buck took a deep breath. The last thing he'd wanted today was a shoot-out on Main Street.

Chapter Fifty

The sun was setting as the caravan pulled into the justice center in Walden and parked by the back door to the sheriff's office. Marty Womack, Bax and Paul were standing outside the door waiting. The group parted as Buck approached with the chief of police and followed him inside. The two holding cells were empty since the doctor and Billy Wilson had been transported earlier to Fort Collins, so Buck processed Chief Anderson.

The entire time Chief Anderson was being fingerprinted and photographed, he never said a word, just looked stunned. Buck put him in the cell and locked the door. He closed the door to the lockup area and walked over to the group. He thanked Marty for the assist and wondered how he had been able to get it set up so quickly. He also wondered about Victoria James, who he now noticed was wearing a sheriff's department badge clipped to her belt. Marty sat at the open desk he was leaning on.

"Pop had just gone up the hill to get Lars, so they could help Bax reach the mine. I caught them just before they got to the turn for the highway. Victoria here, that's kind of an interesting story."

Buck looked at Victoria, who nodded her head. The sheriff said, "Victoria spent her early career working for the FBI. When she retired three years ago, she moved up here and took over the family business, kind of."

"My great-grandfather and grandfather," said Victoria, "ran a brothel out of the house. I think my dad kept the tradition alive, but I was never sure. It was a boardinghouse when I was a kid, but there were always people coming to our house at all hours of the night. When Dad passed away, Mom wanted to sell the place, but I was coming up on retirement, so I took it over and turned it into a B and B."

"Victoria noticed some odd things going on in town and was concerned," said Marty. "So she approached me about helping her investigate. When I told her I wasn't allowed to have anything to do with the town, she had an idea. I would make her a reserve deputy, and she would keep an eye on things in town and gather as much information as she could, so eventually, we could get someone to listen. We felt we were getting close, and then that kid committed suicide, which is why I called your director, and he put me in touch with the governor."

Bax, Paul and Buck looked at each other. Buck finally broke the silence. "You called the governor about the suicide?"

"I knew it wasn't a suicide," said Victoria. "And I saw an opportunity to get someone to come up here and look around. The governor told Marty he would send you up to look into the suicide and nothing else. You have a reputation for finding clarity amongst the crap. I had no idea the wheels were going to come off the bus and everyone in town was going to panic about why you were here. I seem to have created quite a mess."

Buck looked at Victoria. "When I get the prints I just lifted from the camera, where Kevin Ducette died, they're gonna come back to you, aren't they?"

"Yes. I put the camera there, and I left the pictures and the thumb drive in your room. I knew you were getting stonewalled by Chief Anderson, so I thought I'd help."

"Victoria," said Bax. "Kevin Ducette isn't the only person you have pictures of, is he?"

Victoria looked at Marty and then back to Bax. "No, I have video of at least a hundred people who used that room regularly. Most are locals, but some others are pretty well known. I know the videos are not admissible in court. I was hoping that if the time came, they might be used to help persuade some folks to tell the truth. I can send you the cloud link for the file if you would like."

Buck put up his hand to cut everyone off. "Let's not go there yet. If we don't see the videos, then we can't testify that they exist. You hold on to them, but I would recommend that you go through them, and any that do not show criminal activity, unless they are pertinent to the investigation, you delete. Autoerotic asphyxiation is not illegal. Let's let the locals have their privacy."

Buck's phone chimed with an incoming message, and he unclipped it and looked at the message. He closed his phone and clipped it back on his belt. He addressed the group. "I went back a little while ago and lifted fingerprints from inside the control box where Kevin died. The fingerprints belong to Josh DiNardo. Surprise, surprise, he has a juvenile record, so his prints are on file. I'm gonna write up an arrest warrant, and then I'm gonna have a conversation with Chief Anderson. Bax, you guys better head for the mine. We're running out of daylight."

Bax, Charlie and Lars Gunderson left the office.

Buck looked at his watch. "We've got a couple of hours until the state police and the drug dog from Larimer County arrive. Paul, how did you make out with getting a ground-penetrating radar team up here, and do we have a backhoe available?"

Paul told him the judge had no problem signing the warrant to search the plaza on campus and that he had a GPR company from Steamboat Springs heading over the pass as they spoke. Marty told him that he had one of the county's heavy equipment operators heading over to the maintenance shed to load up a backhoe.

"Great. I may want you to back me up when I go to pick up Josh DiNardo, so stay close to your phones."

He looked at Victoria. "Looks like a lot of things are coming to a head. I hope we didn't blow your cover today, but thanks for the help. I'd like you to go back to the B and B and wait in case we need some backup again."

Everyone headed out, and Buck sat down with his laptop and pulled up the arrest warrant request. He sat for a minute and thought about how the day had gone so far. He pulled out his phone and speed-dialed the director.

Chapter Fifty-One

Charlie Womack drove his truck up the narrow switchback-laden road that led to the Gould number one mine. To call it a road was an understatement. The dirt road disappeared halfway up the mountain. What they were driving on now was nothing more than two depressions in the dirt and rocks. Charlie had dropped down into granny low and pushed ahead. They rounded a sharp bend with breathtaking views, and there was the mine. Charlie stopped on the most level piece of ground he could find and parked.

Bax wasn't even sure there was a mine here, except for the mine tailings that created the flat ground they were parked on. The mine entrance was hidden behind some trees and overgrowth.

Lars pushed his way through, holding back branches so the others could pass. The mine entrance had a metal gate covering it that was bolted into the side of the mountain. The lock was a heavy chain and a big padlock. A new-looking padlock.

Bax pulled her lockpick tools from a pocket in her backpack and made fast work of the padlock, which they pushed to the side with the chain. The gate squealed as they swung it away from the entrance.

Lars opened the duffel bag he was carrying and handed them each a hard hat with an LED lamp attached to it.

"I'll go first," said Lars as he turned on his light, picked up the duffel bag and walked into the mine.

Bax followed, and Charlie brought up the rear. He wanted to be able to keep an eye on the entrance in case they had been followed.

"This mine was never a good producer," said Lars, as they walked along the rough-cut floor. "Original mining claim belonged to the McTavish family, way back in the eighteen eighties. According to what I was told growing up, they worked it for about two years until it played out altogether. Sat empty for years until the late sixties, when some young fella from Denver bought the claim and tried working it. It never paid off, and Martelli bought it a couple of years later for next to nothing."

The mine was not very deep, maybe two hundred feet or so, and they continued until Lars held up his hand to stop Bax from walking past him. Bax looked down, and her light disappeared into what looked like a bottomless pit.

Bax, who had never been claustrophobic, was glad they could still see a little bit of light from the entrance. She had always heard that nothing was darker than cave dark, and she was beginning to understand that sentiment. Lars pulled a glow stick out of his duffel bag, cracked it and waited for the full glow. He dropped it into the pit.

Bax was relieved to see the glow stick land on

the bottom, only about fifty feet below. They could see several piles and lumps from where they stood.

"I need to get down there," said Bax.

Lars reached into the duffel and pulled out a climbing harness and a length of rope. "Do you know how to use this? Borrowed them from my son. Thought they might come in handy."

Bax, who had done a lot of climbing with her dad, slipped on the harness while Lars took the rope back to the entrance and tied it to the gate. He walked back and threw the rope into the pit, and they were relieved when it landed on the bottom with some to spare. Lars laid his coat under the rope at the edge of the pit so it wouldn't chafe on the floor and <u>Bax</u> clipped in.

Bax rappelled into the pit and hit the bottom in three jumps. She unhooked and picked up the green glow stick. She walked towards the one lump she saw and stopped. The lump was something wrapped in a large black tarp, and it was sitting on a bunch of bones. Human bones.

She took off her work gloves and pulled a pair of nitrile gloves out of her pocket. She pulled out a pocketknife and cut the rope holding the tarp together. The body flopped onto the dirt floor as the tarp unwrapped itself. She stepped back with a start. Between the glow stick and the headlamp, everything took on a weird glow. Pulling herself together, she took out her phone and started snapping pictures of the body.

The body was a young male. Decomp hadn't started yet, and she lifted one of the arms. Rigor was still evident, the body stiff and cold, so she figured he had been killed sometime in the last twelve to thirty-six hours. A full autopsy would be able to give her an exact time of death. She looked and spotted one bullet hole in the chest, his shirt covered in dried blood. She took some close-up pictures of the wound and then threw the tarp back over the body.

She took pictures of the other bones on the pit floor and then worked her way towards the other bundle. She cut the rope and folded back the tarp. She was prepared for another body, but the face of the once-pretty blond girl was startling, especially since her eyes were wide open. The dark marks around her neck indicated that she had probably died from strangulation. The young woman's clothes were torn and had been stuffed in next to the body. Bax figured she had been raped.

She took pictures of the body in situ and then checked for rigor. The body was cold but not as cold as the previous body, and the arm still had a little movement to it. This young woman hadn't been here as long as the guy had.

She put her camera away, walked back over to the other side of the pit, clipped into the rope and, using the ascender, made her way back to the top of the pit. Lars reached out his hand and helped pull her up. She was amazed at the strength of the seemingly frail older man as he lifted her one-handed out of the pit.

"Bad?" he asked.

"Someone's been dumping bodies down there

for a long time, but there are two new ones, one male, one female."

Lars helped her out of the climbing harness and rolled up the rope as they walked back to the gate. Charlie was leaning against the wall, just inside the entrance, and he stood when they walked up. Bax stepped into the light and pulled out her phone. She showed them the pictures of what she had seen. Neither man recognized the two newest victims.

She closed the camera app and was thrilled that she had cell service. She called the lead forensic tech. They were just loading up after finishing with the doctor's house. She gave them directions to the mine. She hoped their van would make it. She knew the van had four-wheel drive, but that was one tough road they'd come up on. She hoped they could make it before the sun went down. She knew she didn't want to drive on that so-called road after dark.

Charlie walked over to his truck and came back with a couple of water bottles and some trail mix bars, and they sat on a couple of rocks and waited for the forensic team. While they waited, Lars told them more stories of the old days in Jackson County. Bax leaned back and watched the sun touch the top of the mountains to the west. She never got tired of the beauty of Colorado, and it helped to clear some of the ugly out of her head.

Chapter Fifty-Two

Buck kicked back in the sheriff's chair and enjoyed the quiet. He needed to be careful. He hadn't slept in the last thirty hours, and if he closed his eyes, he wasn't sure he'd wake up. He had pulled a cold Coke out of the sheriff's little office refrigerator and was sipping it.

Paul and the sheriff had left earlier to meet the ground-penetrating radar technician, and he'd called Buck to let him know they were getting set up in the courtyard behind the campus hospital.

Buck had emailed the judge upstairs the arrest warrant for Josh DiNardo, as well as search warrant requests for Josh's apartment and Chief Anderson's house and office. The judge was hesitant to sign the warrant for Chief Anderson's office, but he emailed back that he would review them and get back to him shortly. He was waiting for the chief of police's attorney to show up when his phone rang.

"Hey, Bax. Anything in that old mine?"

"Yeah," said Bax. "We need to give Billy Wilson a gold star."

She described what she'd found and then told Buck she was sending him the two victims' pictures. Buck's phone chirped, and he pulled up the pictures of the young man.

"Looks like the story Billy told us about the kid

being shot by Martelli is true. Timing works, and so does that hole in the kid's chest—two gold stars for Billy."

He opened the next picture and sat staring at it for a long time. "Damn," was all he said.

He heard Bax calling him, and he snapped out of his thoughts. "Sorry, Bax. That's Nadia, the girl I ran into that night behind the old school building. Shit."

"Buck. I think she was raped or brutalized before she was killed. Whoever did this is one sadistic, twisted son of a bitch. It looks like she was strangled."

"Okay, make sure forensics does a rape kit on her. I don't want to wait for the pathologist. Send those by secure courier if you have to, but get them to the lab tonight, and call Max and let her know they're coming, and I need a rush job. Make arrangements to get both bodies to the Larimer County coroner tonight. We'll pay for the overtime, but I want those autopsies finished as soon as possible. I'd like you to be there when those are done. Call me with the results as soon as you have them."

"You got it, Buck. We'll get the prick who did this," she said just before she hung up.

Buck looked up as the door opened and a short, bald man in an oversized suit walked through the door. He introduced himself to Buck and handed him his card. Robert Silvestri, Attorney at Law.

"I'd like to see my client before you question him," he said.

Buck led him back to the holding cells and grabbed a desk chair as he passed. He set the chair in front of the first cell, walked out and closed the door. He gathered up his laptop and notepad and carried them into the interview room. He placed the laptop and pad on the table and cued up the items he wanted. He walked to the closet next to the interview room, turned on the video recorder and adjusted the audio. He was all set to interview Chief Anderson.

An hour later, and just as Buck was starting to nod off in the sheriff's chair, the lawyer banged on the outer door to the cells. Buck got up, stretched and unlocked the door.

"My client is ready," he said as he walked past Buck.

Buck walked back to the cells, handcuffed Chief Anderson and escorted him to the interview room. He looked outside as they passed through the office and saw it was getting dark. He would need to hurry if he was going to get the drug bust set up. He sat him down in one of the metal chairs and took his seat opposite the lawyer.

"Can you remove the handcuffs, please?" asked the attorney.

"No, sir. There is no one else in the office, so protocol dictates that he remain cuffed."

The attorney didn't look pleased, but he held back his comment.

Buck pulled his Miranda warning card out of his pocket. "For the record, I read Chief Anderson his Miranda rights when he was placed under arrest. I told him to remain quiet, which he did. I am going to read him his rights again, in front of counsel this time."

Buck read the rights and asked him if he understood them. Chief Anderson looked at the attorney and the attorney nodded. Chief Anderson said he did, and Buck asked him if he wanted to waive his right to counsel. The lawyer looked at Buck, but Buck waved his hand and told him it was procedure.

Buck introduced the three people at the table for the video and then clicked a button on his laptop.

"Chief Anderson, you are being questioned for falsifying documents, hindering a criminal investigation, conspiracy and as an accessory to murder after the fact."

The lawyer and Chief Anderson looked at each other, confused. Chief Anderson figured there were a dozen things he could have been arrested for, but he had no idea where these charges came from.

Buck continued. "Once we have completed this interview, the district attorney will determine which charges will be filed against you or if more charges will be added."

The lawyer stopped him. "My client is unaware of what these charges stem from. This is absurd."

Buck ignored the lawyer and looked at Chief Anderson.

"Did you advise Detective Cummings to declare the death of Kevin Ducette a suicide?"

Chief Anderson looked surprised. "It was a decision made by Detective Cummings and me.

It was a suicide. The evidence and the medical examiner agreed." He looked at the lawyer, and the lawyer indicated for him to be quiet.

"Would the medical examiner be Dr. Griffin, who was arrested earlier today for operating without a license and is being investigated in connection with the deaths of multiple young women over the past fifty years or so?"

The lawyer quickly intervened and told him not to answer that.

"What evidence indicated that the death of Kevin Ducette was a suicide?"

Chief Anderson spoke about the noose, the locked doors and the suicide note.

"That would be the suicide note that came from Kevin Ducette's computer, which has still not been found, despite the fact that it was in police custody."

The lawyer pulled Chief Anderson's arm. He didn't like where this was heading, since he had no idea what was going on. When James Martelli had called him earlier in the day and told him to get to the sheriff's office, he'd suggested a couple of things that Chief Anderson might have been arrested for; this was not any of those things.

Chapter Fifty-Three

Buck took a sip of his Coke. "Chief, why were you at the scene of a suicide? Doesn't seem like the kind of crime your detective would call you out on."

"This is a small town," said Chief Anderson. "I try to get to any unusual crime scene. In case my people need advice or help."

"Why were no fingerprints taken of the doorknob or the controller button for the winch?"

"It was a suicide. It wasn't needed."

"Is that the same reason you didn't send the victim's clothes or the rope to the state lab for DNA analysis?"

Chief Anderson answered that it was, but he looked at the lawyer more confused than ever. The lawyer asked Buck where this was all going, and Buck ignored him.

"Chief, had you visited the scene before the official emergency call came in?"

Chief Anderson sat back in the chair, his face suddenly ashen. The lawyer looked at him, not comprehending what was happening and why Chief Anderson reacted the way he did.

"Chief, please answer the question. Were you called to the scene of the suicide before the emergency call was received?" Chief Anderson still didn't answer. "Okay, we'll come back to that. Did you re-dress the suicide victim, remove a terry cloth wrap from the noose and then rehang the victim?"

Buck thought the lawyer was going to come unglued. He demanded to know what the questioning was all about, but Buck held up his hand.

"Chief, were you aware that the down button on the winch had been tampered with, as had the knot, so that neither one could be released or lowered to help the victim?"

Chief Anderson, ignoring the lawyer, jumped on the question. "We lowered the winch just fine when we arrived at the scene. This some kind of trick question, Taylor? What the hell are you trying to pin on me? We did everything by the book. It was a suicide, for Christ's sake." The lawyer pulled him back into the seat.

Buck smiled at him. "For the record?"

"Damn straight," he said. The lawyer sat back in his chair and sighed. He knew Buck had followed the age-old legal adage: never ask a question you don't know the answer to.

Buck pulled his laptop closer and clicked on a couple of buttons. He spun the screen to face them, and then he watched Chief Anderson's reactions as the video of that fateful night unfolded.

Chief Anderson sat in stunned silence, as did the lawyer. The first portion of the video was hard to watch, but the second and third parts were the most revealing. Tears formed in Chief Anderson's eyes, and he started to hyperventilate. The lawyer reached over to try to calm him down. When the video ended, there was silence in the room.

Buck spun the laptop screen back to face him. He gave them a minute to compose themselves.

He finished his Coke and looked at his watch. "Chief, did you interview the young woman in the video?"

"No," was the only reply.

"Well, just so you are aware, the young woman is now missing, and we are concerned for her safety. If anything happens to her, you will be charged for your part in not securing her or her testimony."

"What?" said Chief Anderson. "No. Wait a minute. I had nothing to do with her disappearance." He looked at Buck pleadingly. "You have to believe me."

"Why did you cover up the murder of Kevin Ducette?"

"I had no idea it was a murder. The lift did work fine when I met Josh at the scene. I was trying to protect the club."

Chief Anderson spent the next few minutes telling Buck about the sex club they had formed a long time ago. The club, which many of the townspeople were involved with, was a social group, and nothing that went on was a crime. If word got out that someone had been murdered, it would destroy everything. The members paid a hefty membership fee to belong and for privacy, and no one wanted to be named as being part of the club.

Chief Anderson's face turned white, and his hands trembled. Buck asked him what was wrong. "I lied to James Martelli. I told him it was just an accident, which I believed it was at the time, and that the kid was into some kinky sex and had strangled himself during an autoerotic episode. Fuck." He looked startled. "You have to protect my family."

The lawyer told him to shut up and asked Buck where the videotape had come from. Buck told him it was a long-running investigation. "The video camera had been placed in the space to record who in the city was involved and determine if any of the young women filmed were either underage or here illegally." Chief Anderson looked like he wanted to vomit, and he started to cry.

Buck stood up, walked behind the lawyer and helped Chief Anderson to his feet. He released the one cuff from the table and hooked it around his other wrist.

"Chief Anderson, you are being arrested for the charges outlined before. You will be remanded to the Larimer County Sheriff's Office and be placed in their jail until your arraignment."

The sheriff, who had arrived back at the office sometime during the interview, opened the door to the interview room, and Buck handed Chief Anderson off to him. He placed him in the holding cell and had him remove all his clothes. He handed him a yellow jumpsuit and a pair of yellow Crocs, and he locked the door behind him.

Buck checked his phone messages and watched

the lawyer leave the office, his phone already to his ear. He figured James Martelli was getting an earful of what had just happened. He had two messages from the judge. The arrest warrant and search warrant for Josh DiNardo were attached to the first one, and the search warrant for Chief Anderson's home and office was attached to the second. Buck let the sheriff know, and the sheriff asked him what they were going to do.

"The warrants will have to wait," said Buck. "We need to set up a traffic accident, and we're running out of time."

Chapter Fifty-Four

Buck's phone rang, and he answered. "Buck, it's Charlie. They're loaded up and on the move. Just leaving the mine. I'll be right behind them."

"Okay, Charlie, but don't get too close, we know where they're going, and we don't want to spook them."

Buck hung up and addressed the group. "Okay, folks. Just like we planned it, and everyone goes home tonight. And remember, they are cops, and they are armed. It's possible they already killed one Carbon County deputy, and I don't want to get into a shoot-out tonight."

The sheriff had remained at the office to wait for the transport from Larimer County, so Buck was in operational control of the stop. He had positioned two state troopers right at the Colorado–Wyoming border on Highway 125. There were two Carbon County deputies on the Wyoming side of the narrow border.

Farther down the highway, on the Wyoming side, and just over a ridge out of view, the Carbon County sheriff waited with several additional deputies. They had their lights flashing to help make the story of the accident more realistic. From where Buck stood, he could see the flashing blue, red and white lights in the night sky but could not see the supposed accident.

Lying in wait off the side of the road were two Jackson County deputies and a third state trooper, who would pull in behind them and block the rear retreat. Everyone was in position, and several pedestrian cars were let through the barricade. They wanted the two cops in the drug car to be the first in line at the barricade.

Buck's phone rang. "Go, Charlie," he said.

"Five minutes out. You ready?" asked Charlie.

Buck told him they were good to go and hung up.

"Five minutes," he yelled, and everyone took their positions.

Buck slid down into the dry culvert next to the road. He was glad that traffic was light. The troopers let two more cars through, and then they waited. Two minutes later, they spotted the headlights of a car moving fast. The car slowed as it approached the two state troopers and pulled up to the spot the one trooper pointed to.

The trooper walked to the driver's window, which rolled down as he approached. "Evening, sir. Got an accident up the road just a piece. Fire department is telling us shouldn't be any more than five or ten minutes till they get the road back open."

The passenger rolled down his window and the driver shut off the car. They both lit up cigarettes and waited. A white heavy-duty pickup truck pulled up behind the Camaro. The trooper walked to the driver's window and repeated the same speech. The driver turned off his engine and opened his door. He yelled to the trooper, who was walking away. "Trooper. Okay if I let my dog out to take a pee? Been in the truck awhile."

The trooper told him it was fine but to stay near the truck. The driver climbed down out of the truck and opened the back door of the crew cab. The dog, a black lab mix, jumped out of the truck and sat while his owner hooked up the leash. They walked around the truck and passed behind the Camaro.

Buck watched Boomer as she passed behind the Camaro. If the dog didn't alert, they were screwed on probable cause. Deputy Everett Harcourt walked Boomer along the side of the road, let the dog pee and then walked her back between the car and the truck.

This time the dog sniffed around the Camaro's bumper and then sat down. While all this was going on, Charlie Womack arrived and parked his truck behind the deputy. He climbed out of the truck, and with his hat pulled down to cover his face, he met the trooper halfway. Deputy Harcourt gave Buck the signal, walked around the truck, unhooked Boomer and placed her in the back seat. Harcourt moved to the front of his truck and pulled his pistol from under his coat, concealing it behind his leg.

Buck and the others were ready, and the trooper walked back to the Camaro, said something to the driver and started to walk away. The trooper turned back around and drew his pistol, the second trooper pointed his pistol at the passenger and Buck and the others swarmed the car.

The driver and passenger were caught off guard. The driver dropped the cigarette from his mouth and started to reach for it but thought twice about making any sudden moves. He slowly raised his hands and placed them on top of the steering wheel.

The passenger started to reach under his seat when Charlie shoved his big .44 caliber revolver in the window and pointed it at the passenger's head. That close, the barrel must have looked like a cannon to the passenger. He kept his hands in his lap.

"I wouldn't do that if I were you. Let me see your hands," said Charlie.

With several pistols and several AR-15s pointed at them, the driver and passenger surrendered without a fuss. The driver was ordered out of the car. As he did, he reached into his coat and was immediately slammed to the ground. "I'm a cop. I was getting my ID. Copper Creek police."

Buck helped him up, frisked him and handcuffed him. He removed his gun from the holster on his waist and pulled his ID from his top pocket.

"What's this all about?" said the cop, his hair blowing in the wind. "We're the good guys; call our chief."

Buck was relieved that it appeared they didn't know Chief Anderson had been arrested. He looked across the car and saw that Charlie and Deputy Harcourt had secured the passenger. Charlie nodded.

Buck reached into the car and hit the trunk release button. The driver looked like he wasn't sure what to do or say, so he stood there with his mouth open.

"You're being held because a drug dog alerted to something in your trunk. That gives us probable cause to look in your trunk." The third trooper walked behind the car and lifted the trunk lid. Inside were several cardboard boxes loaded with small glass vials marked fentanyl. Buck immediately closed the lid without touching anything and walked back to the driver.

The driver started to stammer and object when Buck pulled out his Miranda card and read him his rights. He did the same for the passenger and then told them to remain quiet until they got them processed back at the sheriff's office.

The Carbon County sheriff walked up and stood next to Buck. He had arrived with several deputies, just as the bust was going down.

"Any chance you can give me five minutes with them?" he asked, with a smile on his face.

Buck laughed. "I wish I could. We'll interview them tonight and see what we get. I'll let you know what we find."

The sheriff thanked Buck and headed back to his SUV. Buck walked over and thanked Deputy Harcourt and patted Boomer on her head, which was sticking out of the back window. The dog's tail wagged furiously, and she licked Buck's hand.

Buck told everyone to load up and head to the sheriff's office. They still had more work to do. The troopers loaded the driver and passenger into separate cars and headed south, followed by the rest of the team. So far, the night had gone smoothly. Buck was pleased. He dialed Marty Womack as he slid into his Jeep.

Chapter Fifty-Five

The small sheriff's office felt even smaller with all the people standing around, and Buck was amazed they all fit. The sheriff took the two Copper Creek cops back to the holding area to begin processing them. He had handed Buck the warrant to search the mine as soon as Buck entered the office. The judge had been good enough to wait around the office, so he could sign the warrant if they found drugs in the car.

Buck was in the process of gathering everyone together for a quick briefing when Pam Glassman walked in and asked him if she could have a minute.

Pamela Glassman was about forty years old, short and had shoulder-length mousy brown hair. Her brown pantsuit looked like she had slept in it, which was probably the case since she had been in the office for the past eighteen hours working on search and arrest warrants with the sheriff and Buck's people.

Pam was the resident assistant district attorney for the Eighth Judicial District and was assigned to the district attorney's Walden office. She'd taken the position in Walden to get away from the rat race and spend time with her two daughters. That was before Buck Taylor came to town. Today she felt like she was back in the rat race of the big city.

"What's up, Pam?" asked Buck.

"Chief Anderson wants to talk to you and me, in private. I think he wants to trade information for some consideration."

"What's his attorney say?"

"That's the funny thing, Buck. He doesn't want me to call his attorney. What do you think?"

"I think James Martelli is paying his attorney, and he's scared to say anything. It can't hurt to listen, without offering anything, right?"

"Okay. I'll have Marty bring him up to our conference room and we'll see what he has to say. When do you want to do this? I just gave Marty the search warrant for the mine."

"I'll come back as soon as we hit the mine. I've got a forensic unit working not far from there, and I can get the troopers to keep an eye on the place. I'll call you when I'm heading back."

Buck started back to the sheriff's office, then stopped and pulled out his phone.

The director answered right away. "Buck, what's up?"

"Sorry to call so late, sir. I'm gonna need some help up here. We are now working multiple crime scenes, and I think there's gonna be more to come, and I only have a handful of forensic techs. Can you scare up some forensic guys from Denver? I'm gonna call Loren Hatch and see if she can lend me her team and a couple of deputies. I'll also call Jess Gonzales after we hit the mine and have her take on the drug case."

"Sounds like you have a good plan, Buck. Let

me make some calls and see what kind of help I can dig up."

Buck hung up and called Loren Hatch and explained what he needed, and she promised to send up her forensic unit and as many deputies as she could spare. Buck thanked her and hung up.

He walked into the office and got everyone's attention. The plan was simple. Charlie had already headed up to the mine to keep an eye out. If Charlie didn't see any guns, the plan was to drive up and raid the mine building. Two of the troopers would block the road to the mine to prevent anyone from leaving.

Someone in the back yelled, "What's plan B?"

Buck knew it was a serious question, but he was running on adrenaline, and the answer came out before he realized he had said it: "Plan B is to not let plan A fail."

There were a couple of laughs, and they all headed for their cars. Since they were all still geared up from the takedown on the highway, there wasn't a need to prep. Everyone checked their weapons and headed for their cars.

Buck was just about to his car when Deputy Harcourt pulled into the lot. He rolled down his window. "Heard you could use some help?"

"Yeah. I'm spread a little thin right now. I'm short a deputy and a trooper who are watching the Camaro until we can get it towed to the Highway Department garage, where they can secure it. You looking for a little more fun?"

Deputy Harcourt looked over the seat. "Boomer, you ready?"

Boomer barked once, and Buck laughed. He told the deputy to fall in line, and the caravan pulled out of the parking lot and headed for the mine.

Buck hit the phone button on his entertainment console and told the female voice on the other end to call Charlie Womack, cell phone.

"I'm here," he said. "Looks like the night shift is getting ready to leave; they seem to be locking the place up. What do you want me to do?"

"Stay put. We're ten minutes out. Any weapons?"

Charlie told him there were no weapons visible and that he would scoot down the hill and get a little closer, so he could be ready when they got there. They hung up, and Buck focused on the drive. He spotted the turn ahead for the road to the mine and took it without slowing down. As soon as the last vehicle made the turn off the highway, he hit his flashers, as did everyone else. They tore up the dirt road and swung into the parking lot.

Several of the workers were heading for their cars when all the flashing lights hit them, and then the sounds of people running everywhere, yelling, "Police, we have a warrant," and, "Hands where we can see them."

Buck spotted Charlie heading into a small office at the back end of the parking area, and a few seconds later, he came out the door, gun in hand, following a man dressed in a white Tyvek jumpsuit who stumbled his way across the lot.

Before Buck could ask, Charlie said, "Caught this one trying to make a phone call." He pushed him in the back with his revolver and told him to turn around so that Buck could place the Flexicuffs' on his wrists.

Buck asked Charlie to keep an eye on his prisoner, and he headed into the metal building that fronted the mine entrance. Deputy Harcourt and Boomer were in heaven as Boomer alerted at every box he passed. The deputies and troopers he had left were handcuffing everyone in the place. Buck pulled out his phone. His first call was to the forensic unit. His second call was to Jess Gonzales.

"A little late, Buck. Do you know what time it is?"

Buck laughed. "Hey, Jess. Time to wake up and go to work."

"Not funny, cowboy. I'm gonna take a wild guess that this is not a social call."

Buck told her about the car they'd intercepted tonight and about the warehouse he was now standing in. He told her he could use her help. She promised to start rounding up the troops.

"You know," she said. "The last couple times we were together, people tried to kill us. I sure hope this is going to be different." She laughed and hung up.

Buck clipped his phone to his belt and looked around. There were crates of drugs all over the warehouse. It looked to Buck like they were being sorted out for delivery to parts unknown.

He stepped out of the building and ran into a

state police sergeant, who had just arrived. He asked what he could do to help, and Buck asked him to take charge of the scene until the DEA arrived. He asked him to arrange transportation for the seven people they'd arrested back to the sheriff's office. "We're gonna need a bigger jail," he said to himself as he walked back to his car, slid in and headed back to Walden. He wondered what information the police chief was willing to trade to try to stay out of jail.

Chapter Fifty-Six

Officer Terrell was parked back behind the dumpsters down the street from the old school building. The same dumpsters Buck had hid behind a day or two before. She had left her patrol car back at the station, and though still in uniform, she was sitting in her personal car. She hoped it would be less conspicuous.

All had been quiet for the two hours she had been sitting there. She had driven by the school building several times while she was on duty but didn't see anything that attracted her attention. This was the first time she had been on a stakeout, and she realized it was nothing like the ones you saw on television. There was no fun-loving banter between partners, no jokes about peeing in a Styrofoam cup and she found it to be boring.

She was just finishing up a peanut butter and jelly sandwich, which she had made at home when she'd stopped to take care of her nana, when she noticed three men approaching the front door to the school. She couldn't see their faces from her position, but she recognized one man right off from his walk and his gestures while they talked. It looked like Detective Cummings. She was having a hard time understanding why Detective Cummings was about to enter the old building.

She watched as one of the men pulled out what must have been a key and unlocked the door. She was confused. When she was first hired, her training officer had told her that the old school was never used and sat abandoned. She wondered what was going on inside the building. No lights were visible from any of the main-level windows, and she found that curious.

Curiosity got the better of her, and even though Buck had told her to watch the building, she decided to see what was going on. She sent Buck a text telling him that three men had entered the building and she was going to get closer. She slid out of the car, grabbed her big Maglite flashlight and started towards the school.

She walked around the perimeter of the building and looked in some of the windows to see if she could see anything, but all she saw was black. Her next stop was the front door, but it was locked. She was beginning to think it was her imagination and that the three men were just shadows or something. She decided to check one more place.

On one of her patrols, she'd caught some neighborhood kids trying to get into the building through an old coal chute that was boarded over but not secure. She had sent the kids away with a stern warning to stay away from the school, and even though they never got into it, they had partially pried off a piece of plywood that was screwed to the chute frame. She wondered if anyone had gotten around to securing it after she filed her report.

The chute was behind some shrubs and hidden

from view. She walked around the building and pushed through the shrubs. She shined her light on the plywood and was surprised and pleased that it was still loose. She grabbed the plywood and pulled. It took several pulls before the plywood ripped past the screws. She stood still for a minute, holding her breath, hoping no one had heard the noise. After a couple of minutes, she started to breathe again and shined her light down the old chute.

The bottom of the chute was about eight feet below her, and other than a lot of dust, she didn't see anything that might stop her. She slipped her flashlight into the holder on her belt and climbed into the chute.

When she emerged at the bottom of the chute, she was covered in gray dust. She wiped herself off as best she could and pulled the flashlight from her belt. She shined it around the space. She was in a storeroom, with a bunch of old decaying boxes sitting on metal shelves. She opened the cover on one box, which disintegrated in her hand, and looked inside. The box contained old math textbooks. She figured the rest of the boxes contained the same thing, so she headed for the door she saw along the center of one wall.

She stopped at the door and listened. She didn't hear anything, so she opened the door, which gave a slight squeak as she pulled it. She stopped halfway and slid past the door, pulling it closed behind her.

It looked like she was in a long corridor, and the light from her flashlight was barely enough to cut through the darkness, but she continued forward. She walked past several doors that had signs for the various maintenance functions they served.

When she arrived at the end of the corridor, she had a choice to make: left or right. She turned off her light and looked down the left corridor but didn't see anything in the dark. She looked down the right corridor and spotted a thin line of light coming from under a door, about halfway down the hall. Leaving her light off, she headed that way.

The door she stopped at had a sign that said kitchen. She placed her ear against the door and could hear voices, but she couldn't make out what they were saying. She tried the door handle and found it was unlocked, so she pushed the lever down and pushed the door open, an inch at a time.

The voices seemed to be coming from somewhere in the back, so she squeezed through the open door and looked around. She was amazed to see that, in such an old building, the kitchen was shiny and modern. Most of the equipment looked brand new. She wondered why.

She took the aisle along the inside wall and moved towards the sound. She stopped as the voices grew angry.

"There must be a better way. Why do we have to kill her?" a male voice pleaded.

"You can't be that stupid. She knows everything. Dad says we have no choice. Now, either screw her one more time, so I can get this over with, or get out of the way, and I will. I've got a lot to do today."

"You can't do this. I won't let you."

Officer Terrell heard a muffled thump and then an even louder thump, like something heavy hitting the floor. She stepped out into the back service area with her gun drawn. "Police, freeze."

Jimmy Martelli was in the process of removing his shirt when she jumped around the corner. He looked at her standing there with her gun out and looked at Detective Cummings, standing next to him. There was a body lying on the floor and a naked girl lying on the floor with her hands and feet tied to a couple of shelving units. The girl looked terrified as she struggled against the ropes. She tried to scream, but the tape across her mouth prevented anything from coming out.

Detective Cummings saw the confused look on Officer Terrell's face. He held up his hands in surrender. "It's okay, Terrell. I have everything under control. Nothing for you to worry about."

She was about to say something when the blow struck her behind her right ear, and the lights went out.

Chapter Fifty-Seven

Buck walked into the DA office's conference room and pulled up a chair. While he waited for Pam Glassman and Chief Anderson, he pulled out his phone to check messages. He had two calls, one from Bax and one from the director. He also had one message from a number he didn't recognize.

He read the text and jumped out of the chair. He dialed the number, and it went straight to voice mail. Pam Glassman was just coming out of her office as he ran past. "I'll be back," he yelled as he flew through the door with his phone to his ear.

As he raced down the stairs, Paul answered.

"Paul, are you still on campus?" Buck yelled into the phone as he sprinted towards his Jeep.

"Yeah, we just started . . ."

"Officer Terrell may be in trouble. She was watching the old school building and texted me that she spotted something. I can't reach her. Get to the old school building, fast as you can. I'm on my way."

Buck didn't wait for a reply. He jumped into the driver's seat, flipped on his flashers and blasted out of the parking lot. Charlie Womack was just pulling into the lot when he saw Buck fly by with his emergency lights on. He spun around in the parking lot and hit the street. He pulled out his phone and called Victoria James. He didn't know what was happening, but Buck was in a damn big hurry. She told him she'd watch for Buck if he came through town. Charlie hung up and stomped down on the gas.

Paul hung up and yelled for the forensic tech, who was watching the backhoe pull up huge pieces of concrete patio. The CBI forensic techs were all certified law enforcement officers, and even though they usually had their hands in something ugly, they were still cops. The tech rushed to catch up to Paul as he sprinted across the lawn, towards the old school building.

By the time he caught up, Paul was standing at the back corner of the old building, catching his breath.

"What's going on, Paul?" the tech asked while he caught his breath.

"We may have a cop in trouble. She was supposed to be watching the building, but she may be inside." They started walking to the front of the building, looking for a way in. As they went, they heard five gunshots in rapid succession. They raced towards the front door, guns drawn. Paul didn't wait to see if the door was locked. As he hit the top step, he charged forward and hit the door with all his bulk. It was just like the old days, playing football.

The front door gave way as the hinges broke free from the frame, and Paul smashed through and landed hard on the floor. Jerry, the forensic tech, came in behind him, looked at the smashed doors and smiled. "You sure know how to make an entrance," he said.

Paul stood up. "Shots sounded like they came from the basement. We need to find a door." They split up and went searching. Jerry found the door along the side of the main room, hidden behind a velvet curtain. He yelled for Paul and opened the door, staying to the side as the door opened and hit the wall. Paul pulled out his flashlight and headed down the stairs. They stopped for a second at the bottom of the stairs and looked down the dark corridor. They moved down the hall following Paul's light until he signaled to stop. He cocked his head to one side. He had heard something in the stillness. He waited. This time Jerry heard it too. Someone was screaming out of control. They raced down the corridor and stopped outside a door marked kitchen.

Paul looked at Jerry. "Go left," he whispered. Jerry nodded. He pushed open the door and moved to the right while Jerry moved to the left. The sound was coming from the back of the kitchen area. They moved along opposite walls and entered what looked like a service area.

They could hear someone sobbing. They stepped through the entrance, guns forward and stopped. The scene was a bloody mess. Officer Terrell was sitting on the floor covered in blood, holding a naked woman in her arms. There were four male bodies, three of which were covered in blood. Paul put away his gun. He walked over and kneeled next to Officer Terrell. He took the gun from her bloody hand and said, "It's okay, Terrell. The cavalry is here." He looked up at Jerry, who was already on the phone calling for an ambulance.

Chapter Fifty-Eight

Officer Terrell couldn't have been out long. Her mind had started to clear, but the pain in her head was intense. She could hear voices around, but she didn't move.

"What the hell are we going to do with her?" said one voice.

"Who cares," said another voice. "What's one more body? We'll kill her and take her with us."

"She's a cop. I can't kill a cop. It wouldn't feel right."

A man laughed. "No problem, I'll take care of her when I'm done with this bitch."

Officer Terrell was lying on her side. She realized her hands weren't tied. They must have figured she would be out for a while, she thought. She couldn't feel her gun belt, which they must have taken off before they dumped her back on the floor. She assessed her situation and decided she needed to do something because she was going to die anyway. Her only regret was that she would never be able to say goodbye to her grandmother, and she wondered who would take care of her.

She moved just slightly and felt a lump in her front pocket. Her knife. They must not have frisked her after she hit the floor. Cummings would have known that she didn't have another weapon stashed on her person. The chief had a strict rule that the only weapon that could be carried while in uniform was the service weapon. He must not have thought about her carrying a knife.

She'd never understood, until now, the importance of carrying a knife, since she always carried a gun. Now she knew. She thought back to one of her favorite cop shows that she and her grandmother watched together. The show's main character had a lot of rules that he lived by, but the one that stood out most in her mind was, "Never go anywhere without a knife." Now she was glad she had followed that sage advice.

She slowly slid her hand under her hip and started pushing the knife up with her fingers. She was relieved when it finally popped into her hand. She knew it was easy to flick open with one hand; she prayed she would have the opportunity.

She could hear the girl who was tied up struggling and heard a man grunting, and then her prayers were answered.

Detective Cummings stood over her. "I've been looking at this one since she was hired. Would love to see what's under that uniform." He laughed.

He kneeled next to Officer Terrell and grabbed her shoulders. He turned her so she would be flat, and as he did, he heard a slight snick and saw a flash of light. The knife plunged deep into his throat, and blood gushed all over Terrell. He reached up to grab his throat, and Terrell reached under his jacket, grabbed his pistol and fired twice into his chest. He flew backward and smashed onto the floor.

The bodyguard, who she hadn't seen coming before he knocked her out, came around the corner with his gun drawn, and looked around in disbelief. With blood covering her face, she aimed as best she could and fired twice, hitting him in the chest with both shots.

She turned and saw a naked Jimmy Martelli start to roll off the girl, reaching for the gun on the floor next to him, and she fired a fifth time, hitting him in the throat. Blood poured all over the naked girl as he slumped on top of her. Terrell sat up and scanned the room with the gun in front of her.

Seeing no other threat, she slid across the floor and pushed Jimmy Martelli off the girl. She pulled the tape from the girl's mouth and wrapped her arms around her, holding her tight. The girl let out a couple of screams from deep inside and then started to cry.

Terrell looked up as Paul and Jerry stepped into the room with guns drawn. She didn't know who these two guys were, but she felt safe. The big man in the suit jacket had a badge hanging around his neck. It was the same badge that she had seen clipped to Buck Taylor's belt.

The big man walked over, kneeled beside her and took the gun from her hand. He told her everything was going to be okay, that the cavalry had arrived.

She started to cry.

Chapter Fifty-Nine

Buck pulled into the parking lot, slammed the Jeep into park and jumped out. Charlie was just pulling in behind him, as was Victoria James. He didn't wait. He'd spotted the smashed-in front doors as he pulled in, and he raced across the lawn and up the stairs. He stopped at the side of the doors and shined his flashlight into the room. Victoria James moved into position on the other side. Charlie was just coming up the stairs with his revolver in his hand.

Victoria caught his eye and pointed to the right. Buck nodded. He did a silent count to three in his head, moved through the door and slid right, while Victoria slid left. Charlie moved into Victoria's position and held his gun at low ready.

They both scanned the room and then lowered their weapons. Charlie saw the open basement door and pointed. Buck shined his light down the stairs, and they headed down one at a time. There was light coming through an open door down the hall and Buck headed that way.

He stopped outside the open door and looked inside. He noted the shiny kitchen equipment with a "What the hell?" look, and Charlie shrugged his shoulders. They moved quickly into the space and heard the sobbing coming from somewhere in the back. Jerry was standing just inside the entrance talking on the phone, and they lowered their weapons and stepped into the space.

Buck looked around. With blood everywhere, he could only imagine what had happened. Paul, who was kneeling next to Officer Terrell, stood up and walked over to him. Jerry walked over and told them that the ambulance was on the way. He had also called the Larimer County coroner's office, and they were mobilizing.

Buck looked around the room and then at Terrell; she offered a weak smile. Melanie Granville squeezed in tighter and buried her head in Terrell's shoulder. Victoria James walked over and kneeled next to the two women.

"What the hell happened?" asked Buck.

"From what little I could get out of Terrell," said Paul as he stepped over to Detective Cummings, who still had a knife sticking out of his throat. "Someone struck her from behind as she confronted the men. When she came to, they had taken her weapon and gun belt but hadn't checked her for a knife. Cummings got close, and she stabbed him, and then used his gun to shoot him and the guy by the door."

Buck walked over and looked at the body by the door. His jacket was open, and Buck could make out the shoulder holster. The gun that belonged in that holster was lying a couple of feet away. He had two small red holes center mass.

"Who's the naked guy?" asked Buck.

Paul walked over and turned the naked guy's head. Buck whistled, as did Charlie.

"I'll be damned," said Charlie.

Jimmy Martelli's open eyes were glassed over, and he had a jagged bullet hole in the left side of his throat. Blood had pooled on the floor under the body and, from the looks of it, all over Melanie Granville too. There was a pistol on the floor next to the body.

The other lump on the floor was starting to come to, moaning and holding his head. Buck could hear sirens in the distance; he asked Jerry to meet them. He also told him to keep all the local police away.

He walked over to the other person, and Paul saw the look of recognition in Buck's eyes. "You know this kid?"

"Josh DiNardo," Buck said.

"Didn't we get a warrant for this kid earlier tonight?"

"Yeah." Buck reached over and placed his handcuffs on Josh's wrists. Josh was out of it and couldn't even keep himself upright. He knew it would be pointless to read him his Miranda rights in this condition, so he called over one of the paramedics, who had just entered the room.

"This one is under arrest. Make sure he keeps his mouth shut on the way to the hospital, and do not remove the handcuffs," he said to the paramedic.

Victoria James stood up and told Buck she needed to get some air, and she walked through the kitchen and out the door.

Buck walked over and kneeled next to Terrell.

"Officer Terrell, are you okay? Is any of this blood yours or Melanie's?"

Terrell shook her head. "I'm sorry, Agent Taylor. I should have stayed in the car like you told me." She looked past Buck to the dead Jimmy Martelli. "I had to shoot him. He was raping and strangling this girl, and he went for his gun." Tears rolled down her bloodstained face.

"It's okay, Tracy, whenever you're in a fight and you come out ahead, it's a good day."

Several more paramedics arrived, pulling gurneys. Buck moved out of the way, and they put a blanket over Melanie's shoulders and helped her up. They put her on the gurney and started talking to her while the female paramedic checked her over for injuries. Buck walked over and told the paramedic that she had most likely been raped. She nodded and told Buck they would run a test as soon as they got her to the hospital.

Another paramedic was talking to Terrell. She was sitting on the edge of a table, and he was running a neurological test on her. Buck walked over.

"She might have a mild concussion," said the paramedic. "We'll take her along and get her checked out."

Buck thanked him. He spotted Terrell's gun belt lying on the floor under a table, walked over, picked it up and carried it back to her. She took the belt and pistol. Her hands shook. The paramedic laid her on another gurney, strapped her in and they rolled both gurneys through the kitchen.

Buck asked one of the paramedics to check for vitals on the three bodies. He checked each one and shook his head no.

Chapter Sixty

Buck was starting to feel the effects of not having slept. Hell, he couldn't remember when he'd slept last. He was about to pull out his phone when Jerry came back into the room.

"Forensic team from Denver just pulled in," he said. "I called them and rerouted them from the mine. There's also a woman outside, says her name is Jess Gonzales, DEA. Said you know her. I asked her to wait by the door."

Buck nodded and looked around. What a mess. He should have never left Terrell alone. He'd never considered that she might go off on her own. He admired her spunk, but she could have been killed, and that would have been on him. He stepped aside as the forensic team arrived, and he asked everyone to step out of the area. This was now a crime scene.

"You look like shit, Buck," said Jess Gonzales as he walked out of the kitchen door. "When was the last time you slept?"

"Not sure, Jess. What year is this?"

She was about to say something when Charlie and Victoria walked up. The concern on both their faces was evident.

"You're gonna want to see this," Victoria said, and she turned and walked away. Charlie tipped his hat to Jess and walked off, following Victoria.

Buck, Paul and Jess followed behind. They turned down another short hall, and he saw Victoria stop in front of a closed door. Someone had been kind enough to turn the lights on, so they weren't fumbling around in the dark. Buck walked up to the door and looked through the small glass window. Two young women looked back. Everyone looked young at Buck's age, but these girls couldn't have been more than fourteen or fifteen at the most. They were huddled together against the back wall and looked scared to death.

Buck moved to the next room and saw the same thing. It was the same in the next eight rooms. He looked at Victoria.

"Looks like the stories were true," she said. "We had heard this was going on, but I couldn't find any information around town. These are just kids, for Christ's sake. What the fuck is wrong with people?"

Jess, standing behind Buck, pulled a small leather pouch out of her back pocket and removed two lockpick tools. She started working on the first door lock. Buck pulled a similar case out of his pocket and started on the second door.

Charlie watched them work on the locks. "Do we want to know why you guys have those?" he asked with a grin.

Without looking up and without any coordination, they both said, "In case we lose our house keys."

Charlie laughed, and that laughter helped to break the somber mood. While Buck and Jess unlocked the rooms, Victoria, Paul and Charlie escorted the girls upstairs, where two state troopers stood watch over them. None of the girls said a word.

With the doors all unlocked and everyone upstairs, Buck and Jess had a minute to talk.

"I stopped by to let you know my team is all over the Camaro and the mine. I've ordered a couple of large trucks to gather up all the equipment and the existing pills. We found a bunch more back in the mine. They had a storage area back there."

"Any idea how they were getting the drugs in here?" asked Buck. "All I saw were tables that looked like they were used to sort the fentanyl into travel-sized packages. It didn't look like they were manufacturing."

"They had the equipment back there to manufacture as well as distribute. It was still in crates, so they hadn't gotten that far. There's two possibilities. It came in through the Walden-Jackson airport, or it came in by highway from Laramie or Rawlins. I called the FAA on the way over, and they are looking into all the flights that come in and out of the airport. My guys in Laramie are looking for connections up that way. We'll figure it out."

She hesitated for a minute. "Fuck, Buck. What the hell have you gotten yourself into?"

"I wish I knew, Jess. I think the entire town is just one big criminal enterprise, and it's been going on since the town was founded. So far, we have drugs, murder, mob connections, criminal conspiracy, prostitution and human trafficking.

There might be illegal gambling, and there's an old doctor who was performing illegal abortions and removing babies from unwed mothers to adopt out, sometimes resulting in the death of the mother. Strangest of all is that I think the whole town or a good percentage of it is being paid from the proceeds, so no one is talking. I've already arrested five members of the police department, and now I've got a dead detective and the dead son of the guy who runs this whole town, and I have to get back to Walden to work a deal with the chief of police. It's a wacky world, and we're not finished yet."

Jess slapped him on the back as they headed down the hall. "I don't envy you your job right now, but if you need anything, you yell. I got your back."

Buck smiled at her, and they headed up the stairs. Paul was waiting for him, so he said goodbye to Jess and stepped outside with Paul. As he walked through the main room, he could hear bits and pieces of foreign languages being spoken as the young girls and women sat waiting for something to happen.

"I called the director, and he has more help coming. I got to tell you, Buck. I'm concerned. In a couple of hours, the sun's coming up, and this town will wake up to a lot of things going on. The local cops will realize that bad things are happening when they can't locate their chief, the lead detective or some of the other officers. I've got three of them outside champing at the bit to find out what happened to Officer Terrell and why they aren't involved. We need a plan."

"I know. I'm working on that. What's going on at the plaza?"

"Jerry headed back over. Ground-penetrating radar picked up twenty-seven disturbed areas. He's got the backhoe guy digging down to within six inches of the anomalies, and then his team is digging by hand. So far, they've uncovered bones of what appear to be a woman's body and also a baby's skeleton. Buck, this is going to be tragic if every anomaly is a body."

"I know. Let's keep our heads on a swivel. I need to deal with the chief of police. Can you head over to the hospital and formally arrest Josh DiNardo? I had two messages from Bax, so I'm gonna call her now and see where she's at. I'll be back quick as I can."

Paul headed off, and Buck pulled out his phone.

"Hey, Bax. Sorry about not getting back. Things just got a little nuts around here."

"No worries. I should be there in an hour or so. Two things. Nadia was raped. We got a good sample, and it's at the lab. No matches, but Max will hold it till we have something to match it to. Second thing. That second body we found, the male, was dead twenty-four to thirty-six hours—one gunshot wound in the chest. Bullet was in good shape. If we can find the gun, we can get a match."

"Great job, Bax. I'm heading back to Walden.

Chief Anderson wants to talk a deal with the DA. I'll fill you in on the rest when you get here."

Buck hung up and slid into his Jeep. The Coke sitting on the center console was warm, but he drank it down in one gulp. What he needed was food and sleep. What he had to do was get back to the DA's office. He pulled out of the lot and headed north.

Chapter Sixty-One

James Martelli stood behind his big wood desk in his bathrobe. County Commissioner Bob Stewart stood in front of the desk. Bob had never seen Martelli this angry.

"How the fuck did they find out about the drugs? That operation was protected. Only a handful of people knew about it."

He looked out the window at the touches of pink and red that were starting to fill the sky. His family had controlled this valley for over a hundred years, and it was all coming apart. He spun around and, in one move, swept everything off his desk onto the floor.

"I want that motherfucker dead! Do you hear me? Dead, dead, dead!" he screamed.

He yelled for his bodyguard, who came in looking like he had been awake for hours.

"Where's Jimmy?" he shouted.

The bodyguard shook his head.

James Martelli looked at him. His face was pure evil. He started speaking softly. "Well, maybe you should find him, or do I have to do everything myself?"

His voice got louder. "Now, shithead. Find him, now!"

The guard left the room with his tail between his

legs, and James turned to Bob Stewart, the county commissioner.

"Did they get the shipment?"

Bob was afraid to answer, so he nodded his head.

"That state cop is gonna pay for this if I have to kill him myself!"

James Martelli stormed out of the office, and Bob Stewart could hear doors slamming as he went. He was bellowing uncontrollably. Bob knew this was bad. Maybe it was time to hit the road. He had plenty of money stashed away. He could run home right now, grab the kids and his wife and head south. He could be safely away before James knew he was gone. He walked out the front door and headed home, calling his wife as he went.

James Martelli, now dressed, stood in the doorway to his office. He looked at the mess on the floor. He didn't care. He had tried calling Chief Anderson but gotten his voice mail. Jimmy wasn't answering, and neither was Cummings. "Where the hell is everyone?" he said to himself.

He sat in the chair behind his desk and rubbed his temples. He needed a plan, but right this minute, he felt alone. He had called police headquarters and gotten the night dispatcher. She told him she had been trying to reach Chief Anderson for a couple of hours but had gotten no response. She wasn't sure if he was aware of the incident that had happened at the old school building.

He asked her for more details, but she didn't have any. He hung up and threw his phone against the wall. Not the school too. He needed to find out what was going on, so he started calling everyone he knew.

No one seemed to know anything, and he was concerned with the lack of cooperation he was getting. All anyone would say was that there was a large police presence at the old school building, but no one had any details.

A thought crept into his brain. A thought he didn't like. He had told Jimmy to take care of the girl and the DiNardo kid last night. They were holding the girl at the old school building. "Oh, shit! What if the stuff going on at the school was because of that? Maybe that's why Jimmy wasn't answering his phone."

His anger welled up inside, and he was suddenly afraid to leave the house. He turned around in his chair and looked at the valley below. His hands were shaking.

Chapter Sixty-Two

Buck pulled out a chair in the conference room and sat opposite Pam Glassman and Sheriff Womack. He filled them in on the evening's events, picked up the cold Coke and held it against his head. Pam Glassman shook her head.

"What the hell happened to that town?" she asked.

Buck set the Coke bottle on the table. "My guess is this has been going on for a long time. Like one of those old factory towns you read about, where the company owns everything. After a while, no one cares anymore."

"Buck, what are we gonna do? I don't have the jail space or the manpower for this."

"I spoke to the director earlier. He is sending up some help. Should be here in an hour, give or take. My biggest concern is the cops still on Martelli's payroll. We need to disarm them before things get out of hand."

"What about Martelli?" he asked. "He's gonna go ballistic when he finds out his kid is dead."

"You've got nothing on him," said Pam. "We know he's connected to everything going on, but all we have is the word of a bad cop, who heard from somebody that he shot a guy in his office. You have a dead body of a college kid shot in the chest, but nothing that proves Martelli was the one who shot him. Did you get anything at the mine or from the Camaro drivers that connects him to the drugs?"

"No," said Buck. "The driver and passenger lawyered up. Their lawyer won't be here for a couple of hours. Robert Silvestri is representing everyone we arrested at the mine. So far, we found nothing to connect Martelli to the drugs or the girls in town."

"Okay, let's bring up Chief Anderson and see what he has to say," said Pam.

Marty Womack left the room and headed downstairs to get the chief of police.

Pam looked at Buck. "I woke up the DA and filled him in. He's having a hard time dealing with all this, but as soon as he gets to the office and can get organized, he is sending up a team to help out."

Buck nodded and took a long drink from his Coke. Chief Anderson walked in, in handcuffs, followed by Marty Womack. He sat in the chair next to Pam.

Pam pulled out a voice recorder, pushed the on switch and set it on the table. "Chief Anderson, you asked for this meeting, but I have to tell you, I am not comfortable doing this without your lawyer present. I also want to remind you that your Miranda rights still apply. What can we do for you?"

"He's not my lawyer. He works for Martelli. Anything I say in front of him will go straight back to Martelli. Now, I'm ready to talk to you and tell you anything you want to know, but I have some conditions."

"What conditions?" asked Buck.

"First, I want my family protected. Martelli is nuts, and if he even thinks I've talked, he'll go after them. Second, I want immunity, and third, I want witness protection. You agree to those terms, and I'll fill a book with what I know."

Pam sat thinking about the terms, but Buck needed answers, and he needed them now. "Before ADA Glassman calls her boss, we need something from you. Call it good faith, so we know what you plan to tell us is real."

Chief Anderson sat for a minute thinking. He knew this was a dangerous game, but he had to see it through for the sake of his family. "Okay," he said. "One thing, and then you call the DA."

Pam nodded to Buck. "We were told that you were in James Martelli's office a couple of days back and that Mr. Martelli pulled a gun from his desk drawer and shot a young man in cold blood. Is that true?"

Chief Anderson looked at Buck in disbelief. He was trying to figure out how Buck could have known that. There were only five people in the room.

"Come on, Anderson," said Buck. "You want a deal; we need to hear the truth. Did James Martelli kill a young man right in front of you, and you did nothing about it?"

Chief Anderson bowed his head. When he looked up, he had tears in his eyes. "Yes," he said.

"He killed that young man right in front of me. I thought I was next. I can still hear the shot ringing in my ears."

"Why did he kill the young man?"

"He was supposed to be watching a girl who ran away. Martelli was angry."

Buck smiled. "We already know about the girls in the old school building. We rescued them about two hours ago, along with Officer Tracy Terrell and Melanie Granville. Detective Cummings and Jimmy Martelli were going to kill them. Both Cummings and Martelli are dead."

Chief Anderson looked at Buck as if he couldn't comprehend what Buck was saying. He wondered how much else they knew about what went on in town.

"Did you kill them?" asked Anderson.

"No, they got sloppy, and Officer Terrell killed them both, along with a bodyguard."

Chief Anderson was stunned. "I gave you what you wanted," he said. "Now I want my deal."

Buck signaled for Pam to step out of the office, and they walked out and closed the door.

"Can you wake up the judge and get me a warrant? He just corroborated the story we got from Billy Wilson. When you talk to your boss, bear in mind that we don't know the full extent of Chief Anderson's involvement in all of this. There will most certainly be other charges dropped on him after the investigations are complete."

"Don't worry, Buck. I'll be careful how I word the agreement. Mr. Anderson is going to spend a long time in jail. Now, go get some backup, and I'll text you the warrant."

Chapter Sixty-Three

Buck stepped out into the cool morning air, snugged his jacket against the chill and watched as the sun crept over the mountains to the east. He was about to call Paul when he saw his Jeep pulling into the parking lot. He walked over and waited as he walked around the Jeep and pulled Josh DiNardo from the car. Josh had a white bandage wrapped around his head, and he looked a little glassy-eyed.

Paul explained that Josh had a mild concussion and a large headache, but the doctor felt he was okay to be released from the hospital. They walked up the stairs and into the sheriff's office. Marty Womack was upstairs with Pam Glassman and had left two of his reserve deputies to watch the jail. They were still waiting for the transport to take the Camaro duo to Fort Collins.

Charlie Womack was sitting at one of the three desks, with his feet up and his Stetson pulled down over his eyes. He snapped to when they walked in. Paul processed Josh and put him in the cell that had previously held Chief Anderson.

Buck told everyone about the conversation he'd just had with Chief Anderson. It would have been hard not to notice the looks of pleasure on their faces. Buck was about to say something else when Bax walked in. She looked as tired as Buck felt. She had overheard the conversation when she opened the door.

"So, when do we go get Martelli?" she asked.

Buck told her he was waiting for the warrant to come through. The door opened, and Kevin Jackson walked into the room. He was wearing a CBI windbreaker over his ballistic vest. He looked around at this tired bunch of do-gooders and smiled.

"You guys are all amazing," he said.

"Sir, are we glad to see you," said Buck. "We were just about to put our heads together and come up with a plan to round up the local cops before they find out what's gone on, and things turn ugly."

"No need to worry," said the director. "The governor had the same concerns. He appointed Darcy Glover as the interim police chief. For those who don't know Darcy, she retired last year after thirty years with the Colorado Springs Police Department. She left the job as the assistant chief. She accepted the governor's request. She has taken over police headquarters and has twenty state troopers and CBI agents rounding up all the remaining officers. The night shift has already been detained, and the day shift folks are just waking up. We should have the town secure before most people have their breakfast."

Buck's phone chimed, and he pulled it from his belt and read the text. "Good news?" asked the director.

"Yes, sir. The arrest and search warrants came

through for James Martelli. Let's go see if Mr. Martelli has had breakfast yet."

Bax, Paul and the director headed outside and hopped into Bax's Jeep. Buck, Charlie and one of the two deputies headed for Buck's Jeep. Charlie was the resident expert and knew where the Martelli ranch was located, so Buck led the way, with Charlie acting as navigator. They had been driving down Highway 125 for fifteen minutes when Buck signaled a turn onto the ranch road. The director had called ahead, and two state police cars were waiting outside the gate. They fell in line as Bax passed them.

Buck pulled up in front of the main house, and everyone exited the car. Buck directed the two troopers and Paul to cover the back of the massive house. He gave them a few minutes to get into position, and he approached the door, followed by Bax, Charlie and the director.

Buck pounded on the door with the side of his fist and waited. The door was opened by a young woman in a purple maid's uniform, who asked what they wanted. Buck didn't respond but pushed open the door and moved her out of the way.

Bax took her into the first room on the left, which appeared to be a living room, frisked her and handcuffed her to a heavy-looking wrought iron floor lamp. She asked her how many people were in the house, got her answer and rejoined Buck.

"Mr. Martelli," Buck yelled. "James Martelli, police, we have a warrant for your arrest. Please show yourself."

With guns drawn, they moved down the hall, checking rooms as they went. They reached the end of the hall without incident, and Charlie walked over and unlocked a back door, whistling for Paul and the troopers. As they entered, Buck told them to check upstairs, and they headed for the staircase.

Two cooks were found in the kitchen, and both were searched, Flexicuffed and cuffed to a couple of chairs. They reached the last room on the right and split up to opposite sides of the door. Buck pushed the door open and signaled for Bax and the director to go left. He and Charlie entered and moved right.

James Martelli stood with his back to them, looking out the window. He didn't move.

"James Martelli," said Buck. "We have a warrant for your arrest. Please turn around and show us your hands."

James Martelli remained where he stood and continued to look outside. "I just love this view. It never gets old. I hoped someday to have grandchildren to share the view with. All this would have been their legacy. But now I've been told that my only son is dead, so I guess that dream got shot to hell along with him."

"Mr. Martelli, I'm not going to ask you again. Please turn around and show us your hands."

Paul and the troopers slipped into the room and waited. Buck took a step forward. Bax moved a little more to the left. Martelli glanced over his shoulder. His shoulders slumped, and he slowly turned around.

The gun was in his left hand, and, without aiming, he fired as soon as he was lined up with Buck. His aim was off, and the bullet hit the doorframe. Bax was the first to react and fired twice. Two red roses blossomed on his white shirt as the gun dropped from his hand, and he fell into his chair. His last breath escaped his lips, and he was silent.

Buck moved around the desk, checked for a pulse and shook his head. He pulled a pair of nitrile gloves out of his pocket, put them on and picked up the pistol by the barrel. He laid it on the desk, and that's when he noticed a stack of old and new ledgers, just sitting there in the open. The director flipped open the top ledger with a pen tip and read the first page. They had hit the mother lode.

The director pulled out his phone, called the Denver forensic team he had brought along with him and directed them to the house.

He walked up to Buck. "Why do you think he gave up so easily?"

Buck thought about it for a minute. "I think when he found out his son was dead; it meant the end of his legacy. Something inside him died, and I think he realized the futility of fighting. He would never have survived in prison. The mob would have seen to that, and he had nothing else to live for, so I think he figured this was the only way out."

"Suicide by cop," said Bax, as she walked over and stood next to Buck. "Lucky me."

"Could have been any one of us," he said. "Sorry it had to be you."

They spent another hour at the house, looking for more evidence. When the forensic team arrived, they had already found enough evidence to fill several banker's boxes. The forensic team took over the evidence gathering, and the director ordered everyone out of the house, so they headed out the front door.

Charlie walked up to the group. "I don't know about the rest of you, but this old goat could use a good breakfast and a week's worth of sleep. How about it, folks? I'll even buy."

"That won't be necessary. Breakfast is on me," said the director.

They climbed into the two Jeeps, left the troopers to guard the house while the forensic team worked and headed back to Walden.

Chapter Sixty-Four

Buck woke to the sun shining through the opening between the curtains and to the smell of bacon cooking. He realized he was starving, so he grabbed a quick shower, dressed, clipped his gun and badge to his belt and left his room. He checked his phone and saw he had fifteen messages and seven missed calls. He also noticed that he had slept for almost twenty-four hours. The exhaustion had won. He couldn't remember crawling into bed, but here it was, twenty-four hours later, and he couldn't remember the whole last day.

He walked into the lounge and spotted Bax, Charlie and the director sitting at the table for four.

"Well, look who finally woke up," said Bax. The group laughed.

"We thought maybe you'd left without telling us," said Charlie.

Victoria James walked into the lounge with a plate of scrambled eggs and bacon and a large cold Coke. It seemed that the already huge group of people who knew about Buck's legendary Coke drinking had grown even larger over the past couple of days.

She set the plate down on the table in front of Buck.

Charlie stood up and said to Victoria, "We should get going."

That was when Buck noticed that Charlie had put on his black Stetson and had his retired sheriff badge hanging from a lanyard around his neck. He looked at Victoria, who had on jeans and a Carhartt jacket and her reserve deputy badge clipped to her belt. She had her holster clipped next to it.

"What's going on?" asked Buck in between bites of eggs and bacon.

Charlie laughed. "Until they finish vetting the cops, we're the day shift." He looked at Victoria. "Ready?"

She nodded her head, wished everyone a good day and they left the B and B. Buck couldn't hide his surprise.

"I go to sleep for a couple of hours, and the whole world changes."

The director finished what was left of his coffee and stood up. "I need to head back to Denver. You need anything, you call." He shook Bax's and Buck's hands. "You guys did great. Take a couple of days off when you get the chance. Bax, I'll let you know as soon as I get the report."

He put on his coat and headed for the door, pulling his suitcase behind him.

Buck asked, "What report?"

Bax put down her coffee cup. "I'm on paid leave pending the shooting report. It shouldn't be too long; the DA is running the investigation, and both troopers were wearing body cameras, so they have two views from different angles. It should be a cakewalk."

Buck put down his fork. "How are you doing?"

Bax smiled. "I'm fine. Nothing to worry about. Thought I'd stick around a couple of days and put the investigation file together." She refilled her cup.

Buck took a sip of Coke. "You're not fine, Bax, and it's okay. Right now, everything looks and feels good. You did your job. What's the big deal? Well, let me tell you from experience. Killing a person is a big deal, and it might not seem like it now, but one night, the demons will sneak into your bedroom, and you'll wake up crying or screaming, or both. It will scare the shit out of you when it happens, but it's okay. It needs to happen. It's the only way to heal. If you fight it and keep it buried inside, it will eat you alive. Trust me. I know. I'm still haunted by the people I've had to kill over the years, and there are nights I wake up crying. Lucy always said it was night terrors, but she had no idea how terrifying it really is. Don't look for it to happen, because it will only happen when you're not ready for it. This is what separates us from the animals that need to kill to survive. If it happens and you need someone to talk to and help you through it, you give me a call. I will always be here for you."

He reached behind him and pulled his wallet out of his back pocket. He pulled out a business card. "The director will make you go to counseling; it's required for any officer-involved shooting." He handed her the card. "Claire is one of the best psychologists I've ever dealt with. She reminds me of you. Very athletic. Does all the things you do. You'll get along great. I still call her once in a while when I just need to talk. Give her a call today and schedule an appointment."

Bax looked at him with tears in her eyes. She stood up, walked around the table and gave him a huge hug. When she pulled away, she smiled and said, "Don't tell human resources." They both laughed.

Chapter Sixty-Five

Bax and Buck spent the next couple of hours sitting in the lounge while Bax filled him in on what he'd missed while he was asleep.

"Jess Gonzales and her crew have pulled out," she said. "They cleared out the warehouse and the mine and took the car back to Grand Junction. She told me to tell you goodbye, and she would call you in a couple of days."

She told him that one of the two guys in the car had caved. She wasn't sure if it was the driver or the passenger, but he'd given Jess contact info for several people involved in the transportation end. "Jess has her guys rounding them up as we speak. They had a whole network of drivers cruising from Chicago to the West Coast."

Buck interrupted. "What made the one guy turn?"

"That's the best part," she said. "We got the warrant for both their houses a little after you headed to your room. Lots of interesting stuff."

She told him that it appeared they were muscle for the organization, besides being the drivers. It turned out they were responsible for some of the bodies in the mine shaft. "But what turned the tide was that in the one guy's garage, we found the laptop, cell phone, dash camera and body camera that belonged to the Carbon County deputy. As soon as Marty Womack showed him the evidence, it was like the dam broke."

"Did he give up why they killed him?" asked Buck.

"They were working with another deputy, who looked the other way when they came through. The Carbon County sheriff was suspicious something was going on, so he changed the schedules. The deputy stopped them for speeding and thought it was odd that two Copper Creek police officers were cruising through Wyoming, late at night, in an unmarked police car. One of them shot him, and they moved the car to hide the scene. Wyoming is filing extradition papers for both of them, and the Colorado attorney general is going along with it."

"Pretty stupid, keeping the evidence," said Buck.

Bax smiled. "No one said these guys were geniuses."

"What about the girls?" asked Buck.

"ICE picked them up last night. They will all be returned to their native countries. They were there to provide sex to any of the big shots who came here for the Friday night party. That old schoolhouse had a full casino on the ground floor and a dozen fancy bedrooms on the second floor."

She slid her laptop so he could see it. "Here's the list of this week's guests. Each guest paid twenty grand for the weekend to do whatever they wanted. Martelli had video cameras in every room. The blackmail came later."

Buck looked up from the list. "Lots of impressive names on here." He pointed to two of them.

"The governor told the director that he would take care of them," she said. "There's three more on there from Washington. When the governor is done with them, they'll wish the mob had blackmailed them. Gonna cost them big in favors."

Buck asked about Nadia.

"One of the other girls knew her mom in Ukraine. ICE is going to have her body shipped back home. She was only sixteen. Got kidnapped from a school party."

"How are Officer Terrell and Melanie Granville?" asked Buck.

"Officer Terrell is covering the night shift. Darcy vetted her first and put her right back to work. She's one lucky and tough girl. You might want to give her the speech about demons in the bedroom. She might need a friend. Melanie copped to the kinky sex, but she had no idea Josh DiNardo rigged the controller button not to work. She couldn't believe he killed Kevin Ducette over her. To them, it was just a college fling and a little experimentation. She's probably still crying."

Buck said she was gonna have a lot to deal with and asked if the DA had said anything about charging her.

"Unless our investigation finds something else, they think that between the death of Kevin and getting raped and almost murdered by Jimmy Martelli, she has suffered enough."

Buck pulled up a copy of the DA's agreement with former police chief Anderson. He read it quietly for a minute. "Looks like Pam was careful in how she worded this agreement. She only agreed to drop the charges associated with the death of Kevin Ducette."

"Yeah," said Bax. "By the time we're done, he'll face a dozen more charges. He'll end up spending the rest of his life in jail."

"Okay," said Buck. "What's our status overall?"

"Once word got out that Martelli had video cameras in all the old schoolrooms, the purge began. The mayor and all but two city councilpersons resigned. We arrested one of the county commissioners; the second one disappeared with his family. We have an APB out for them and alerted Border Patrol and TSA. Josh DiNardo is in the Larimer County jail and wants to make a deal, and the doctor suffered a stroke in jail. He's in the hospital and is expected to recover. Probably the stress that got to him. We have five forensic teams working, ten troopers maintaining law and order, along with Charlie and Victoria, and James Martelli's ledgers are in the hands of the forensic accountants."

"Speaking of the doctor. Where's Paul, and what's going on at the plaza?"

"Paul's still at the site. That's where two of the forensic teams are. He would like you to stop by the site so he can fill you in."

"It's been a hell of a week," said Buck. "You guys did a great job. We all did a great job. Let's finish up the investigation, and maybe we can go home in a week or two."

Bax got a serious look on her face. "Buck, one thing I don't get. Why did they try to cover up Kevin Ducette's murder? That's what led to all of this. It doesn't make sense. Shit's been going on here for a hundred years. Why now?"

Buck sipped his Coke and thought about the question. "You're right, Bax. If they had been honest about what happened to Kevin Ducette, none of this would have happened, and you and I would be investigating something else. The truth would have been embarrassing for Kevin's parents, but they would have accepted it. When I asked Anderson why he covered up the murder, he said he didn't know it was murder. He swears, and the video backs him up, that the winch worked fine when he got there. If you believe he had no idea, then Josh DiNardo was the one who set all this in motion, out of jealousy."

"I buy all that, but he's involved in only a small portion of what went on here. How did the rest come apart?"

"I think it was coming apart long before you and I showed up. I don't think James Martelli, for all his ruthlessness, had the same kind of control over the people of this town that his father or grandfather did. He let his psychopath of a son deal with the people, and I think the townspeople resented his behavior and the way he handled things. You spoke with several of the people. They didn't like what their town had become. They were ready to fight back. The dynamite was already here. We were the spark. Since no one knew what we were looking at, they thought we were looking at everything."

Bax hesitated for a minute. "Did the governor set us up?"

Buck laughed. "I think the governor had an idea of the kinds of things that were going on in this town. There had been rumors for years that this town was stuck in the Wild West of old, but I don't think anyone had any idea how bad things were. When Marty Womack called him about Kevin's suicide, it gave him the opportunity to send us in here to see what we could see, without looking at anything specifically. My guess. He would have been fine if all we got were some answers for the Ducettes because I think he was touched deeply by their convictions. I guess we'll never know."

Buck stood up, stretched and finished his Coke. "Rest up a day or two, and then we'll hit the paperwork. I'm gonna head over and see Paul." He grabbed his coat, patted Bax on the arm and headed for the door.

Chapter Sixty-Six

Buck zipped up his ranch jacket and looked down the main street of Copper Creek. From the outside, it looked like nothing had changed, but on the inside, there were going to be significant changes in the lives of these folks. Some would survive and adapt, and some would fail and leave. He hoped the majority would stay, because he had met a lot of nice people, and this town was gonna need all the nice it could muster.

He looked at the bright bluebird sky and the dusting of snow that had covered the grassy areas overnight and decided it was too nice a day to rush through, so he started walking towards the campus.

Paul was standing talking with Jerry, the forensic tech, when Buck walked up. Buck asked them if they had gotten any sleep, and they both said they had, but the rings under their eyes told a different story.

Buck looked at the holes in the field once covered in concrete, where the students would sit and enjoy their days on campus.

"How many?" he asked.

"Too many," said Jerry. He walked away to talk to one of the other techs.

"Everyone's taking this one kind of hard," said Paul. "We had thirty hits from the ground-penetrating radar. So far, the techs have excavated seventeen graves. We have eleven young women and six infants. The Larimer County coroner is taking them as we find them. They'll issue a report as soon as the forensic anthropologist and the pathologist can get them cleaned and inspected. This is a real tragedy, Buck. The anthropologist thinks some of these women were only girls. Maybe fourteen, fifteen. Who the hell does this to a kid?" Paul stepped away, and Buck saw him wipe his eyes with the sleeve of his jacket.

He walked back to Buck and stood staring at the field. "Look, Paul, you've been at this for days. Let me take over. You head home for a couple of days and see the wife and kids. I got this."

Paul reached out and shook his hand, said thanks and headed for his Jeep. Buck stood there for a minute and looked at the holes. A shadow appeared on the ground next to him, and he turned. Tracy Terrell walked up and gave him a big hug. She stayed there for a long time before she let go and stepped back.

"I didn't think I was ever gonna see my nana again. I was never so scared in my whole life. I killed three men."

"Yeah," said Buck, "and you saved a woman's life. That's what's important." He gave her the same speech he had given Bax and told her to call if she ever needed someone to talk to. She took the business card for the psychologist and promised she would call. She gave him another hug and headed off across campus.

Buck smiled. He was hopeful that a lot of good was going to rise out of the bad. His phone rang, and he looked at the number. It came up as a restricted number. He answered. "Buck Taylor."

The gravelly voice on the other end of the call was distinctive, and Buck knew right away who was calling. "I hear you arrested my son for murder. Tell me about it."

Buck told Frank DiNardo what he felt he could, about the fake suicide, the video evidence, the prostitution and gambling and his son almost being killed the other night by Jimmy Martelli.

There was silence on the other end of the phone, then Frank spoke. "I thought sending him to a small, exclusive, expensive college would be good for him. I tried all my life to keep that boy away from my way of life. Somehow, he always ended up gettin' dragged in. So, this kid he murdered. This was all about some kinky sex thing and gettin' a little pussy? What a fucking idiot. Maybe jail will do him some good. I heard that both Martellis were killed, that right?"

Buck told him they had been. "That's too bad," said Frank. "I was supposed to be there last night. You know he was planning to kill me too?"

Buck told him that he had heard that from one of the cops they'd arrested.

"Son of a bitch wouldn't have had the balls to do it himself. He would have sent that psycho kid of his to do it. Good thing he's dead. Wouldn't have lasted long in prison."

There was silence for a minute, and Buck thought he had hung up.

"You and your people saved my kid. Even if he is an idiot and will spend a lot of years in jail, he's still my kid. I owe you. You need anything, you call me. I always pay my debts."

The line went dead, and Buck clipped his phone back on his belt. The sky had clouded up, and it had started to snow. Buck headed for the campus cafeteria to grab some lunch and call his kids. It was a good day.

Epilogue

Buck sat in the leather chair opposite the Ducettes and told them about the investigation. He knew the lifestyle Kevin had lived on campus would hurt his mom, and hurt the beautiful black girl who sat next to her and held her hand. All three of them had tears in their eyes.

Buck didn't leave anything out of the story. He had promised that he would tell them the truth, whatever that may be, and he fulfilled that promise.

Marcus Ducette stood and thanked the governor, who was standing behind him, shook hands with the director and thanked Buck for all his efforts. He walked out of the room, wiping tears out of his eyes as he left.

Mary Ducette rose slowly with the help of Kevin's fiancée and walked over to where Buck stood. She took his hand and patted the top of it. "You told us you would tell us the truth about how our son died, and you have done just that. For that, we will be eternally grateful. Thank you, Agent Taylor." She pulled herself up straight and proud and headed for the same room her husband had entered.

Buck shook hands with the governor, and they all left the building. Once outside the hotel lobby, the governor slid into his car and disappeared into the beautiful fall day.

The director looked at Buck. "The Marshals Service would like us to stop by their office. Something about paperwork. You know the government. Wouldn't run at all if it didn't have paperwork."

They walked the three blocks to the building housing the U.S. Marshals Service and stepped up to the reception desk. The young woman made a call and directed them to a conference room down the hall.

They reached the door, and the director opened it and nodded for Buck to go first. He stepped through the door, and a room full of marshals applauded. Buck looked around. He had no idea what was going on. U.S. Marshal Keating walked up and reached out his hand, and Buck shook it. He led Buck up to the front of the room as the applause continued.

Buck felt embarrassed.

"Buck Taylor," said Keating. "You stepped up and did the right thing four weeks ago when you confronted three heavily armed terrorists set on killing our friends and colleagues. You looked the terrorists in the eye and did what had to be done, and you saved lives. We wanted to honor you in some small way, but since you don't wear a uniform, a medal would have no value, and a plaque hanging on your wall just wouldn't do it. So, we came up with something that we hoped would be of real value to you."

He took a small leather wallet off the table next to him. "We cleared this with your boss and the governor, and we're awarding you this because, on that sad day, you lived up to the highest traditions of the Marshals Service." He handed Buck the wallet.

Buck opened the wallet and was speechless. Inside the wallet were a silver U.S. Marshals Service badge and an ID card with his name on it.

Keating continued. "Raise your right hand and repeat after me. I, Buck Taylor, do solemnly swear . . ."

After repeating the words, Buck lowered his hand and still didn't know what to say. Keating got serious. "Besides being a CBI agent, you are now a deputy U.S. Marshal. You keep that badge with you always, and if you need something during an investigation, you know that you will always have help." The applause rose again, and everyone held up their drinks. It took Buck a second to realize they all held up bottles of Coke. Buck smiled and wiped a tear from his eye.

The director walked to the front of the room. "Don't let this go to your head. You still work for me." The director laughed. "Congratulations, Buck." He stepped away to talk to Keating.

Buck was accepting congratulatory handshakes and pats on the back when Chief Deputy Marshal Harvey Willets walked up and congratulated him. He took Buck aside. "This is real," said Willets, tapping the wallet. "Even though you don't officially work for us, you have all the power and authority that comes with that badge. Use that power wisely, Buck. What that badge does is extends your range of jurisdiction, if you ever need it, and know that we will have your back."

He handed Buck a card with a number on the back. "Put that number in your phone. Whatever you may need during one of your investigations, be it information, a federal warrant or a couple of door kickers, you call that number, twenty-four seven, and a nice woman named Harriet will answer the phone. You tell her what you need, and she will make it happen." They talked for a few more minutes, and then the party broke up, and everyone started leaving.

Buck walked out of the building with the director and his new badge in his pocket.

"How did you manage that, sir?" asked Buck.

"You've always shied away from publicity and praise, and we never really get to thank you and your team for the great jobs you do. When Keating called the governor, the governor told him the same thing I just told you. Keating suggested this instead of a plaque or a medal, and the governor made some calls to Washington to make it happen. It seems there might have been a couple of highly placed people on a list somewhere that owed the governor a favor or two. Or a hundred."

The director slapped him on the back. "We're proud of you, Buck. Now, head home and take some time off. You and your team deserve it."

The director walked away and left Buck standing on the sidewalk. Buck thought for a minute, looked up at the sky and smiled. He knew

Lucy was looking down on him and she was smiling.

About the Author

2019 Pacific Book Awards Best Mystery Finalist . . . *Crime Delayed*

2020 Pacific Book Awards Best Mystery Winner . . . *Crime Denied*

Chuck Morgan attended Seton Hall University and Regis College and spent thirty-five years as a construction project manager. He is an avid outdoorsman, an Eagle Scout and a licensed private pilot. He enjoys camping, hiking, mountain biking and fly-fishing.

He is the author of the Crime series, featuring Colorado Bureau of Investigation agent Buck Taylor. The series includes *Crime Interrupted, Crime Delayed, Crime Unsolved, Crime Exposed, Crime Denied* and *Crime Conspiracy*.

He is also the author of *Her Name Was Jane*, a memoir about his late wife's nine-year battle with breast cancer. He has three children, three grandchildren and a Siberian Husky. He resides in Lone Tree, Colorado.

Other Books by the Author

"*Crime Interrupted: A Buck Taylor Novel by Chuck Morgan is a gripping, edge-of-the-seat novel. Right from page one, the action kicks off and never stops, gaining pace as each chapter passes.*" Reviewed by Anne-Marie Reynolds for Readers' Favorite.

Finalist . . . 2019 Pacific Book Awards Best Mystery

"*This crime novel reads like a great thriller. The writing is atmospheric, laced with vivid descriptions that capture the setting in great detail while allowing readers to follow the intensity of the action and the emotional and psychological depth of the story." Reviewed by Divine Zape for Readers' Favorite.*

"Professionally written in the style of a best-selling crime novelist, such as Tom Clancy, Crime Unsolved: A Buck Taylor Novel by Chuck Morgan is a spellbinding suspense novel with an environmental flair. *Intriguing subplots of fraud, survivalist paranoia, and murder weave their way through the fabric of the plot, creating a dynamic story. This is an action-filled, stimulating tale which contains fascinating details that are relevant in our present climate." Reviewed by Susan Sewell for Readers' Favorite.*

"Chuck Morgan has a unique gift for plot,

*one that makes **Crime Exposed: A Buck Taylor Novel** a hard-to-put-down book.* From the start, readers know what happens to Barb, but they become curious as they follow the investigation, wondering if the characters will find out what happened to her. The descriptions are filled with clarity, and they offer readers great images. The prose is elegant, and it captures both the emotional and psychological elements of the novel clearly while offering vivid descriptions of scenes and characters. This is a fast-paced thriller with memorable characters and a criminal investigation that is so real readers will believe it could happen." Reviewed by Romuald Dzemo for Readers' Favorite.

Winner . . . 2020 Pacific Book Awards Best Mystery

"It's really progressive to see a female serial killer portrayed with such intelligent writing and depth of character, and the cat and mouse chase dynamic is thrown off nicely by the switching of genders. What results is a really enjoyable thriller and crime mystery novel, and overall Crime

Denied is certain to please fans of both hard-boiled detective tales and action/adventure crime novels." Reviewed by K.C. Finn for Readers' Favorite.

"This makes for a truly dynamic story where anything is possible, and a hero you can root for even when it looks like all is lost." Reviewed by K.C. Finn for Readers' Favorite.

"This is a book you can't put down, which will entertain you on many levels, and at times make your skin crawl; the kind of book that remains in your thoughts long after you finish reading." Reviewed by Steven Robson for Readers' Favorite.